HOUSE OF LEIGHTS

SECRET KEEPERS SERIES #3

JAYMIN EVE

Jaymin Eve

House of Leights: Secret Keepers Series #3

Copyright © Jaymin Eve 2018
All rights reserved
First published in 2018

ISBN-978-1-925876-05-5

STAY IN TOUCH

Stay in touch with Jaymin:
www.facebook.com/JayminEve.Author
Website: www.jaymineve.com
Mailing list: http://eepurl.com/bQw8Kf

For Lola and Silvie.
My sunshine.

NOTE FROM AUTHOR

I changed landmarks, schools, and locations used in this book to fit the story. You should assume all errors were deliberate (even if they weren't). ;)

1

____

"Hey, Maya. Wait up!"

At the shout, I swung around to find Brad loping across the front of the redbrick science building, heading for me. As I waited, I shifted my pack to the other shoulder. The thing weighed a freaking ton. The teachers here were taking this "prepare us for college" thing a little too seriously. It made me tired just thinking about the rest of the year. I really just wanted to cheer, hang out with my friends, and occasionally attend school for my senior year. Not cool that the teachers were making it such hard work.

"Sooo..." Brad drawled, stopping in front of me, towering over my five-foot-two frame. "Are you hittin' up Owens' party tonight?" His dark brown hair was rumpled, which he did deliberately because he thought it made him look hotter. As usual, his very blue eyes were twinkling.

He was a linebacker for our football team, and he used his height and broad shoulders to pummel the other team. Our team had yet to win a game, but they still gave it their all. Dae Academy was a very small, very exclusive private school in Old

Town, Alexandria, Virginia, meaning we had excellent facilities and awesome trainers, but not a lot of students to choose from. They did what they could, though.

Pushing some of my dark hair back, I sighed. "Honestly, I don't think I'm going to make it." I pulled a sad face. "I have two quizzes I need to study for, a history assignment which is over *three thousand words*, and now Mr. Chan wants us to demonstrate our public speaking skills by reciting a twenty-verse poem – without prompt cards."

My sad face morphed into a pout, something I had perfected long ago. Brad just laughed, used to my antics. We'd been best friends since we were little, and I couldn't imagine him not being around, which was another huge reason I wasn't that excited about college. We were not going to end up at the same school. I had to stick around Virginia, as per my parents' rules, but Brad was looking at Texas U.

"I'm sure you can get all of that work done over the weekend," he pushed, reaching out to ruffle my hair. "Friday night is for relaxing ... it's like a rule."

I elbowed him to make him stop ruffling my hair. It took time to get the long, thick strands into order. "I can't argue with you about the Friday rule, but my parents are really on me about dealing with my college choices."

"Still have no idea where you're applying?" His tone was more serious now. He'd heard all my worries before.

"Nope," I said softly. "Nothing feels right. Nothing fits. I keep hoping something will fall into place, but I'm half contemplating just running away for a gap year."

It was a lot more than half, actually, but I didn't want to freak everyone out. I hated the way I always felt so displaced. I tried to do all the "in" things – I was a cheerleader, had great friends, an awesome best friend, rich parents. I had everything. And, for the most part, I enjoyed my life. But there was this ... emptiness.

Switching my bag to the other shoulder again, Brad reached out to relieve me of the weight. "Holy shit, girl. What the hell do you have in here, bricks?"

Wrinkling my nose at him, I let out a sigh. "Pretty much. Textbooks should be used to build walls. That would be a better use for them."

"Come on," he said as he started to walk. "Gracie will be waiting for you. She hates when you're late."

Gracie was my nanny, like a second mother, and she was pretty strict. She expected me out in the parking lot at 3:20 P.M. and not a moment later. That way our chauffeur could beat the majority of school traffic.

I picked up the pace, and Brad easily kept up with me. I had to take three steps to one of his. "Have you asked your 'rents why they won't get you a car?" he asked me, before he leapt down a set of five stairs.

I hurried after him, skipping just the bottom two steps. "They told me that we have Bruce to drive everywhere, so I really don't need to worry about that yet. And my safety or some crap."

My parents were diplomats. I pretty much knew nothing else about their job, because that knowledge required a clearance level just below God. Or maybe it was above God? Seemed that way at times. Suffice it to say, security was high on their list of priorities. While their jobs sounded cool and provided us with all the material things, it did require them to be away from me a lot, hence the need for Gracie.

Brad had his thinking face on, my bag swinging lightly against his back as he walked. His brow furrowed. "I just wish we knew more about their jobs. Like, they're legit crazy about security. Extraaa strict. I mean, my parents work for the government, too, but they've never been on my case like yours."

This was true. His parents were pretty relaxed. And while they were gone a lot, it was nothing compared to my parents. Brad was their only child and they indulged him to ridiculous levels. Which meant he was the epitome of a rich playboy: fast car, fast girls, lots of freedom. Under the playboy exterior, though, there was a reliable, loyal, caring friend. So, I forgave the rest. He was definitely the brother I had never had, and without him and Gracie, I would have been a hell of a lot lonelier growing up.

"The extra strict is probably something to do with Mom's upbringing," I guessed. "Apparently her parents had a lot of rules, which definitely influenced her way of raising me."

My mom, Konami Lewis, was second-generation Japanese. It was from her that I got the brown skin tone and long, straight black hair. In most other ways, I looked like my dad, Samson Lewis. He was a blue-eyed, Texas-born Southerner. His family was from old oil money, and they were very proud of their son the diplomat. They loved my mom, so the cultural differences never mattered to them.

Mom's family wasn't as proud, because we didn't uphold a lot of Japanese culture in our house anymore, but on the nights Mom was home, we always ate the best food. Homemade sushi, tempura, and edamame. With vegetables only – we were not into the meat thing.

When we reached the parking lot, a familiar black Mercedes was idling in the same spot it always was, dark tint hiding Gracie and Bruce, who I knew were inside.

"So, I'll pick you up at nine tonight?" Brad said as he handed me my bag back. Before I could protest, he ruffled up my long hair again and strode off toward his Aston Martin. I grumbled while waiting for Bruce to hurry around to open my door. I could have gotten it myself, of course, but he liked to do his job properly. So, I waited.

Bruce and Gracie were two of the five permanent staff my parents employed. I'd known them most of my life and it was a comfort to have some stability. When he reached my side, I smiled, and he gave me a nod in return, always polite. At sixty years old, he was nearing retirement age, and I was afraid that one day soon his kind brown eyes, grizzled face, and wiry salt and pepper hair, would be gone from my life.

"Thanks, Bruce," I said as I slid inside. He closed the door after me and I settled back into my seat.

If Brad was your typical rich playboy ... I wasn't much better. Spoiled would be an apt description. It was my thing. When I was younger, I'd been into school and grades, but then I discovered friends, and I ditched those "nerdy" things to focus on that part of my life. It took me a long time to realize I was just playing a part. Pretending.

Except for Brad. I never had to pretend with him. He knew about my secret anime obsession, not to mention that I was still waiting on an owl to tell me I was a wizard.

I was coming to realize, though, that it was more than just college choices that confused me. It was the very essence of what made up Maya Lewis.

"How was school?" Gracie asked this same question every day. It was our tradition.

After dropping my bag down, I turned in the leather seat to face her. She had her light blond hair up in a tight ponytail, which made her look younger than her forty-three years. Her hazel eyes were very brown today, only a hint of green, and she wore not a slick of makeup.

"It was hectic," I said truthfully. "The teachers are piling on the work, and college applications are due or overdue. It's insane."

She patted my arm, tilting her head to the side as she gave me a sympathetic smile. "Don't push yourself so hard that you burn out. Just keep going the way you are."

The urge to hug her was strong. I had no idea what I would have done without Gracie's calming presence in my life. Like most kids, I adored and forgave my parents for their flaws. But Gracie was there every day. I was eternally grateful for that, even if she was getting paid to do it.

Her words resonated with me and I made a sudden decision. "Brad wants me to go to a party tonight. I wasn't planning on it because I have so much work to do ... but maybe I should try to relax before jumping into my assignments."

She nodded, her brow tightening minutely. "Sure, I can cover with your parents."

Technically, I wasn't allowed out at night, especially not to parties, but Gracie didn't agree with keeping me completely locked up. She said she trusted me, and that as long as I never broke that trust by drinking or doing drugs, among other things, she would allow me small freedoms.

For the most part, I never *really* broke her rules. A few drinks here and there, but I never lost control.

"Especially if Brad is there to keep an eye on you," she added, turning back to the front and sinking into her seat.

"He's going to pick me up and drop me back off, so he'll definitely be keeping an eye on me."

He'd disappear through the middle of the party, off hooking up with half the cheer squad, most of whom were my friends, but then he'd find me again before we went home. He never left me behind. He was a great friend ... and a really shitty boyfriend. Luckily, I'd never had any romantic interest in Brad, because that would have gotten awkward really fast.

Traffic was heavy, but we made it home in decent time. Our mansion was in a gated community on S Lee Street, just a few blocks from the school. It took a minute for the huge front gates to open, and then Bruce drove up the round drive, pulling up at the door to let us out. This was the only house I'd ever lived in: three stories, cream and tan exterior, with brick-work, climbing ivy, and two pillars framing the front entrance.

My room was on the second floor, and I went straight up to ditch my uniform and change into something more comfortable. It had started getting cold last week – the middle of November – so I settled on some jeans, a white, fitted, knit pullover, and my fluffy socks. The dark purple streaks in the end of my hair were very prominent against the white of my top, and I was glad I'd talked my mom into letting me get it done.

My cell rang as I started down the stairs, heading for the kitchen. Whipping it out, I slid my finger across. "Hey, dude. I'm in for tonight."

Deep laughter came back at me. "I didn't even need to pull out my persuasive tone of voice," Brad said.

I scoffed. "You know your *tone* doesn't work on me. I've seen you naked and covered in paint."

"I was three," he said with a huff. "You can't keep using our childhood against me."

I shrugged, even though he couldn't see me. "Perks of a friendship with me. A lifetime reminder of every mortifying moment you've had."

It sounded like he was counting to ten – there was a lot of breathing – before finally, he said, "I'll be there later. P.S. you're a shit friend." I laughed and we hung up at the same time.

Downstairs, I moved through the wide hallway and into our kitchen. The large room was designed for catering, because on occasion my parents hosted events here for the people they worked with. In secret. Only not always so secret because they all liked to eat hors d'oeuvres together. Francis, our chef, was already at work on dinner, but he'd popped a plate with my favorite afterschool snack on the bench.

"Thanks, Frannie," I said, snatching up the sandwich.

"Out of here." He waved me away. "I have dinner to prepare."

I gave him a wink, because he was a cranky bastard, but he always made me my snack, so I was pretty sure he kind of liked me. Or at least tolerated me. Which for him was a big deal.

I bypassed the formal lounge – no food allowed in there – which was cool with me; I preferred the rumpus room. Gigantic flat screen, a bunch of squishy couches, a mini-fridge for my drinks and snacks, three different gaming consoles and more games than I could count.

What else could a girl need?

As a double bonus, it led into the outdoors games room, which had our pool table, ping pong, and all the pinball machines. The games room opened up to the pool, so ninety percent of the time this is where I hung out with my friends.

As I ate, I tried not to think about all the schoolwork waiting for me upstairs. It felt like a waste. I couldn't for the life of me decide on a career path I was interested in. I should just pick a college, hopefully get accepted, and then worry about the rest later. That would get my parents off my case. I just ... kept waiting for a sign to point me in the right direction.

At some point in my deep contemplation I must have dozed off, because when I opened my eyes again, it was dark. *Shit!* I jumped up, my eyes flicking across to my watch. 7:15 P.M.

Double shit! I had two hours to get ready for tonight, and considering I hadn't even showered yet, that was barely going to be enough time. Just my hair took forty minutes to dry and style. I rushed past Gracie as I took the stairs two at a time. "Slow down," she called after me. "You're going to break your neck."

"Why didn't you wake me?" I shouted back, almost up the stairs.

Her laughter followed me. "I tried. You were so out of it, I figured you needed the rest."

"Ugh." I threw my hands in the air and she laughed again.

Running into my room, I was already stripping and flinging clothes around as I crossed to the bathroom. Quickest shower in history, shaved my legs and all the other hairy essentials. I might meet my soul mate tonight. Always had to be prepared for that.

Once I was out, I battled with the hair dryer. Having hair almost to my waist was a real pain at times, but I couldn't imagine cutting it. My childhood goal had been to be Rapunzel when I grew up, and I'd given it my best shot. I no longer wanted her life, though, thanks to Brad who had almost scalped me when we were ten by trying to use my hair to climb over a fence.

When my hair was dry, hanging in thick lengths over my shoulders, I used a bit of product to keep it smooth and shiny. Then it was makeup time. The winged eyeliner took me the longest, but after all the years of practice, I had a very firm hand. Within fifteen minutes, my almond-shaped eyes were lined, mascaraed, shadowed, and ... I was ready to go.

I expected Brad to be waiting for me when I got downstairs, but apparently he was late, too. I really shouldn't be surprised; he spent almost as long on his hair as I did. Gracie strolled out of her office, a small room off the formal living area where she did all of the coordination of schedules and other bits and pieces for the entire family. "Have you got everything?" she asked, looking over my outfit.

I was wearing a black skirt with black knee-high socks. I'd put my boots on when I stepped outside. I was short, so I loved to wear the highest heels I could. Tonight, the ones I'd chosen were only four inches ... so I'd be almost average height. My top was a dark gray shirt dress, with long sleeves to combat the cold.

It was casual but dance-ready. My bag was small. I could only fit in my phone, cash, some cards, and lip gloss.

"I've got everything," I told her.

She smiled, rubbing her hand across her eyes. She hadn't taken any time off this year at all – she needed a holiday. Maybe this year she'd go to her parents' place for Christmas, back to California. "Text me periodically," she finally said. "Home by one, and don't drink anything except what you poured." She turned to go into her office, before pausing and looking back. "You look beautiful," she added, and then pointed her finger at me. "Be careful. Stay close to Brad."

I didn't complain about her rules. It was nice to have someone who worried about me but still let me have a little freedom. It was the best of both worlds. I grabbed my coat from the hall closet, pulled my boots on, and then stepped out onto the porch to wait for Brad. It was cold; the wind whipped around me, and even though what I was wearing was not exactly suitable for winter weather, there was no way I was changing. It'd be warm once I was inside the party.

A car was slowly making its way up the drive. I knew it was Brad because he'd installed these stupid blue-toned bulbs in his lower light. Plus, my parents were gone for a conference for three days and wouldn't be back until Monday or Tuesday, depending on travel time.

They had this entire world and life I could never be part of, which always meant there was a huge space between us. It used to hurt a lot, made me feel like they didn't want to be around me, didn't trust me with their secrets. Now I understood that it was their job and they were legally unable to share the details with me, but just because I understood didn't mean I liked it.

"Hey, Maiz," Brad said through the open window as he pulled up. "You look smokin'. Seriously. But you're gonna freeze your tiny ass off."

I wrinkled my nose at him while hurrying down the steps to get out of said freezing winds. It hadn't snowed yet, at least; that would definitely have ruined my suede boots. Brad had the window back up by the time I slid into the passenger seat, his heater sending delicious bursts of warm air across my half-frozen body.

"This party is inside, right?" My teeth chattered slightly. I seriously didn't think it was this cold in November last year. Mother Nature was kicking in her cold snap early.

"Yep, Owens has an entire basement decked out. His dad just finished the renos and this is the christening."

I nodded, settling back into my seat. I wasn't a huge fan of Mitchell Owens – a soccer star at our school who thought he was top shit. He was blond, ripped, and had biceps for days, because he basically lived at the gym. His ultra-confidence didn't bother me as much as the vibe he gave me. I had a decent douche-radar, as I liked to call it. If there was a guy around who made me even slightly uncomfortable, I made sure to never be alone in a room with him. It was one thing my mom taught me, something she learned after being raped at a party when she was fifteen.

Her parents never allowed her out at night, so she'd snuck out one time and the worst had happened. It shaped her entire world for years, basically until she met my father and learned to trust men again. She finally found the happiness she deserved.

"I'm surprised you don't have a date tonight," I said to Brad, needing to think about something less stressful.

He shrugged, focusing on the traffic we were slowly moving through. "Honestly, the girl drama has been a bit much lately. I'm thinking a nice, relaxing night with my best friend and a few drinks is the ticket."

I laughed. "Yeah, okay." This wasn't the first time he'd started with those intentions, but by the time "a few drinks" happened, he always managed to get snared by one of the scantily-clad chicks there.

Brad flashed me his trademark crooked grin, the one he pulled out to get him out of trouble at school, and into trouble with women. "Scout's honor."

My laugh turned into a snort. "You're no Scout, my friend. Not even close."

He didn't argue, because as usual, I was right.

2

It took us about twenty minutes to make it through traffic and reach the very nice development that Mitchell's house was in. Cars were everywhere on the side-walks, down the street, and across the road. Brad didn't even bother looking for a spot, he just drove right down the main driveway, which was off the side of the house, and parked behind Mitchell's car.

"Owens told me that it was cool for me to bring my baby closer to safety," he explained as he switched the engine off.

I nodded, because I seriously didn't care what the reason was. I was just happy I didn't have to trek for miles in the cold. It also meant I could leave my coat in the car – I could brave the cold for a few minutes.

As soon as I stepped out, I wasted no time heading for the house. "Come on, the new entrance is this way," Brad told me, leading me past the path I thought we would take.

I'd been heading for the front porch, but apparently that was not the way in now. We walked around the side of the house and there were people scattered everywhere, smoking and drinking. Brad waved and greeted most of them as we continued toward a set of open double doors that lay almost flush with the ground. Basement entrance, I would assume.

Loud music could be heard before we were even close. We took the stairs down to the ground level, and ... I could admit it, it was impressive. The area was huge; an entire floor had been cleared out and redesigned in a similar setup to a club: couches, tables, a designated dance floor – even a bar, which was packed with people. I recognized a ton of kids from school, but there were also a lot I didn't know.

"Big party," I shouted over the music.

Brad pushed a hand through his hair, ruffling it up a little. "Yeah, I kind of expected he would go all out now that his party space was ready, but this is pretty insane."

It was hard to hear him – I never quite understood why the music had to be so loud at parties. But after a few drinks I wouldn't care. I'd just be dancing and dancing until my legs gave out.

Brad wrapped an arm around me, semi-protecting me from the crowds. "Let's get a drink," he said, leaning down close to my ear.

I nodded, letting him steer me toward the bar. Despite it being thirty people deep, we managed to get near the front quickly. I was surprised to see three people behind the bar wearing black and white and taking orders. I mean, my parents hired staff when they had their little parties, but I'd never seen it at a school thing.

Brad noticed my wide-eyed stare. "Remember, Owens' family owns a catering company. That's where their money comes from."

I wrinkled my nose at him. "I'm sure this will come as a

shock, but I don't remember every little detail about Mitchell and his family."

Brad shot me a smirk, turning to order from the waitress. He got a beer, and I ended up with a pre-mixed bottle of something pink with vodka. I'd sip on this one drink for half the night, because if I came home too drunk, Gracie would never let me out again. Brad and I both watched closely to make sure the bartender opened it in front of us and that nothing shady went down. It was the reason we went for something in the bottle or can every time.

The woman serving us looked to be about our age. She smiled as she handed the drinks across the bar, not even blinking an eye at serving alcohol to minors. I wondered if they were paid extra to break the law.

As long as I got a drink, I didn't care.

"Maya!"

The scream had me spinning around to find Courtney and Lace swaying before me. They were both cheerleaders on the team with me, the two I considered to be my closer friends. "You didn't tell us you were coming!" Courtney yelled as she hugged me. She was almost a foot taller than me with heels on, her long blond hair smacking me in the face.

As I hugged her back, I was hit with a strong smell of alcohol and I realized they'd been here for a while. Or they drank fast. Because they were halfway to wasted already.

Lace stepped in for a hug next. "Love your makeup," I said when she was close. She'd gone for a sparkly red eyeliner to match her short, pixie hair. This week's hair color was a rich blood red. Her large brown eyes almost looked vampiric against it. Not to mention her skin was even darker than her eyes, so the red really popped.

I could never pull off the fashion choices she made, but

she rocked them hard. Half the guys at the school pursued her, while she continually brushed them off. College or older for her; she didn't date high school "boys," as she called them.

After my last disaster of a relationship, I was starting to come around to her philosophy.

Brad, who had been chatting to a friend nearby while we caught up, gave me a wave. "You go dance," he said. "I'll find you in a few hours, and then we can head home."

Waving back, I turned to my girls. "You both ready?" I shouted, my hips already moving. The warmth from the vodka was spreading through my body. I was so ready to let loose. No more thinking about papers and college and being thousands of miles from my friends when we graduated. No more trying to figure out why my life felt empty even when it was full. Nope. Not tonight.

Tonight was about the music.

Despite my plan to go slow on my drink, by the time we reached the area set up as a dance floor, it was already gone. I dropped the bottle on a nearby table, smiling stupidly. I was always a lightweight with alcohol.

Lace dragged me out onto the floor. She out-danced us without even trying, her moves a natural rhythm that could not be learned. But all of us were gymnasts, flexible and used to moving with the beat. Hugging in close, I moved my body with theirs, all of us smiling and throwing our heads back and arms up. The music was really working for me tonight, a great mix of dance and pop, without too much techno. I wasn't a fan of too heavy a beat.

Guys crowded in close, but they were useless to us on the dance floor. All they wanted was to slide up on me, and that threw my moves right off.

"No!" I said firmly, pointing my finger at a dirty blond-headed guy I didn't recognize. "No touching."

He held both hands up and backed away. As I was just turning back to Lace, who was shaking her ass like the next Beyoncé, I caught a glimpse of someone who gave me a moment's pause. He was half in the shadows, leaning back against a nearby wall, and I could have sworn he was looking straight at me. There was a light rolling sensation in my tummy, but instead of the usual reticence I felt with strangers, the feelings inside of me this time were ... different.

My feet moved, heading toward him. He looked very tall ... taller than most guys I knew, and considering my best friend was on the football team, that said a lot. He had one leg propped up, casual and relaxed. I sensed a coiled lethalness about him, which should have made me nervous.

But it didn't.

I took another step closer. At the same time his leg slid slowly down the wall so he was standing on two feet again.

"Maya, everything okay?" Lace asked. It took me a beat to register her question. With effort I turned to answer her, but before I even spoke one word, I was already turning back to him. He stepped out of the shadows and my heart clenched so tightly that I actually gasped in my next breath.

"Maya!" Lace was more forceful this time. "What's wrong? What did you see?"

Still no words emerged, because I was trying to figure out if he was real. Was it possible any man could be that unbelievably gorgeous? His face ... it had been the most perfect thing I'd ever seen. Dark and exotic, full lips, a strong jaw ... it was the sort of face movie stars would kill to have.

A body bumped me hard; the dance floor was getting so crowded. I stumbled forward. By the time I regained my footing and turned to the wall, he was gone. Without thought, moving in a frantic, almost trance-like state, I ran to where he'd been standing. But there was no one even close to this spot now.

What the hell just happened?

Had I literally just imagined that? Could my drink have been spiked after all?

"Maya! For shit's sake, girl." Lace reached out and grabbed my arm, startling me. "You're gonna give me a heart attack. Don't just run off like that, lookin' like you just saw an axe-wielding psycho."

I blinked at her slowly, and she examined me closer. "Was there actually a psycho?" she asked, her eyes roving around just like mine had done. Courtney joined us then, face creased in concern.

I shook my head. "I thought … I thought I saw something … or someone. Never mind … I might just be losing my mind." I shook my head again, more vigorously, and hoped some sanity would return with it.

I didn't feel drugged, just a little buzzed. But maybe this was something new, undetectable except for weird hallucina-tions of fantasy men. My burst of laughter did nothing to ease the concerned looks on my friends' faces.

I waved it away, shaking my head. "It's all good. Come on, let's dance again."

Neither looked convinced, but they did turn to head back toward the crowd. As I took the first step, I noticed something on the ground, almost hidden in the darkness. Leaning down, I picked it up, praying it wasn't a used tampon or something equally as gross.

Lifting my hand toward the light, I blinked a few times. It was a leaf, but not like any leaf I'd seen before. The stem was a bright golden color. At first I thought it was one of those artificial plants, but as I closed my hand on it crushing the leaf, a strong scent of pine and mint drifted to me.

With a shake of my head, I dropped it back into the darkness. There was too much weird happening for my liking. I needed to go back to my normal life.

There were no more glimpses of gorgeous strangers for the rest of the night, just the standard Dae students and a few newbies from neighboring schools. I found Brad later, playing poker with Mitchell and a few other football and soccer jocks.

He caught my eye as I stepped into their corner of the room. I lifted my wrist and pointed to my watch. He picked up his phone, and realizing it was almost 1 A.M., threw down his cards and gathered up his money.

"Ready to go, Maiz?" he said when he reached me.

I nodded. "Yep. My feet are killing me. I've hit my dance quota for the night."

As we walked toward the stairs – the place was still mega-packed – I asked him, "Are you fine to drive? How much did you have to drink?"

"Totally fine," he told me. "I only had that one beer when we first got here, and I didn't even finish it. I've been on water since."

I wasn't surprised. If there was one thing Brad would never do, it was drink and drive. He'd lost his cousin a few years ago; the college junior wrapped his Beemer around a pole. Now, if Brad caught any of his friends even thinking about getting behind the wheel after drinking, he was right in their faces until they gave him their keys.

The further up the stairs we got, the colder the air was, and by the time we stepped out onto the lawn I was shivering. "This weather is the worst," I whined. "I'm probably going to get a chill and die."

"You're so dramatic," Brad said with a shake of his head. "You're not going to die in the two minutes to the car."

"How can you know that for sure?" I countered.

If he didn't think it was completely unmanly, he'd totally be rolling his eyes at me right now. "Come on, you annoying brat."

He ruffled my hair, and I bit back the curse words just waiting to be flung at his annoying ass. It took longer than it should have to reach the car, because Brad had to high-five and fist bump every idiot along the way. At least my glare and chattering teeth kept him from lingering any longer than the bare minimum.

Once I was inside, I started bouncing in my seat. "Hurry up and get the heater on!"

The car started with a roar, and I got a deadpan look. "Anything else, your majesty?"

Considering it for a beat, I finally shook my head. "No, I'm good. Just get me home in one piece."

He winked at me. "Consider it done."

As we pulled out of Mitchell's little subdivision, a bunch of police cars and dark SUVs screamed past us. "Think they're going to break up the party?" Brad asked, turning a confused face in my direction.

"Um ... four police cars and four undercover cars is a little excessive, don't you think?" Guess it was possible. There were a lot of kids there.

Brad shrugged, before inclining his head toward his phone in the center console. "Can you text Owens, just in case. Let him know he needs to shut down the underage drinking."

Opening up the app, I quickly sent out a text to Mitchell, explaining what we'd seen. Brad's phone buzzed almost immediately with a "thx dude."

I gave Brad the message and he relaxed. "You're a good friend," I told him, sinking back into the heated seat. "Despite my continued annoyance at your inability to treat women decently."

He ruffled my hair. I swiped his hand away and he laughed.

"And because you won't leave my damn hair alone."

"You know I respect women. I just don't want to settle down. Something I make very clear far in advance of our hookups."

I would grudgingly give him that point. He made no false promises, but that didn't mean he didn't leave broken hearts behind. The ones who cared always hoped he'd change for them. And he never had.

I was just opening my mouth to ask him if it was possible that he hadn't settled yet because he hadn't found the right person, but before I could say anything he hit the brakes hard and I threw both hands out toward the dash to brace myself. My seatbelt saved me from faceplanting at least.

"Dude..." I said, pushing my hair back and glaring at him. "A little warning before you slam on the brakes like..."

I trailed off as I finally registered the look on his face as he stared out the front windshield. Swinging around, I followed his line of sight, and blinking a few times, let out a low gasp. "What in the ever-loving world is going on?" I murmured.

Four black SUVs, looking very similar to the ones we'd passed on the way to the party, were blocking the road.

"I almost hit them," Brad growled, looking slightly less shocked. "They overtook me and then swerved right in front of me, blocking the road."

"What do you think they want?" I asked, trying not to let

the fear I felt creep into my voice. "Late at night, unmarked vans. Is this a carjacking?"

"I'm going to reverse and get the hell out of here," Brad said grimly. "I don't like this. Your parents are important. Mine are also in the government. We're definitely prime targets for kidnapping."

He was right. Even though I knew nothing about what sort of work my parents did, it had to be important. Why else would there be so much secrecy?

Brad shifted the gear to reverse, but when he turned his head to look he realized a few cars were close behind us, blocking us in. There was literally no way for him to go backwards, and the street was too narrow to turn around quickly.

"Shit," he growled.

Pulling out my phone to dial 911, I thought about the argument I'd had last year with my father about assigning a permanent bodyguard to me. I told him it was a definite *no*. I would never be okay with someone following me around every day. I was kind of regretting that decision right about now. Damn my stubborn teen tendencies.

As I went to dial, I noticed that I had fifteen messages and dozens of missed calls. My phone had been on silent because I never heard it at parties. Still, that many notifications was unusual enough that I opened the app, finding that they were all from my parents and Gracie.

"They're getting out of the car," Brad warned me, his voice low and rough. "They're in suits, but criminals dress nice too, so don't let your guard down."

I was too busy reading through my messages to check out the "suits."

Maya, you need to call us ASAP!!! This was from my father.

The next was my mom: *There has been an emergency at*

work. You are in danger. Do not go home. Do NOT let anyone take you anywhere. Tell us where you are and we will come for you.

Gracie: *Maya, parents looking for you. Very worried. Please call.*

I jerked my head up and stared at the suited men who were twenty feet from our car. "I need to run," I said to Brad. "My parents just texted. I think I'm in danger."

Brad opened his mouth, no doubt to ask a million questions I didn't have time to answer, but I was already moving. My belt was undone and I was out of the car in almost the same instant. "Follow me," I said to him through the open door before I took off.

I picked a direction the opposite way to the men and started to run without looking back. I knew my city well, but I also hadn't spent much time in this particular area, especially late at night.

Maybe the darkness would give me an advantage. I could put some distance between them and then hide until my parents got me.

"Maya!" I heard Brad's shout. He didn't sound like he was too far away, so I slowed slightly to let him catch up. He was a hundred times fitter and stronger than me, which might come in handy if I needed to scale a fence or something.

"What the fuck is going on?" he said, as he reached my side.

Our feet hit a rhythm together. He had to slow his run to keep up with my shorter legs. Not to mention I was in damn heels. "I have no idea," I said, breathing hard. "Parents said danger and not to get taken by anyone, so I'm running and hiding."

I hit my mom's number on the phone, which I'd thankfully

not dropped in my haste to run. It rang in my ear, over and over, but there was no answer.

"Shit."

My father's number was next, and I had no expectations that he was going to answer either. But he did: "Maya, little one, where are you?"

I could have cried at the deep, rich drawl. "Dad, I need your help. Some men tried to stop us ... they're after us now." I assumed they were anyway. I had not looked back yet.

Brad did glance over his shoulder as I spoke, and when I met his gaze it looked grim. They were definitely after us.

"Maya, get out of Alexandria immediately. I can't speak to you on the phone about it, but you're not safe right now."

"Where should I go?" I asked, my heart sinking as I realized no help was coming for me. "Why aren't we calling the police?"

"No!" came the forceful reply. "The police cannot be trusted. Do not trust anyone until you find us and we explain it all."

The police had been with those black SUVs before...

"So where do I go?" I asked, wondering if the "anyone" included Brad. Because it was far too late not to trust him, he was my family.

"Maya..." That low call from Brad had the blood pumping faster through my body. "They're gaining on us. You need to get off the phone."

My talking was too loud, which was not helping me "hide" in the darkness. Not to mention it was slowing us down. "I have to go, Dad. They're catching up to us."

I heard his low rumble of anger and knew it was frustration at being so far away from me. "Ditch your phone as soon as you hang up," he told me. "Brad, too. They can track your cells. Then get to the place where I took you last summer. Close to my work. Meet in our favorite spot."

The line went dead, and I let out a sobbing gasp before lifting the phone and pitching it as hard as I could against the wall. "Get rid of your phone," I told Brad, my voice wavering as I tried to keep it together.

Brad didn't even question me. He pulled his cell from his pocket and did the same thing I had, smashing it against a nearby wall.

"How far back are they?" I asked, picking up the pace. My legs were starting to ache, mostly because I was sprinting in heels. Sure, I was excellent at walking and even running in heels, but not for long distances. Plus, I was freezing.

"About twenty yards."

Trying not to panic, I said, "We need to get to Washington. If you see a cab, grab it."

My bag was slung across my body, so I still had plenty of cash on me. And I knew exactly where my father wanted me to go – to the park near the White House. He always joked that his next-door neighbor was a very stately, shiny sort of fellow. Looked like I was going to find out exactly where he worked.

3

———

"We need to get to a more populated area." Brad didn't sound remotely breathless. "There are not going to be any cabs down these side streets."

He was worried, and I knew why. If we didn't get out of the back alleys, we were going to find more trouble than just the guys behind us.

"I think I know where we are," I added, recognizing a little vintage store that I loved to visit. They got in all the best vinyl records, plus an eclectic mix of bags and boots.

Unable to stop myself, I glanced back, and I almost gasped at how close the men were. The only reason they hadn't caught up to us yet was because we'd had the head start. But we'd lost almost all that advantage now.

And we were outnumbered. I could see at least five of them … and it looked like they were holding guns.

"Holy fuck. We're going to die. I'm so sorry, Brad. I didn't mean to get you killed."

He let out a low laugh, and I could have punched him in

the face for being so casual. "We're not going to die. I won't let that happen."

Awesome sentiment, but the odds were stacked against us. Still ... I liked optimism. "We might have a chance," I decided, my breathing growing more labored now, "if we can make it to the street. Even at this time, there will be people around. And taxis."

It was only another half a block to the well-lit main street and there were still about twenty feet between us and the assholes ... so there was a chance. As I had that thought, three shadows burst out of a side alley and blocked the path. I stumbled, trying to skid to a halt. Brad grabbed my arm at the last moment to stop me from face-planting.

The other five slowed, while still closing in on us. We were trapped between them. The street was not narrow, but there was no way we could get around them surrounded like this.

"What do you want?" I yelled, trying to buy some time. We needed to come up with a plan. I could not let myself get taken. My father's voice was still ringing in my head. His warnings.

"Our boss needs a word with you," one of them said. "If you come along without fuss, you will not be hurt."

Yeah, sure.

"My friend goes free?" I asked, deciding on the spot that it wasn't worth both of us dying. I would do whatever I could to protect Brad, even if the thought of being dragged off by these men had my insides twisting like crazy.

"Yes..." This came from a different thug. It was almost impossible in this low light to differentiate any of their features, so he could be thug number four.

"Not going to happen, Maiz," Brad bit out. "If you think for one second I'm letting you go alone, you're insane."

"No point in us both dying," I murmured. "Plus ... they need me for something – you're expendable. It's better if you get out of here. Tell someone what happened to me. Find my parents."

He shook his head and stepped closer, one hand wrapping around my wrist to prevent me from running off. "Never."

That was the final word from him; he was as stubborn and unmovable as a bull when he set his mind to something. The men moved closer; we had only seconds to decide what to do. "Don't fight them," I whispered. "There are too many and they have guns."

Brad didn't answer me, which generally meant he was going to ignore my plan completely. With not much left to lose, I opened my mouth and started to scream for help. The main street was close by. Maybe someone would hear me...

The eight continued closing in on us, uncaring that I was screaming. Despite my words not to fight, I brought both hands up closer to my face and clenched them into fists. I couldn't just go quietly; I wasn't raised that way. I screamed again, shouting for help, but there was no one coming to our rescue.

The man closest to me was not that tall, but he was very wide. Broad shoulders, a little bit of extra fat on him, but it was clear there were a lot of muscles under that layer. "Shut up," he growled. "I'm not supposed to kill you, but there is a lot of pain between healthy and dead. Don't push me."

I swung both of my fists around and flipped him off. "Kiss my ass, asshole," I spat out.

Shut up, Maya.

My mom hated me swearing; my father had no issue. So I had a weird tendency where I mostly didn't swear, but when I was freaked or stressed the worst kind of cursing known to pirate and Texan would fall from my lips.

He lurched forward, arms outstretched. Instinct kicked in and I swung my fist toward his brick-like head, but just as I was about to connect, he made a weird grunting sound and was jerked backwards, away from me. I blinked a few times, wondering what had just happened. It hadn't been my punch, because it didn't actually land. Had one of his friends pulled him back? Were they fighting over who was first to grab me?

"You okay?" Brad asked, his back pressed against mine.

"Yeah," I nodded. "Something weird is happening, but they're backing up."

The remaining men were looking between themselves, trying to figure out what happened to their friend. After a moment, one of the others let out some very inventive swears of his own, before he came toward me. "Stupid bitch, what did you do to Leroy?"

I held both hands up on either side of me, palms up. Whatever happened to Leroy, it had nothing to do with me. Or apparently the other four confused kidnappers standing before me. Thug number one reached for me, and just as I braced, he was swept away, quick as a flash. I didn't see anyone behind him. There had been no clear sign of what happened. Just one moment there and the next gone.

The remaining three on my side looked nervous, and when Brad turned around, I realized there were none left on his side. "What is happening?" I asked, reaching out for his hand. I needed something to hold onto.

"I have no idea," he said, not sounding very happy about it. "Before I could even land a hit, they just disappeared."

Despite this, the final three did not give up. They each came for us, and each time they were gone in the same instant.

I took a step down the alley, back the way we'd originally run, trying to see in the dark. All of a sudden, my stomach did a twirl, and as I pressed my palms to it, I recognized the sensation. I'd felt it only a few hours ago at Mitchell's party from that guy leaning against the wall, the guy who seemed to have created a plethora of emotions inside of me from across the room of a crowded party.

Was he here somewhere? In the darkness?

"Thank you," I called out, not sure where that came from, but needing to say it all the same.

Brad was confused. "Who are you thanking?" he asked, pulling me back toward the main street.

Not wanting to leave, but knowing I had no choice, I reluctantly followed. "I have no idea," I told him. "But I think we might have a guardian angel."

Brad didn't ask anything else, his focus now on hustling me toward the street, his face tense and stressed. That expression reminded me that we'd almost been kidnapped. Which was completely insane, and yet, I still couldn't stop thinking about the guy from the party. Was it even possible to have chemistry that strong? Strong enough to feel in the dark, even though I could not see him to confirm he was even there.

Maybe stress was finally causing me to lose my mind. That'd make just as much sense.

When we reached the main street I hailed the first cab we found. Normally Uber would be the way, but since our phones were dust, this was where we were at. "Where to?" the driver asked when we were both in the back seat.

"Washington, D.C.," I told him, trying to keep the urgency from my voice. "Will the train still be running at this time?"

According to his front console it was 1:36 A.M. How could so much have happened in forty minutes?

"Nope, last train left just before."

Dammit. "Can you take us?" I asked, one of my legs jittering with impatience. I really just wanted him to move it.

There was a beat of silence. "Well, sure, I can take you, but the round trip for me will be quite expensive."

I didn't even hesitate, pulling out the wads of cash from my bag. "Here you go. I'm sure this will cover it."

The driver looked down, his eyes widened, and he immediately pulled out onto the road. I felt somewhat better now that we were moving, relaxing just a touch.

"Where to in Washington?" he asked, maneuvering through an intersection.

I opened my mouth to reply, but then decided I would take the "trust no one" thing seriously. "I'll let you know when we're closer. Just head into the main downtown part."

He nodded and then fell silent. I dropped back against Brad, who hadn't said anything since we got in the car. Stretching out my aching feet, I tried not to think too much about what we'd just gone through. Two hours ago, I'd been a normal teenager at a party. Now I was on the run, I had no idea where my parents were, and part of me was wishing I was back in the alley. The feeling in my chest and stomach was gone now, the rushing of hormones through my body fading.

I wanted it back.

The ride was fast and quiet. I was a combination of exhausted and freaked out, but there was no way I'd even close my eyes until I found my parents. What if I fell asleep and the driver was somehow a bad guy too, and decided to drive us to some remote location and knock us off?

Trust. No. One.

Brad and I didn't talk, both of us locked in our own thoughts. I mostly spent my time trying not to freak out further. Not knowing if my parents were safe was the hardest part. What if they had run into the same trouble I had? What would I do if I got to the National Mall and they weren't there?

Before I could descend all the way into the depths of madness, familiar sights distracted me. Washington, D.C. The driver swiveled to see us. "So ... have you decided where you'd like to be dropped off?"

Leaning forward, I nodded. "Yes, as close to the White House as you can get." I wasn't sure about security at this time of night. I figured he might be able to drop us within a few blocks. Brad gave me a look but didn't say anything.

"No worries." The driver glanced back again, and it looked like he wanted to ask more questions but refrained. No doubt he was wondering why two teenagers were trying to go to the White House at almost 2 A.M. In the end though, he stayed quiet as he drove on.

When he pulled up I could just see a few buildings and a lot of trees. I didn't know the area, but as soon as we were out, the taxi driving away, Brad said, "I've been here a few times to visit my parents. The Mall is just over there." He pointed.

The street was quiet. I couldn't see another person around, which made me uneasy. "Do payphones still exist?" I asked as we walked. I was trying to come up with a backup plan if my parents were not waiting for me. "Can they be traced ... payphones?"

Brad shot me a sad attempt at a grin, the first I'd seen from him in a while. "In the movies they can. I have no idea if that's real life, though."

Hopefully I wouldn't have to risk it. Maybe I'd get my second stroke of luck tonight, if you counted the stranger in the alley as the first, and we'd find my parents waiting exactly where my dad said. It was plausible, right?

Brad took my hand as we walked along the street. If we had to speak, we kept our voices just above a whisper so we didn't draw attention to ourselves. Brad remained quite short with me, saying only what he had to, and I knew him well enough to know when he was angry. Or upset.

"What's wrong?" I finally asked after the tenth one-word answer.

His hand flexed on mine for a beat, and then he said, "You were going to sacrifice yourself for me. I'm not okay with that. You were almost taken right out from under me. I should be able to protect you."

Snuggling in closer to him, I snaked one arm around his back, mostly for comfort, and a little for warmth, because I was absolutely freezing. "You're my best friend," I told him. "My family. It's my job to protect you as well. The truth is, they wanted me. There was no point in you dying, too."

He made a sound, part devastation and part anger, and it had my heart clenching painfully. "We're a team, Maiz. You and me. If there is no you, then what the hell is the point of me?"

Everyone expected that Brad and I would get together one day, that we couldn't be this close without romantic feelings coming into it, but they were all wrong. We were family: brother and sister, best friends, a team. But there was never, and would never, be anything romantic. Even if I'd wanted that from him – which I definitely did not, I'd seen him through every single disgusting stage of his life – I would never risk what we had.

"You're my people," he said to me.

"The one I'd call to help me hide a dead body," I finished, sucking some deep breaths, the freezing air chilling my mouth and throat. "I'm sorry. I shouldn't have tried to leave you behind."

"Damn right," he exclaimed, hugging me tightly. He wore only a shirt, but he at least had pants on so his butt wasn't freezing. Still, if we didn't get out of the cold soon, both of us were going to be in trouble.

Thankfully, we were in the Mall now. I'd never been here at night, and as darkness closed in around us, I realized how super creepy it was. There were a few people around, but not many. I'd never seen White House security out this far in the daytime. I was half expecting at night there would be some, but so far it looked clear.

"The Lincoln Memorial, right?" Brad murmured close to my ear.

I twisted my head to see him better, shooting a smile in his direction. "How did you figure that out?"

He shrugged. "I know you and your family pretty well by now, Maya. You mentioned the trip to the memorial multiple times. I saw the way your eyes lit up when you talked about that time with your dad."

I nodded. "It's our special spot. He's a little obsessed with history ... especially the presidents. He used to take me here all the time when we were kids, tell me that I needed to learn and love our history."

"It's kind of spooky here at night." Brad shook his shoulders like he was preparing for battle. "Feels like we're about to star in a thriller movie."

My fists clenched tightly. "I really hope not."

We fell silent, moving in the shadows – which there were a lot of – creeping our way closer to the monument. My father would be around the outside somewhere I expected. Even though the memorial was open 24/7, he would not wait in an obvious place.

I wondered where my mom was. I really couldn't picture her slinking in the darkness like this. She was very proper and formal ninety percent of the time, so she was probably holed up somewhere. Hopefully in a safe house.

Brad grabbed my icy hand and I almost moaned at the warm relief his palm provided. His other hand went across my mouth then, silencing me as he yanked me behind a large bush. I had no idea what he was doing, until a small group of men strolled past our spot. None of them looked in our direction, and when they were gone we hurried off again. I picked up the pace, paying better attention this time.

No one crossed our path again before we reached the steps of the Lincoln Memorial. Staying in shadow as much as possible, we crept up the first flight of stairs, darting in toward some nearby bushes. When no one jumped out and there was no obvious sign of any other people around, we moved toward the next flight. The lights shining in and around the memorial were almost scary after so much darkness. I liked being hidden away in the shadows.

Brad leaned his head right down near my ear. "Someone is in the bushes over there," he breathed.

I followed his line of sight, and it took me a few moments, but I finally made out the shape of a person. I really didn't want to go over there, especially since I would have to expose myself in the light to get there, but there was no other choice. No way would I find my dad if both of us continued to hide in the shadows.

Taking a deep breath, my hand still firmly held in Brad's, I pulled him along as I moved toward the man-shaped shadow. My heart was pounding so hard I almost couldn't breathe over the clenching of my chest and stomach. When I hit the light, I expected my father would step out of his hiding place, but the shadow didn't move.

"Something isn't right," I whispered, pulling Brad to a stop.

From this angle I could see that the human shadow was just part of the tree and building, which was nothing to be alarmed about, and yet the feeling that something was "wrong" still wouldn't leave me. Maybe my nerves were frayed and I had reached the end of my ability to handle this cloak and dagger routine.

"Let's keep moving." Brad tugged on my hand, reminding me we were standing very exposed out in the open.

Trying to breathe through my fear, I allowed him to pull me off to the side. Once the darkness wrapped around me again, some of my panic eased and I was able to think. *Where would he be waiting?* There had to be a specific spot that he thought I'd know. Where did we go last time we were here?

I was trying to remember, but either the situation was too tense for deep thought, or I'd forgotten whatever small detail my dad thought I'd know. The last time we'd just sat on the steps and talked for ages about all the history here.

"Didn't you get lost in this building as a child?" Brad asked, leaning back against the wall. "Your dad tells that story all the time. He loves it. Where did he find you?"

I straightened. "Yes." I nodded. "That's his favorite story because he found me sleeping at the feet of the statue. I crawled over the barrier and was kind of hidden out of sight. Do you think he might be waiting for us there?"

Brad darted his head left and right, looking around. "Coast looks clear. Let's check inside."

He took off and I was right on his heels, past the pillars and into the white hall. There were low lights scattered around, and no sign of any other people. I moved without pause toward the huge statue

Disappointment hit me hard when there was no sign of my father. He was too large to hide like I had, and I fought against the pressure in my throat threatening to burst free. If I started to cry now, I would not stop for a week. I was a loud, ugly crier, which was definitely not the way for us to stay under the radar. I needed to keep it together. At least for now.

"He's not here," I said, my voice thick.

Brad stepped around the side of the barrier, looking all the way to the back of the statue. Everything was very white in here, so I paused when a splash of red caught my eye. For a second I thought it was blood, and I almost died right then, freaking out that my father had been here and was hurt.

But as I stepped closer, straining against the barrier, I realized it was a piece of paper. Right at the base of the statue.

4

—————

*L*eaning out, I scraped the edge of the red paper with my fingertips, pulling it back toward me. As I straightened, note in hand, Brad made his way to my side. "What did you find?" he asked, eyes locked on the note in my hand.

I quickly opened the folded sheet and we silently read it together.

13 steps toward the sun. 13 steps toward the east. A broken shoelace will not hurt. A gilded cage of the sea.

Brad's brow furrowed, but I let out a low chuckle. "Tell me you know what the hell that means..." he said, frustrated.

I nodded. "This is a poem I made up when I was seven. It was a class project. They gave us a list of five words and we had to use them in a poem. Mine made no sense at all, but my mom laughed and said it was perfect. She put it on the fridge." My hand tightened in the paper. "Then one day, it was gone. Dad told me he took it to his work and put it up on the wall as a reminder of everything he had at home. A reminder of his funny, smart, and silly daughter."

Don't cry, damn it.

"What does it mean, though?" Brad said, and I swallowed my emotions down.

"I don't know." I cleared my throat. "I guess that he was here, and that ... his work is here somewhere. Maybe he wants me to go to his work..."

Only I had no idea where it was.

"Maiz," Brad said, urgency in his tone. I flipped my head up and looked at him. He was pointing toward another red flash. I hadn't seen it in my haste to read the first letter.

He reached out, scooping it up and handing it to me. I opened it and held the letter so we could both read it.

Hansel and Gretel.

Brad growled. "I still don't know what he's trying to tell us."

I blinked a few times, a thought coming to me. "What if he's telling us to follow the breadcrumbs? Hansel and Gretel style." I reread the first note, looking for clues. "There's no sun right now, so it has to be the east thing. But where is the starting point?" A direction was no good if we didn't have a starting point. "Which way is east in general?" My sense of direction was terrible. I couldn't read a map. During orientation at school I'd gotten my entire team so lost they had to bring in trackers to find us.

Brad turned in a circle once, stopping and pointing. "I think that way." We started to walk, counting the steps. We were still in the memorial at thirteen and my confusion was growing. Why couldn't my dad just make this easy on me? I was tired, stressed, scared, freezing. I didn't have time for riddles.

"Found it," Brad said, startling me from my moment of feeling sorry for myself. The note had been wedged into a small space just across from us.

Opening it, I read the next cryptic clue.

A president's job is never fun. Eighty-seven steps down and you're almost done.

Well, that was at least a little clearer.

Brad and I wasted no more time. We rushed out of the building and took the steps all the way down to the reflecting pool. It was barely visible in the dark, and I took care not to overstep into the water. On the last step there was another red note:

Take a left and then a right. Find a bush that looks like spike.

"Spike, your old dog?" Brad asked.

I nodded. "Has to be."

We hurried left first, and then when we reached the end of the water, turned right. There were no signs of any people around, but I was worried that our strange behavior might draw the attention of security. Sooner or later, someone was going to investigate.

As we moved, I kept an eye out for something that might look like a dog.

"There?" Brad asked, sounding unsure.

He was pointing at a plant, huge and bushy, and almost completely hidden in the darkness. But there were a few pinpoints of light behind it that sort of gave it a canine shape.

"I hope so," I said breathlessly as we changed directions and went further into the shadows.

Our steps slowed as we got closer, and I was holding my breath, silently hoping that this was the last stop. I couldn't handle the suspense any longer. As we crept around the edge of the bush, a shadow straightened from where it had been crouched.

"Dad!" I exclaimed, managing to keep my voice low even though my tone was excited and relieved.

I threw myself at him and he wrapped his arms around me. "Where's Mom?" I asked as I pulled back.

He pressed a finger to my lips, before his eyes darted up to Brad. They exchanged a look and my best friend nodded, not saying a word. Holding my hand tightly, Dad led us through the Mall, always looking over his shoulder. He was acting paranoid – but I hadn't forgotten my very recent kidnap attempt, so I understood.

We continued ducking in and out of buildings, moving randomly, before we left the Mall and crossed into a street. I knew we were heading away from the White House, but other than that I'd never have been able to retrace our steps.

There were lots of fancy buildings around us, the kind with an abundance of character: stone and marble fronts, small detailing etched into their front doors, and lots of metal accents. I'd never been here before, and in the dark I couldn't tell if they were houses or condos, but either way, there was some serious money here. You couldn't live this close to the White House without being in the billionaire club.

A cold breeze hit me, the temperature dropping the closer we got to sunrise. I shivered violently and my father let go of my hand to shuck off his jacket, wrapping it around me. He wore a sweater beneath, blue and striped, so I gratefully accepted his coat. My skin prickled and hurt as the warmth seeped into it, and I realized how close I had come to being seriously frozen.

We resumed our fast walk again, staying in the shadows. When my dad stopped abruptly, I almost crashed into him. He entered a front yard and led us to a set of stairs that seemed to disappear into darkness. If I didn't trust my father immensely, there was no way I would step one foot on those creepy concrete stairs. But I knew he would not lead me into danger, so down we went. My eyes adjusted, and as we neared the last step, I saw the door.

It was black. Simple looking. My dad reached into his pocket and pulled out a key. As he fit it into a keyhole – the only thing on the door – there was a click, and I almost gasped as a panel opened up. It was like a huge peephole with a computer screen on the other side.

My father leaned forward and there was a flash. I blinked, waiting for my vision to clear. When it did, I saw another flash, but this time I realized what was happening.

The machine was scanning his eyes. After that it was his palm, then there was a small shelf that slid out and he pressed his fingertip down onto a small pin.

Shut up! Well, I was definitely forming a complete picture of what "top secret" really meant. When all the identity confirmation was done, he reached for me, pulling me forward and positioning me in front of the screen, which had to tilt down to see me. I got the same treatment as my father, and as soon as my eyes were scanned, all of my details appeared on the screen. My full name, date of birth, address, phone number, and blood type.

Speaking of blood … I flinched at the prick of the pin, but it really didn't hurt too much. The anticipation was worse than the reality. Then it was Brad's turn, and when he was done the door finally slid open.

Stepping into the warm building, I could have cried with relief. After being cold for so long, the heat felt like a luxury. Dad wasted no time striding forward, along the plain hallway. He led us toward an elevator at the end of the hall. A man was sitting in a chair just in front of the silver doors, wearing a suit and dark glasses.

"Good morning, Sam," the guard greeted my father, acting like he was legit right out of a Will Smith movie.

My dad nodded in return, but no other words were exchanged. The guard didn't ask what Brad and I were doing here, and it felt slightly awkward as we all waited in silence for the elevator to arrive. How that was going to happen when there was no button on the outside to press was anyone's guess. I jumped when it dinged, and then the silver doors slid open. As we filed inside, I met Brad's eye. He pulled his "what the hell is going on here" face, and I returned it with one of my own.

I had no idea what was going on, outside of the fact that I'd had to run for my life tonight.

"You can talk." My father's somewhat amused voice startled me so much that I almost stumbled into the wall. Only Brad's arm, which shot out quickly, stopped me.

"What the freak is going on, Dad?" I asked as I straightened, finally letting my fear and anger loose.

His expression turned forlorn. The moment I saw that look, the rage coursing through me lessened. I never could stay mad at my parents, no matter how much they hurt me.

"I'm so sorry that we've kept you in the dark for so long," he said slowly. "I know you won't believe this, but we were preparing to tell you everything within the next few months – closer to the end of high school. We held off as long as we could, but you're eighteen now, and the responsibility of your world is something you will have to deal with."

Say what now? This was about me? *My world?*

"What does that mean?" Brad asked with bite to his words, his arm still wrapped around me. He probably sensed I needed the support.

My dad shot him a measured look. "It means that Maya is

not fully aware of her life and destiny. That her mother and I undertake this work here so that we can keep her as protected as possible. And that everything we feared has come to pass."

"Protected from what?" I stepped out from under Brad's arm and closer to my father. I wanted to see his face when he answered. Before he said anything though, there was another ding and the elevator stopped moving.

The doors opened. On the other side there was another security guard sitting in the same position as the one before. Same suit. Same glasses. Same greeting to my father.

"Good morning, Sam. They're waiting for you in conference room one."

My dad nodded, and we trailed after him along a short hall to a door. He ushered us through, and as I stepped to the other side, I gasped, far louder than I would have liked. But ... seriously. The room was huge and well lit, with what looked like at least thirty desks spread out around it. There were big screens flashing numbers and images, and despite the very early hour, people were everywhere. After so much quiet and dark, this was incredibly disconcerting to step into.

"Definitely government," Brad said with a snort. "Always the same décor, no matter what department you work in."

Since he occasionally got to visit his parents at work, he'd know better than me.

"Come on, your mom is waiting." My dad inclined his head to the right. "She wants to be there when you find out."

We ended up in a long glass-walled room. It was set up like a conference room: huge table, at least fifty chairs spread out around it. There were half a dozen people waiting at the far end from us.

I ran toward my mom; she stood to greet me. She was smaller than me, barely topping five foot. In my heels I had to bend down to wrap my arms around her.

"Little one," she said, squeezing me tightly. She was strong; her hugs always made me feel special. "I have been so worried about you."

My mom had no accent, having been tutored by Americans. Her parents had wanted her to integrate in every way possible while still maintaining their Japanese values. When we finally pulled apart, she led me to a chair next to the one she'd been sitting in. With a relieved sigh, I sank down and tried to shrug off everything that had happened that night.

Easier said than done, unfortunately. It was too big to just bury.

Brad and my father took two chairs on the opposite side of the table to us, and then my dad leaned forward. "Maya, it's time for you to learn what we do here," he said, before gesturing to an older, gray-haired man at the head of the table. "This is Peter Mattinson. He's the head of our division."

I examined Peter, wondering if I'd seen him at the house before. His face wasn't familiar, but there was no hiding he was government. From the well-fitted and expensive dark suit to the face completely devoid of all emotions, the high-up government officials always appeared the same: efficient, controlled, and sticklers for rules.

"It's nice to meet you, Ms. Lewis," Peter said smoothly. "As your father said, I'm the director of this sector. We deal in Daelighter and Human relations." He pressed his fingertips together in front of him like a steeple. "Sorry to drag you in here like this, Ms. Lewis, but there have been some breaches in our sector, so for your safety, there was no other option."

Okay, then... "What exactly does Daelighter and Human relations refer to?"

I didn't like the use of "human" in that title, because that made me think Daelighter was something non-human. There was a beat of silence. None of the other members of the team spoke either.

Peter straightened, his hands coming down to rest flat against the wood desk. "I can't say anything until we get clearance on your friend. You have already been vetted, but we are waiting on Mr. Thornton."

All eyes turned to Brad. His face was devoid of expression. He didn't seem surprised by what was going on. Meanwhile I thought I was going to burst not knowing what this sector of the government dealt with. And how it all involved me.

BRAD'S CLEARANCE took two hours. Apparently it had to be vetted by the Secretary of Defense or someone high up in the Oval Office. While we waited, I contacted Gracie, assuring her I was fine, and mentioned that my parents had gotten me and were taking me on their next trip. I could tell she thought this was strange, but after speaking with Mom and Dad, she seemed to accept it without too much fuss. My father suggested she take that holiday back home, with full pay, and for once she didn't argue with us.

During the wait I also had a chance to change my clothes – my parents luckily had some of my stuff in their cars. I was now in jeans, a white shirt that hung long over my pants, and my Converse. Casual with style, as I called it.

By the time we retook our place around the long table, I was munching on a sandwich and feeling somewhat more normal. "I can't believe you were so close to being taken," my mom said for the tenth time, before she reached out and grasped my hand tightly. "We should never have let it go so long without filling you in. We just wanted you to have a normal life for as long as possible."

Using my free hand, I shoved the last of the peanut butter bread in my mouth before leaning forward to hug her. "I know you were just looking out for me, and while it was really scary tonight, I'm happy to finally be learning more about your world..."

I was cut off when Peter breezed through the door announcing that Brad's clearance was through. Within thirty seconds, the rest of the suits were back as well, all of them taking the same seats as before.

"This is going to be difficult for you to believe, what we have to tell you," Peter started, his eyes locked on mine. "But ... aliens are real." He let that statement hang in the air for a beat. "They exist, and some of them walk among us on Earth."

It felt like I stared at him for ten hours while I tried to process my thoughts. I was a big fan of sci-fi. It was my go-to in books and movies, and while the concept of aliens was something Brad and I had discussed ad nauseum, I wasn't sure I'd ever actually believed they "walked among us." Hearing him confirm it so bluntly, the very real fact that we were not alone, hit me hard in the chest. I braced myself against the table, knuckles white as I clutched the side.

I knew my parents were watching me, but I couldn't bring myself to look away from the director. "Sources are murky," he continued, "on the date that Daelighters first started to explore our world, but we believe they have been coming here in peace for hundreds, if not thousands, of years."

In peace. Two of the best words I'd heard in a long time. But ... I'd been attacked. My father said we were in danger. Someone wasn't in on the "peace" thing.

"In 1875 we formed a mutually-beneficial treaty with the

Daelighters. They needed energy from Earth to power Overworld, their planet, and we needed something – a stone from their world – to calm Earth's unstable weather. It was a crisis point for both of us."

"That was over a hundred years ago," I said slowly. "What has changed now? Why are we being attacked? Do they want their stone back?"

My mother made a small sound next to me, and I turned to find her staring down at her hands.

"Yes," Peter replied, and it took me a beat to remember what he was answering.

"They want the stone back?" I breathed. "Why?"

He leaned closer to me, his dark eyes glinting in the illumination of the fluorescent lighting. "There is a rogue Daelighter, one who's managed to amass power and followers. He's the one leading this mission to get their stone back."

"Can we just give it to them?" I asked. Yes, I was stating the obvious, but it was my opinion that sometimes the government liked to "win" for the sake of it. "Do we know our weather is going to spiral out of control again? It might have stabilized on its own."

Surely they had a million scientists looking into this. I mean, it was the simplest and easiest of solutions.

He nodded. "There is a possibility that we could survive without the stone. But it's only a possibility. More importantly, we don't know where the stone is, even if we wanted to return it to them."

My face furrowed as I wrinkled my nose in his direction. "You don't know where it is? You lost it!"

Of course they would lose it. Morons.

Brad flashed me a grin from across the table, followed by an eye roll. Yeah, we weren't the biggest fans of the govern ment. They pretty much stole all of our parents' attention and time. All the while making really bad decisions for the average American citizen.

"We didn't lose it." Peter sounded slightly defensive. "Part of the initial security when the treaty was formed was that neither Daelighter nor human would know of its location. Except for four secret keepers. Human children chosen from a select group of one hundred families who were in on the initial treaty. All sworn to secrecy. All part of this sector of government."

My father spoke for the first time in ages: "My family was one of the originals who dealt with the treaty. So, when your mother was pregnant and they called out through our group for any who would have a child born in 1999, we answered the call."

I was on my feet now, staring between my father, mother, and Peter. "Explain everything to me right now," I bit out.

"You're one of the four secret keepers," my mom said in her soft voice, confirming my fears. "I never knew anything until I married your father, and then I had to be initiated into their world. You're the third keeper, born in Overworld, in the waters of House of Leights. Your blood holds energy that could lead the rogue Daelighters to the starslight stone, a powerful object, that in the wrong hand could destroy everything."

"House of Leights is one of the four lands of the Daelighter people," my father added.

I stumbled and almost fell back into my seat. Brad grabbed my hand, but I shook him off. "I need some air. I need..."

I dashed toward the door. I knew where the bathroom was, so I ended up in there, staring at myself in the mirror, breathing in deep gulps. The words *born in Overworld* continued to run through my head, over and over, taunting me with the fact that I was connected to these aliens – to aliens who were trying to kill me.

I was a secret keeper? That didn't feel right. It didn't make any sense to me. I was an ordinary eighteen-year-old girl. School and cheer and stupid boy drama. I had no qualifications to be part of something that could destroy Earth and ... Overworld. I couldn't even choose a damn college!

Panic clawed at my chest and I knew I was very close to hyperventilating. Scrabbling for the tap, I turned on the cold water, dropping my hands under the stream. Splashing my face a few times helped calm me.

I turned at a light knock against the door. "Maya, little one, can I come in?"

My mother would never think to barge in on me when I needed privacy. "Yeah, Mom, you can come in." I managed to keep my tumultuous feelings out of my voice.

She pushed the door open and crossed the room without making a single sound. She was so graceful, which I was thankful to inherit, even though I'd never achieve her level.

"I'm so sorry," she said as she reached my side. "You deserved to know the truth long ago, but I knew that the moment you did, your life would cease to be normal. I didn't want the same responsibilities for you that we have. Not until you absolutely had to deal with the reality."

I lowered my eyes, staring at my black Converse. "This is why you've been gone so much through my life. Dealing with these Daelighters?"

She took a moment to reply. I lifted my head, and when my eyes met hers she let out a sigh. "Yes. For the most part they exist among us in peace, but there are always incidents. We also deal with their business ventures and liaise when they cross over to Earth."

Sucking in more deep breaths, I forced myself not to act like a petulant teenager, even though I was angry that I'd missed out on so much of their lives because of these aliens. Mom must have seen some of that in my expression, because she hurried on to say: "Mostly, it was to keep you safe. Being here allowed us to be at the forefront of every piece of information coming in from Overworld. You're one of four secret keepers, and until today, only your father and I knew how special you are. We hid you in plain sight, as close to the headquarters of our sector as possible."

I should be appreciative of all the years I'd had being normal, but part of me felt like it had been *too* normal for me. How would I adjust to this new reality? I wasn't prepared for it. I couldn't handle it.

"You can handle this," my mom said, and I realized I'd spoken the last part out loud. "You're one of the strongest people I know. You're more than capable of handling anything that comes your way."

I wanted to believe that, but it sure as heck didn't feel that way right now. Maybe if I had more information, it would make more sense to me. "If I'm the third secret keeper, and they're after me now, that means the first two are..."

Please don't say dead.

5

———

Mom shook her head and immense relief hit me. "They're not dead," she told me. "But the rogue – Laous – has taken the secrets from their blood. Secrets that will lead him to you. We can't let that happen. We can't let the stone fall into his hands."

I was still far from being okay with everything I'd learned here today, but I felt some of my natural resilience reasserting itself.

"I'm ready to go back," I told my mom, and she linked her arm through mine.

We left the bathroom, rejoining the room of suits and my family. "So, what's the plan?" I asked the moment my butt hit the seat. "How are we going to stop him from getting his hands on me?"

Peter blinked, and it almost looked like I'd taken him by surprise. His forehead even crinkled slightly. "We're transferring you and your family to a more secure safe house. You'll be under the protection of very powerful Daelighters. Leaders of their houses."

I tried not to show how much that shook me, knowing I'd be seeing these Daelighters soon ... it was a lot. I couldn't even imagine what they looked like, I mean, surely they weren't little green men. They had to look like us. Otherwise they'd never blend in with the human population.

Peter was still talking: "...they're going to try and use your blood to find the final secret keeper. If we can find her first, we should be able to find the stone."

"And move it before this Laous gets his hands on it," I finished.

He nodded. "We'll move and protect it. The old way is flawed, as we've all come to realize, so it's time to rework the treaty and make it even more secure. But we need to find it first."

"Wouldn't her parents be part of this government organization? I know that it's secret and all, but couldn't you just round up all one hundred families and inform them of what has happened. She will come forward then..."

Peter nodded, but his expression wasn't as positive. "It's true that all secret keepers and their families are part of our government sector, but they were given the option to fall off the grid. To hide. Your family were the only ones to stay close and active. As for the others, we had only one way to track them, with a stone that was entrusted to the first secret keeper..."

"And Laous has it now?" I guessed.

He nodded, confirming my thoughts.

"How would you have found the first, then, if she fell off the grid?"

Probably all useless information, but I needed the entire picture. I wanted to know it all.

"I knew who the first was," my father said, startling me. I

was sad to see his eyes so tired and puffy. It had been a long night for us all. "I volunteered to hold that information, because I wanted to know if the first was compromised. If she was compromised, then I knew you would soon be after. Somehow, though, I missed the signs. We grew complacent..."

His voice broke. Peter quickly added, "All of the families were required to check in on occasion through a secure, encrypted phone line. But none made the last call."

Slumping back into my chair, I let this information roll over me. Movement from across the table caught my eye and I realized it was Brad, staring at me like he'd never seen me before. "Why did you let Brad hear all of this?" I asked, sounding disconnected. "Now he has no choice but to be part of this."

"They've seen him," Peter said simply. "He's been compromised. Until we can sort this situation out, it's safer for him to be part of it. He'll be going with you to the safe house."

I'm sorry, I mouthed to him, and some of the shock cleared from his face as he fiercely shook his head.

"I chose this," he said to me, ignoring everyone else. "You gave me the option to stay behind. This was my decision."

Yeah, but he'd had no idea what he was getting into. That sticking with me might turn out to be utterly life changing for him. I was pretty thankful, though, that Gracie hadn't been with me. She might go on to live a normal life, no matter what happened here.

Brad asked the next question: "Will I be able to talk to my parents, at least let them know I'm okay?"

"They've already been informed," the director told him as he got to his feet. "Your transport will be here in twenty minutes. Only a select few will know your new location. It's not going through the normal channels, so you should be safe there. I'll be in touch."

With those final words he left the room, not looking back. The other suits followed; none of them had spoken a word during the entire meeting, and I wondered what the point of them had been. Probably they were the ones behind the scenes organizing things.

When it was just my parents, Brad, and me, we all sat in silence. I was exhausted, scared, and confused, wondering if I'd stumbled into some sort of alternate reality. Or maybe I was dreaming.

Like I'd be that lucky.

"I owe you the hugest of apologies," my dad said to me. His eyes were red, and he seemed smaller than normal. "When the first call went out in our group, I was so proud that I had a child to provide for the cause. But that was before you were born, before I knew the vibrant, funny, clever child who should be free to go out into the world and leave her mark on it." He cleared his throat. "I'm sorry that I never took into consideration how it might affect you. Your life. It was selfish of me."

Pushing myself up, I moved around the table to hug him. "It's okay, Dad," I mumbled against his chest. "Things have been fine for the first eighteen years. I've had more than most kids get." And the truth was, I'd never felt "normal," I'd always been empty and searching. I'd thought it was because of my absent parents, but maybe it had been more to do with the world I was born in but never knew about.

As we went to leave, Dad stopped and spoke to a few of the suits. Brad wrapped an arm around me, offering comfort. When we started moving, he half-carried me all the way to the elevator. Once we were back on the street level, a black SUV –

waiting out the front – took us to a nearby airfield. A helicopter was already powered up and ready to go, blades rotating and sending strong air currents across the tarmac.

My father helped us in, handing us all noise-canceling headphones. The pilot, who I didn't recognize, took off as soon as we were buckled in. The chopper moved so fast that for a second I was afraid we were being chased, but there didn't look to be anyone on the ground below.

I'd never flown in a helicopter; it was far louder and rougher than I had expected. Eventually I got used to it, and watched with fascination as the city passed below. It was early morning, the sun rising in the sky, washing the world in low, golden light. I couldn't talk to my family without everyone hearing through the headsets we wore, but as familiar landmarks disappeared, I really wanted to ask if we'd ever see our home again. I literally had nothing except the clothes on my back and my bag that had two credit cards and my school ID in it.

That was it, like the rest of my identity had been wiped clean. Gone.

A hand wrapped around mine, and I lifted my chin to meet Brad's gaze. Seeing his familiar face, the boy I grew up with, who had been with me through so many of life's obstacles ... it made me feel a little better. Not everything was gone. I still had him. And my family.

I must have fallen asleep, my head against Brad's shoulder, only waking as we landed. Blinking to clear my vision, I tried to figure out where we were. The only things I could see were trees, and I was really hoping that this "safe house" wasn't like a tent or something. Nature and I, we were not exactly simpatico.

We had landed in an open area no bigger than a quarter of

a football field, the only break in the endless trees. We filed out quickly, and then before I could ask what we were doing out here, the metal beast lifted again and was gone over the trees in less than a minute, leaving the four of us standing there like morons.

"Please," I fake begged, hands in the prayer position, "please tell me this is not the safe house. You know how I feel about camping."

My mom tsked at me. "Maya, come now, you need to focus on right now and stop worrying about what you cannot control."

Her favorite mantra: do not waste energy on what you cannot control.

My father took a second to look around; he was clearly as confused as me. "I imagine they needed to land off the grid to leave no record of where we were dropped. No doubt someone else will be by soon to pick us up."

Bet right about now he was regretting leaving the finer details up to Peter.

After a few minutes of waiting, the four of us grew restless and started to walk. I didn't like being out in the open like this. Dad led us toward the closest trees. We stuck close together, stepping into the forest. It was very green, and it felt even colder than Washington, D.C. I had an open sweater on, which was barely keeping me warm.

The forest floor was quite dense in places, filled with messy undergrowth, and no doubt a ton of bugs. I was not a fan of bugs, one of my major reasons for declining every school trip that included camping. Hell, no. Not for me.

My mind flashed to my house and pool, to my soft mattress and organic cotton sheets. Gods, I missed my room. I was a total spoiled brat, but I'd really grown accustomed to the luxury of my life. It felt decidedly unfair that it had all been torn away from me now.

"How are they going to come for us?" I asked, following my father as he pushed further into the trees. "Can you see a path anywhere?"

He shook his head. "No path yet. I don't want to get too far from the drop-off point. Just trying to see if there is a main road somewhere close."

Great. I'd probably get bitten by something that would give me a rash and cause my arm to fall off. "Do you think those men who tried to take me were Daelighters?" I asked my father, gingerly following in his footsteps, trying not to cringe as I brushed against leaves and spiky plants. "Is there a way to easily identify a Daelighter?"

"They would have been Daelighters or humans recruited to Laous' cause," he replied. "And ... they look like human, but in general they're taller, more athletic, and quite intimidating. There's an 'other' feeling about them. Special."

Definitely humans chasing me, then. None of them had seemed particularly "special." My father circled us around the drop-off point, getting a little wider each time. I started to worry that we'd been dropped into the middle of nowhere because the government was cutting their losses. I'd seen enough movies to assume there was some truth to their actions when they needed to tie up loose ends.

Just as I finished that thought, my stomach flip-flopped and my chest got tight and tingly.

It was the feeling...

The feeling from the party and the alley where my attackers had been snatched away. Back in the government lair, I'd tried to explain to my parents what had happened. It

was clear they didn't quite believe me, but I knew the truth –
we'd been saved by my mystery guy.

I turned to stare out into the trees, spinning around to take
it all in. It took me longer than it should have, but I finally
found ... *them?* Three men stood in the shadow of a huge tree,
still and calm.

Stepping closer, I blinked more than once to make sure I
was seeing them clearly. Because they were so ... beautiful. All
of them were tall, with dark skin and long hair. None of them
were the guy from the party though, and I was just wondering
if my stomach feeling had been wrong ... when he stepped out
from behind the other three. Our eyes met and those feelings
in my body intensified. My body almost jerked forward. Just
like at the party, I wanted to move closer to him.

By this stage my father had noticed them, too. When a
relieved smile broke across his face, I figured we were dealing
with friends. He hurried forward, pausing before the tallest of
the four. *The one* – the guy from the party, who I was pretty
sure had saved my life in the alley. His hair, unlike the other
three, was short, dark, and cropped close to his head, save for a
few braids that hung past his shoulders. It also looked like one
side of his head was tattooed, the marks hard to clearly make
out under his hair. Maybe symbols or words.

It was too dark under this canopy for me to tell the color of
his eyes, but they looked light, contrasting beautifully to his
dark skin and hair.

"Chase from House of Leights," my father said, holding his
hand out for him to shake. "It's a pleasure to finally meet you.
Will you be leading us to the safe house?"

Chase acknowledged my father with a nod, but it felt as if
his eyes remained locked on me. I wanted to go forward and
take his hand as well, but something held me back. The pull I

already felt to him was not natural or normal. For someone who'd been pretty lackluster with most things in life, this sort of strong emotion was really freaking obvious.

House of Leights!

I realized then what my father had said. Even though an idiot would know that these four were "special," the reality took a moment to register fully. *Holyfreakingshit.* He was an alien, a Daelighter. Why were the good ones always gay, taken, or aliens? Seriously.

For a brief moment, I contemplated that he might evoke such feeling in me because of some sort of alien power, but the other three men at his sides, who were almost as stunningly handsome, did not make me feel anything except wariness.

There was something more about this Chase. And I wanted to panic about that. But I couldn't seem to produce that emotion around him. He was just ... calming.

Chase finally turned his gaze from me and I managed to suck in some deep breaths.

"We have to walk a small distance, then we can drive to the next destination," he said to my father.

That voice...

If Chase had been looking at me still, there would have been no way I could have hidden my reaction to his smooth, accented tone.

Seriously.

Seductive, sliding across my senses, filling my body with needs. I wasn't sure I'd ever felt this way, and since I'd never even talked to this guy...

"No worries. We just want to make sure Maya is safe," my dad said as he reached out a hand to me. I didn't want to take it. I didn't want to get closer to these Daelighters. None of them.

Liar...

With reluctance, I stepped through the undergrowth, shuddering as a huge ferny-looking plant tried to attack me. Chase's lips quirked as he watched me battle my plant-assailant, and eventually I made it to my father's side.

"This is Maya Lewis," he said. "She's the third secret keeper, the one from House of Leights. She's who we're here to protect."

His eyes were the greenest I'd ever seen, almost luminescent. "It's nice to meet you, Maya," he said, holding out a hand for me to take.

I didn't want to. If his voice affected me to the level where I *almost* moaned out loud, then his touch would probably kill me. Before it got awkward though, the other men stepped forward, distracting everyone. Chase shot me a slow smile, lowered his hand, and introduced the other men. "This is Jordo, Luci, and Manita." He pointed to each in turn. "They're here just as a precaution. We've lost track of Laous' movements, so we err on the side of safety."

I heard what he was saying, but most of my focus was on breathing and trying to stay calm. *We are not compatible species!* I needed to get myself under control. I refused to be *that* girl. The one who fell for the drop-dead gorgeous guy without knowing a single thing about him. He might be the biggest asshole ever, with fifteen wives and a penchant for beating them up when he was drunk.

"Are you ready to leave?" my father asked, and I snapped out of my own head, stepping back to where Brad and my mom were standing.

Chase nodded. "Stay close," he advised, then he moved forward into the trees. The other Daelighters fanned out around us, one going to the back, the other two to either side.

Chase led us further into the trees, and I found myself watching him closely, for no other reason than the way he moved through this forest was unlike anything I'd ever seen. He was at home there, like he'd lived in the jungle his whole life. I could have sworn that trees and plants even got out of his way as he walked.

Got out of his way...

That was brilliant. I just needed to walk close to Chase and I should avoid all branches and leaves. I hurried so I was right behind him – and my dad, who was at his side. It felt slightly dangerous being this close to him, but since I was finally free from leaves and plants attacking me, I could deal.

As an added bonus, I also got to eavesdrop on the conversation he was having with my father.

"Did you have any trouble on the way?" Chase asked. "We heard that Laous and some of the resistance were in your area, which was why we moved with haste."

My father's rumbly drawl sounded coarse against the smooth accent of the Daelighters. "Yes, Maya was almost taken. She managed to escape ... even though she's not sure how. Luckily we got to the government facility before anyone found her again."

I knew how ... even though no one had believed me. There was no doubt in my mind that my escape was all to do with Chase. As if he'd heard my thoughts, I was suddenly staring into those green, pearlescent eyes. *Not human.* Those eyes were definitely not like any human's.

Swallowing roughly, I reminded myself that breathing was not optional. "I'm glad Maya was not hurt," Chase said, holding my gaze for another moment before he turned back to my father. "She's very important."

Those words were a splash of cold water to the face,

reminding me that my life had literally just gone to hell, and that I was an idiot for lusting after an alien. These feelings had to be because of shock or something. That was the only thing that made sense.

Deciding it was better to brave the trees, I fell back to walk beside Brad. He leaned down close to me. "What's going on with you and alien dude?"

He said it very softly, but for all we knew they had super-sonic hearing. We really needed to find out more about them.

"What do you mean?" I muttered. *God, please don't let me have been obvious...*

"I've never seen you stare at anything – except your mom's cooking – like you're staring at him."

There was no way to stop the embarrassment I felt from flooding my face. Luckily, I tended to just get a little color in my cheeks when I blushed, not a full-on red, so it would not be hugely obvious. Except to Brad, who knew me very well.

"I have no idea what you're talking about," I finally said stiffly. "I'm just fascinated ... because they're not human."

He smirked, and it took all of my self-control not to smack him in the face. My mom followed Buddha's teachings. She was all about peace and love. Meditation. Unfortunately, not a lot of her daily practices translated to me. I had a temper that took some time to appear, but when it did, I was like a crazy little ninja, throwing and kicking and breaking things.

Let's just say I was working on it.

And Brad was pushing all of my buttons right now.

"Leave it," I bit out when he opened his mouth to say something more.

His grin grew wider, and I sucked in deeply, trying to calm myself. I thought I might blow when he leaned down again. "Just so you know, he looks at you in the exact same way." My stomach did that stupid flip-flopping motion again, and my chest felt like it might burst from all the feelings in there.

Brad tilted his head to the side, and I thought he looked a little sad. "Be careful of that one, Maiz. He's not human."

Like I was going to forget that anytime soon. But it didn't seem to matter to my hormones. They were on the Chase train, with no intention of getting off.

6

———

$\mathcal{I}$ was pretty fit from gymnastics and cheerleading, but apparently I was not hiking-through-the-forest fit. After thirty minutes my thighs and calves began to ache, and after an hour I was pretty much ready to just hand myself over to Laous. Anything to end the torture.

I'd grown numb to finding bugs on me, the itchy arms from brushing across tree sap and whatever else was on their leaves, the stumbling over exposed roots. Brad was doing a lot better, and he helped me out on more than one occasion. I also managed not to stare at Chase too much. Which was a win.

Eventually the trees cleared and we ended up on a long road. There was a car waiting for us, black and huge, like one of those old army vehicles. I was pretty sure they didn't make Hummers anymore, but this reminded me of that style of car a lot.

"It's specially designed to keep you safe," Chase told our group. "It's bullet and bombproof. Along with being resistant to a variety of Daelighter energies."

"What are Daelighter energies?" Brad asked, and I was

grateful he did, so I didn't have to show how interested I was in the answer to that.

Chase opened the doors for us first and we all climbed in, except the three Daelighters he'd been with. "They'll walk the rest of the way," he told me. "We don't trust transport like this."

Right. Walking was clearly their thing.

Once we were all buckled into the harnesses, Chase started the vehicle and with a rumbly roar we were off. He then answered Brad's question from before.

"There are four houses on Overworld. All of us have different energies and abilities. House of Leights is mine. We have energy derived from the trees in our land. Our powers correspond to that."

I could have guessed that by the way they moved through the forest. Another huge difference between us: he was one with the trees; I was one with my air-conditioned house. Eventually I was going to convince my body that he was off limits. Way off limits.

"House of Darken is a land of beasts and magic. Their powers are to do with nature as well – storms. They can control the lightning and winds. Bring about thunderstorms."

Beasts and magic? I really wanted to ask what sort of beasts they had. Every mythical creature I'd ever read about flashed through my mind, and I was more than a little intrigued to know more.

"House of Imperial is the keeper of the underworld. Volcanic in nature, their power controls fire. The cleanser of souls."

Keeper of the underworld? I was so not touching that one. Brad swung his head in my direction, eyes really wide. I lifted my shoulders in a shrug.

"And finally, House of Royale," Chase said. "They control

water, or as we call it, *legreto*. The energy which runs through the currents of legreto is powerful. It can shape worlds."

I knew he'd given us a basic, one-line description for powers that no doubt needed a ten-thousand-word essay, and I really wanted the essay, because that didn't seem like enough. I wanted to know more.

"And I was born in House of Leights?" I confirmed, my voice barely a whisper. "In the ... trees?"

I was in the back seat, on the opposite side to Chase, so he was able to turn his head and see me. "Yes, you were born in my sector of Overworld. My parents were there. I was also there as a ... teenager."

"You were there when I was born? Like in the same room?" Was that as weird as it felt to me?

Chase chuckled, and the sound was really nice. Too nice. *Focus.* "Not in the same room, but we were close by."

"How old are you?" Brad asked. "You don't seem that much older than us, but you said you were a teenager eighteen years ago."

Right, he had said that. He didn't look more than twenty.

Chase turned back to the road, even though it was still one long stretch of dirt. No obstacles to worry about. "Daelighters do not age as humans do. It's not slow and gradual, more like random bursts of growth. I'd guess in human years I'm around fifty. But on my world, I'm young."

Fifty!

"Daelighters also don't die of old age," my father cut in. "Not really. They age very slowly ... so slowly that technically they could live forever."

I had forgotten that my parents knew a lot about these aliens, having worked with them. My father's family had been part of it as well. The family business I'd never known about.

"You don't age?" My voice sounded a little raspy.

"Just very slowly, as your father said. But we can die from injury and there are a few diseases as well."

I was having trouble wrapping my head around that, but even in my shock, I didn't miss the exchange of a look between my father and Chase. My dad shook his head, answering whatever silent question had been asked, and I really wanted to know what it was. But I kind of felt like I might be at the end of my ability to process any new information right now.

I'd ask later.

After this I shut myself down and stared out the window, trying to ignore the consistent pull in my body to move closer to Chase. If I didn't sort myself out soon, I was going to be labeled a stalker.

At one point we entered a small town, which seemed to pass by in a blink, and then we were back on a forest road. I was about to ask how much longer, when he turned off the main road and drove into the trees. Our ride got very bumpy as we left the cleared path, but Chase easily maneuvered the huge vehicle. I couldn't believe the car fit, but somehow it got through.

Only ... were the trees moving out of his way? I knew I hadn't imagined that when we were walking. It was much more obvious now, because the car required a lot of room. Guess I was starting to understand the Leights powers.

It grew darker once we were under the canopy. I found myself pressing my face to the window, so I didn't miss anything. For the first time in a long time, there was a low level of excitement thrumming in my center. I was invested; I wanted to know everything. Despite the initial dangers I had faced, I couldn't be angry this was happening to me. It felt like my world had opened up so much, and it had only been a few hours.

Even with my vigilance in staring out the window, I totally missed the cabin until the car slowed and we pulled up in front of it. It blended into the environment in a way that was pretty darn impressive.

"It's protected by the land," Chase told us as he opened my door. "House of Leights' power is weaker on Earth, but I still have some pull here."

Yeah, I think we'd all noticed that. No doubt it was this power he'd used when he saved me and Brad in the alley. As everyone exited the vehicle, I struggled to unbuckle the complicated harness, and just when I was about to declare that the car was really nice and I might stay in here forever, Chase leaned in through the door – bending himself in half to fit – and in two swift movements had me free from my restraints.

He hadn't been this close to me before. I could feel energy running across his skin ... as crazy as that sounded. It was bringing every hair on my body to attention. Goosebumps broke out over my arms and a scent of pine and mint invaded my senses. Just like the leaf I'd found at the party. That very fresh smell of nature, mixed with man, created a heady sensation.

My chest heaved as he stepped back, lips parting to suck in air faster. He held out a hand to help me out, but I still couldn't bring myself to touch him. If I touched him, I was pretty sure everything inside of me would cease working, and I needed to retain some bodily function.

"Thank you," I said, deftly ignoring his outstretched hand to slide out on my own. "I appreciate your help."

A flash of white teeth; he grinned in the same lazy way he

had in the forest, like he knew exactly why I was avoiding him. These aliens did not lack confidence, but he wore his without an ounce of arrogance, and that was so seductive.

Chase released me from his magnetic pull by turning away. I sank back against the car for a moment, and Brad, who had just crossed around from the other side, winked and grinned at me. He was silently saying "Told you so." I bared my teeth at him in return, silently telling him "Shut your face or I will break it."

I might be small, but I'd never let that get in my way before.

My parents fell in on either side of me as we made our way toward the stairs that led up to the log style cabin. It looked small and cozy. Front porch, with three rustic, wooden railings, and the walls were layered logs.

As we stopped in front of the large inviting door to remove our shoes, my mom squeezed my hand. "How are you handling it all?" she asked, her face serious.

I shrugged. "Too soon to tell. I'm going to schedule some time for a breakdown soon, though."

My dad chuckled, his loud infectious laughter reminding me of home, of days before worry, of days before aliens. Sure, apparently the aliens had always been there, but I'd been in the dark about it ... and the saying "ignorance is bliss" had come from somewhere.

"That's my girl." My dad ruffled my hair gently. "I'm so very proud of how you're handling yourself. I promise that we will figure this out soon. You won't be a prisoner forever."

Fingers crossed. I was not ready to be caged, that was for sure.

Once our shoes were removed – a tradition my mother instilled in us – we stepped inside. The wood theme continued in here, the floor dark polished. From the entrance it seemed the long planks of wood ran all the way across the entire room.

My father shut the door behind us and I took in the enchanting scene. My favorite interior design style would never change – modern, minimalistic, with white and cream base, and colorful accessories – but there was something completely captivating about this little cottage in the woods.

It was light and open, high windows spanning across the entire living, dining, and kitchen area. The furniture and accessories were cream-colored, and they'd gone for those squishy, comfy styles. I especially liked the way there were no walls at all to separate rooms, just furniture used to create individual and unique spaces.

The couches surrounded a massive fireplace. The hearth was at least six feet wide, the stone of the flue running right up to the ceiling. Its accent, which was dark gray mixed with light creams, was a beautiful contrast to all the wood on the walls.

"Come in. Please, make yourself at home."

I startled, turning to find a Daelighter close to us – a woman. I studied her closely. It was easy to tell she wasn't human. She had the same otherworldly, supermodel look about her. Her skin glowed and eyes shimmered.

"My name is Star," she said, holding her hand out to me, shaking back her long dark hair. "From House of Darken."

I recalled Chase's very fast lesson on their world – Darken was the house with the power to control weather and beasts.

"It's very nice to meet you," I returned, gingerly taking her hand. I wasn't sure what I expected to happen, but thankfully there was nothing out of the ordinary when we touched.

"Emma and Callie will be down soon," she said, releasing her hold on me. "They're just freshening up after their training."

My eyes flicked to my father's and I wondered if I was supposed to know who these two women were.

"Secret keeper number one and two, in that order," he informed me. "They arrived at the safe house a few days ago. Oh, and just so you know, we won't be staying here long. We'll keep moving between safe zones until Laous is dealt with."

Because he could apparently track me no matter where I went. I guess they were just hoping it would take him a little time to find me again.

Star nodded, her smile fading away as a look of sadness entered her eyes. "Yes, we need to make sure he's brought to justice."

Her voice broke and she cleared her throat. I'd seen that look before. She'd lost someone recently.

"I'm sorry for your loss," I murmured.

She blinked a few times. "How did you know...?"

I shook my head, staring at my socks for a minute. "I guess I just recognized your expression ... my friend died last year." She had committed suicide. Katie had suffered from depression, but at that time, I'd thought she was doing okay. When I got the phone call from her parents, I'd refused to believe it. It took me days to come to terms with what happened.

I still thought about her all the time – the sassy girl with long blond hair and gorgeous blue eyes. Technically, she had everything going for her. But depression did not discriminate; it took whomever it wanted and held on for dear life. She had fought hard, but in the end, the battle was too large for her.

It hurt still.

"It was my brother," Star whispered, her almost navy eyes shiny. "He was killed fighting the resistance – members of the four houses that joined Laous' team. We're ferreting them out now, trying to determine how deep it goes in our houses."

Her brother. A lump formed in my throat because her face held untold levels of devastation. "I'm really sorry," I said, wishing there was something better I could say. The thought of losing Brad had tears springing to my eyes.

She nodded at me, swallowing hard. "Thank you, it's ... it's not getting easier. If anything, it's harder than ever, but we're moving forward for Marsil. He would have wanted us to keep fighting."

"We just need to make sure he's the only casualty." The masculine voice came from a hallway leading off the main living area. It was the voice of a rock star, deep rumbly tenors. He stepped out from the darkness, moving into the light where we were all standing.

Holy hell. Beautiful but deadly was exactly how I'd categorize him. His head was shaved, almost completely bald, which showcased his own set of dark red tattoos across one side of his head and down his neck. It looked like they were a similar style to Chase's, the same symbols. That had to be something to do with their houses.

"Daniel, overlord major of House of Imperial." Star introduced us. "He is bonded to Callie, the second secret keeper."

Okay, that was interesting.

"Was Callie born in House of Imperial?" I blurted out.

Daniel paused, tilting his head at me in a completely unhuman way. "Yes, she was. Why do you ask?"

Don't look at Chase. Don't look at Chase. "No reason." I shrugged in an attempt to act causal. "Just trying to piece all of the information together."

Information like ... was there a deeper reason I felt a connection to Chase? Callie and Daniel were bonded. She was born in his land...

"Ask all the questions you want," Star said to me, moving

forward to take a seat on a large one-seater chaise chair. "We have nothing else to do for the next few days until we receive word of where we move to next."

With a sigh, I sank down into the long couch. My parents and Brad joined me, all of us looking exhausted and ready to call it a day – despite the fact it was about 8 A.M.

"Thank you." I attempted a smile. "I have about a billion questions, but let's start with ... what's an overlord?"

Daniel answered: "We have a leadership system which is a mix of your human monarchy and military forces. The overlord major rules over his house, and there are four houses in total. If they have a mate or betrothed, she or he will also rule in supremacy. This title is passed through bloodlines, like a monarchy. Next in line is the overlord minor, then we have admiral major, admiral minor, and it continues down in a ranking system."

I waved toward his head. "So, the marks you wear, they're something to do with being an overlord?"

He nodded. "Yes, a true inheritor is born with the marks, but if there are none to inherit, the marks can be added once you're initiated."

So that means ... I turned toward the silent Chase, who was standing with one shoulder nudged into a nearby wall, observing everything. "Chase is an overlord m..."

"Minor," he filled in for me. "My parents are still alive and well. I'm next in line to House of Leights."

Great, he was a prince – kind of – too. Of course he was.

Star piped up then. "My father is the overlord of House of Darken, my oldest brother Lexen is the next in line. His draygone soul chose Emma as a mate."

My entire world ground to a halt, and I knew I must look crazy, trying to breathe and blink and not pass out. Someone started to talk but there was a roaring in my ears. Eventually, I held both hands up and whoever was talking stopped.

My voice was a breathless whisper: "Are you telling me that the first secret keeper is mated to an overlord of Darken. The second secret keeper to an overlord of Imperial. What? H-how?"

I was destined to be with Chase...

That had to explain why he affected me so greatly. I wasn't weak – it was beyond my control.

"Yes," Star said with a nod. "Both of them are bonded in a way which makes them true mates. A soul-deep bond. We believe it might have something to do with the timing of the secret keepers and overlord minors being born, like all of you were born in a similar year and under the same moon. Maybe the great gods thought this time the secret keepers needed extra security to keep them safe."

No! No! No! No! And hell no! I did not want that. Predestined bull. I controlled my own life. No one else had that right. Unable to stop myself, I looked up to meet glittering green eyes. Chase's expression was unreadable. He didn't look angry, but there was something there that told me he was as confused about this as I was. Neither of us said anything. He didn't confirm that he felt the same connection I did, and I wondered if it was mostly on my side.

"What's a draygone?" I heard Brad ask, and it was enough to pull me from my own head.

I looked down to find my hands clenched, nails biting into the soft flesh on my palms.

"It's like your dragon myth on Earth," Daniel offered. "Lexen can shift his form to a half-beast, half-Daelighter version."

Guess that explained the beasts. They had dragons ... no

big deal. And Lexen was like a ... werewolf but in dragon form. Also ... no big deal...

My breathing was increasing rapidly. I was going to embarrass myself if I didn't calm down soon. "I need a moment," I said, somehow keeping my voice even. "Is it okay if I step out onto the porch?"

My dad took a moment to look at Daniel and Chase, who were no doubt the authority here, being princes and all. Both of them nodded and I shot up in my chair. "Don't wander off," my dad warned me. "If you see anything weird at all, get back inside immediately."

I wasted no time bolting from the room. Brad half-rose from his chair but I shook my head at him. I really did need to be alone.

7
____

Running away to get some air was becoming a thing for me. The excitement I'd felt earlier in the car was fading away again under my panic. I was acting very bipolar in my emotions, freaked out one minute, excited the next. Seriously, how was I part of this Daelighter world? With true mates and bonding. I mean, who even used the words *mates* and *bonding*? This entire thing was too much like a fantasy novel for my liking.

I was not born on Earth!

Technically ... I was an alien? Even if I had human DNA? Wait ... was my DNA still human? I was born in House of Leights for a reason. They needed the secret keepers to be in fetus form for a reason, so that we could be born in the waters of Overworld. Which must have done something to us...

Rubbing at my temples, a headache was threatening to explode behind my eyes. It was just a light pounding now, but I recognized the signs from the few times I'd ended up with a migraine. Too much stress, teamed with no sleep, was taking its toll.

Light footsteps sounded behind me and I turned expecting it to be my mom. She was the only one who moved so stealthily, but instead it was another girl, who looked to be about my age. Her shoulder-length platinum-blond hair was the sort of color that most of my friends spent hundreds in the salon to achieve. Hers looked natural though.

"Oh, hey," she said, blinking a few times as if she'd just noticed me there. "I didn't expect anyone to be out here. I like to escape all the chaos on occasion."

Samesies, strange girl. Samesies.

As she stepped closer, we both examined each other.

"Hi," I said. "I'm Maya."

"Callie." She held her hand out to me.

A sliver of excitement had my stomach flipping. Not in the same way Chase affected me, but in the way that made me think this was someone who understood what I was going through.

"You're the second secret keeper," I said as we shook hands.

She smiled, turning her face from pretty into beautiful. She had a very Jennifer Lawrence look about her, and I could definitely see what had Daniel so enthralled. I hadn't missed the way his face softened when she was mentioned.

"Yes, and you're our third," she declared. "Emma is going to be very excited to meet you. She thinks the four of us have a destiny to be best friends and family. That we're all tied together."

She was blunt in an enchanting way. Like she wasn't sure how to hold a conversation without just saying everything she thought. But there was no malice in her words.

"This destiny business is getting kinda old, don't you think?"

A tendril of curtness crept into my tone, but she didn't

seem offended. She leaned back against the railing and observed me like I was some sort of science experiment. "What do you mean exactly? Being chosen as a secret keeper wasn't a destiny thing, it was just timing. Our families were one of the few in on the alien secret, and our mothers just happened to be pregnant at the right time. All four keepers had to be born in the same year."

Mimicking her pose, I leaned back, keeping a few feet between us. "I'm not talking about the secret keepers stuff, but that still could be destiny if you think about it. What if we were conceived at the exact right moment to fulfill this fate, blah, blah."

Callie chuckled, propping her feet out a little as she leaned further back. I noticed she was wearing black Converse, a mirror to mine that were by the door. She also wore a pair of jeans and a simple white shirt. We were actually twinning really hard right now, and for some stupid reason, that made me feel a bond with her more than any of the destiny crap.

She watched me closely, no doubt seeing the mess I was. "I'm going to guess that just like Emma, you had no idea about this world." Her unusual stormy-gray eyes narrowed on me. The way she was staring made me slightly uncomfortable. Like she was seeing too much.

"I knew nothing," I confirmed. "Which is kind of stupid considering my parents literally work in the government agency which deals with Daelighter and human relations. They said they were going to tell me soon, but that it was important to them that I live a normal life for as long as possible."

Shadows crossed Callie's face. "I spent my days moving every three to four months, living with my crazy mother who blamed aliens for everything that was wrong in the world. I would have liked a few years of normal life." She shook her head, a half-smile back on her face. "Turned out, aliens are the best thing that ever happened to me."

"Daniel?" I guessed.

Her face lit up like I'd handed her a limitless credit card and her own private plane, Christmas and birthday all wrapped into one huge moment. "Having someone like Daniel in my life ... there's no comparing it to anything else. Emma will tell you the same."

I snorted before I could stop the rude sound. She blinked at me, and then raised both eyebrows.

"Sorry..." I said quickly. "I just ... I'm not really down with this whole soul mate thing. I mean, does Daniel love you because of some stupid destiny? Or does he love you because of you?"

"I love her because of both," came the deep voice from across the porch. He'd clearly come in search of her and had heard the end of our conversation.

Despite the fact that he'd been answering my question, his eyes were all for Callie.

"That's the funny thing about fate," she said, moving toward him like she couldn't help herself. "Sometimes it knows better than we do about what is absolutely perfect for us. What will fulfill us. I don't care how Daniel and I found each other. All I care is that we did."

She pushed into his arms then, and as his lips gently brushed across her forehead, her eyes closed and the content-ment on her face...

Turning away, I stared out into the forest again, giving them a few moments' privacy. They were doing nothing but hugging and it still felt like such an intimate moment.

I could have that?

My inner voice, a part of me hidden deep down, the part which was never satisfied with any of the guys I'd ever dated, or with my life in general, made me wonder if I had been waiting for Chase.

"Oh. Em. Gee!" The shriek had me spinning around to find a pretty redhead heading in my direction. She was wearing a white shirt, black jeans with torn knees, and black Converse. What was this, the secret keepers' uniform?

She stopped right before me. "I'm so glad you're finally here," she said with excitement. "And you're totally beautiful, and tiny. Plus, I love your hair. I always wanted to get purple through mine, but it just wouldn't go as well with my red tone."

This had to be Emma, the one enthusiastic about us being one big happy family.

I smiled, and it didn't even feel forced. "It's nice to meet you," I told her with sincerity. Knowing that both of these girls had been through the same thing as me, sent relief through me. I felt less stressed all of a sudden.

"This is perfect..." Emma ran her hands through her long wavy hair, her blue eyes sparkling in happiness. "Now we just have to find the last secret keeper before that asshole Laous. Then the four of us will be a team."

I smiled again. How did these two make me like them so quickly? I'd never had that happen before.

Emma dropped back to lean against the rail next to me. She was taller than me by quite a few inches but wasn't as tall as Callie. I was feeling like a real shorty around all of these people. I mean, the men alone were at least a foot taller than me. Most of them even more.

"Were you a cheerleader, too?" I asked her randomly, wondering where all of her pep came from.

A deep masculine chuckle sent goosebumps over my skin, and I turned to find the second hottest guy I'd ever seen – tied with Daniel – stepping out through the open doorway. Chase was the hottest, but that was not something I was ready to deal with, so I'd go back to the newcomer.

Tall, dark-haired, with a face carved from the gods, and a huge, well-muscled body, he could have been the perfect man, but there was way too much scary there to ever interest me. His intensity, the way he moved in an almost animalistic way, I knew this had to be Lexen. Weredragon.

His chuckle faded off, and he stared at his girl in a way that almost made me blush. "Let's just say that Emma is not exactly athletically-inclined."

Holy hell. The chemistry between the two couples was explosive. Made sense now ... that feeling I got whenever I was near Chase. It was a lot, and I didn't know how to process it. Even worse, I had no real idea if it was the same for him or not. I didn't know him well enough to tell yet; he seemed to be good at hiding his emotions.

Emma distracted me when she sighed. "First Callie is a ninja who can climb ropes, kick ass, and enjoys jogging. And now I find out you're a cheerleader. Let me guess, you can do a dozen backflips and the splits."

I gave a half shrug as a small burst of laughter escaped from me. "You got me. I'm really into the gymnastics side of cheer."

She pouted so dramatically that everyone laughed. And I joined them, feeling like I was part of this world for the first time.

"I've been teaching Emma some self-defense," Callie added. She was no longer in Daniel's arms, but they were still very close to each other. "And she's helping me with my reading."

Emma beamed. "I'm a total bookworm, I love fantasy stories."

"I love to read," I told her. "Sci-fi for me. I've kind of fallen out of the habit in the last few years. Life got busy in high school, but I'd like to find time to start up again."

Her eyes and face lit up, and now she was the one with the credit card and private plane. "I have the best series for you to start with," she burst out. "Oh my God, I have at least six favorite fantasy worlds that are so good you'll never stop reading again. I can't wait to have a book friend to talk to."

Callie groaned. "Don't get her started. She will literally chat your ears off for hours about all the books."

"All the books," Emma chimed in, her smile lifting her cheeks high as she took no offense to Callie's scrunched-up face.

"You're not a reader?" I asked Callie.

She shrugged. "I can't really read. Words get all muddled when I stare at them. Letters move around. I'm probably just too stupid. But ... Emma is determined that I live in these cool worlds, so we've been trying to figure out a way to help me."

Emma left my side so she could throw an arm around Callie. It was clear they were great friends. I wondered how long they'd known each other.

"You're not stupid," Emma groused at her. "You need to stop saying that. You have dyslexia. It's an actual condition which makes reading hard for you." She turned to face me. "Callie is ultra-smart, seriously. She basically taught herself everything, and I'm pretty sure she did a better job than the hundreds of teachers I've had over the years."

Callie pushed her away gently, but there was a twinkle in

her eye. She adored Emma, and I got it. It was hard not to like her. She was funny, and quick-witted, and super-nice. Both of the secret keepers were. I felt like an outsider, the one who didn't know the jokes, who hadn't done the miles to earn her place yet. But a part of me wanted to stick around long enough that I became a true member of this group.

"One of my friends back home has dyslexia," I said to Callie. "She had to do a bunch of therapies, and they use a computer program to change tone and depth and color of letters. It helps her immensely. She told me it never really gets easy, but it does get easier." I quickly hurried to add, "And it definitely doesn't make you stupid. She gets better grades than me, if you're judging on that sort of thing."

When I got a chance, I would try to get Callie an e-reader. Just the simple change of black page and white writing had helped Denise. Also, different fonts could make a huge difference. There were lots of things we could try.

Callie smiled at me, her first real, proper smile. "Thank you. My mom was kind of a bitch. She put the word *stupid* in my head. Called me stupid almost daily. I need to break the habit."

Daniel pulled her back into his arms, fitting her spine to his front, and she let him support her. He leaned down and whispered into her ear, but I was too far away to hear his words. Whatever he said, though, made Callie very happy. Her eyes brightened.

Lucky chick.

"So, have they filled you in on what the plan is?" Emma drew my attention back to her. "I know you only just got here and everything, but time is of the essence."

I shook my head. "Just that we're to stay here for a day or so, then we're moving to another safe house. We have to keep moving while they're working on the tracking down Laous thing."

She rolled her eyes at me. "They never give us the entire story in one go, do they? We're not just passively running around while they deal with Laous. We're going to try and find the fourth secret keeper. We don't have the stone, which would have made it easy, but we have your blood. And the network. Which is more than Laous has."

Peter might have mentioned that, now that I thought about it. Trying not to freak out about people wanting to steal my blood, I asked, "What's a network?"

Lexen beat her to the explanation. "The network is the energy source of Overworld. Sort of like your sun, it runs through the world, giving it life and energy. It's especially strong in our sector."

"A sector is a country," Emma chimed in. "Unlike Earth, though, none of them travel to other countries. They can only come to Earth or stay in their house."

"It's forbidden to visit other sectors in Overworld," Lexen said. "It's also very dangerous. There are a lot of different species throughout the sectors. Most of them are not compatible with Daelighters."

Which meant they were not compatible with humans either. "So, this network is your sole source of energy?"

"Yes," Lexen told me. "It's almost like a grid crisscrossing under the land."

"Like ley lines," I said, the mental image clear in my head. "We did a study session in school about witchcraft and sorcery. They spoke of ley lines and using the energy of the Earth."

Callie nodded, seeming to know exactly what I was talking about. "Ley lines is how I think of them in my head too," she told me.

My natural curiosity about this new world was piquing again. "Can you communicate through the network? Can you find people? What does it do exactly?"

Lexen crossed his arms over the broad planes of his chest. "We're always connected, but when we tap in fully, we can use it sort of like a search engine. We can also communicate within the network, even over long distances. It's the closest thing Overworld has to cell phones."

"Clearly we'll have to go to Overworld to search for the fourth?" Made sense if that was where the network was.

Emma nodded. "Oh yeah, once we know the coast is clear to travel, we'll head to our second safe house, in House of Darken."

I must have gone very pale, because Emma reached out and patted me on the arm. "Seriously, I know exactly how you feel, but don't stress. It's beautiful there. Natural. And Overworld's energy will call to yours, since you were born there."

Callie stepped away from Daniel, not touching me, but seeming to offer comfort with her closer proximity. "You don't have to fear Overworld. I *have* to spend a certain amount of time in House of Imperial, because Laous tried to kill me ... and long story, I am now tied to Daniel and the land of my birth. But I don't think of it as a sacrifice. House of Imperial is more home to me than any place on Earth ever was."

"Laous tried to kill you?" I focused on that horrifying fact. "Remind me not to get captured."

A strong burst of gratitude for Chase lit up inside of me. If it wasn't for him, I'd be in Laous' hands right now. No doubt, as soon as that crazy creep got my blood, he'd kill me.

I could have been dead before the dawn of this day. Gone. Never to see the world, or my parents, or Brad, again. "Are you okay?" Emma's concerned question sounded like it was coming from very far away. My breathing started to come in and out in gasps.

"Maya!" Callie tried this time, but I couldn't focus on anything except the thought of my death and the knowledge that it could still happen, because Laous would not stop coming for me. Not until he got what he wanted.

8

"You all need to take a step back. She needs some space." The low voice, with its smooth accent and deep timbre, finally got through to me.

Chase appeared on the porch like magic and everything inside of me responded. Even in my half freaked-out state, the familiar jumping sensation was in my stomach ... the pull in my body. I wanted to move closer to him.

Emma and Callie exchanged a look, then they grabbed hold of their guys, gave me a wave, and disappeared back into the house. As more clarity returned, the first thing I felt was the ache in my hands. Glancing down, I realized I had them clenched on the railing, white knuckles standing out starkly.

"Do you want me to leave also?" Chase asked, exuding that amazing calm of his. It seeped into me, slowing the racing beat of my panicked pulse. "It can be hard to truly have privacy here in a shared house, but I'll keep them all away if you need."

"No," I stuttered out, not even giving myself time to think about it. "I don't want you to go."

That was the truth.

He didn't say anything more. He crossed the few feet between us, his strides long and even, before he leaned against the wooden rail. We stayed like that in silence for many long moments. "Are my parents worried?" I asked, staring down at the grain of the wood below.

"They are," he said gently. "I told them I'd check on you and that I'd get them if you weren't okay. Brad..." His jaw tightened. "Was a little harder to convince."

That didn't surprise me. Brad was probably freaking out just as much as me, but he'd still be worried and protective. He was a good guy.

Chase shifted slightly, and I surprised us both when I reached out and grabbed his arm. It was the first time we'd touched, and it hit me as hard as I expected. As the jolt of energy went through me, I yanked my hand back, and Chase made this low rumbling sound in his chest. It stirred something deep inside of me also, and I almost closed my eyes to try to hide my obvious reaction to his touch.

"S-sorry," I stuttered.

He held my eyes for a long moment, saying nothing. The energy flowed between us and I eventually had to wrench my gaze away, needing the relief from my strong emotions. As we both sank back against the railing again, I wondered if his heart was beating as fast as mine. More minutes ticked by, and he continued waiting with me. In silence. Eventually the warmth of the sun on my back, teamed with the icy breeze drifting in through the forest, returned some of my natural optimism.

"I didn't die," I said out loud. Needing to hear those words. "I. Did. Not. Die." Turning to Chase, I breathed deeply. "You saved my life ... thank you."

I had to tilt my head back to meet his gaze. God, he towered over me, and I wondered how we could ever be compatible with this sort of height difference. Seriously, get it together, fate. "Thank you for saving Brad and me when we were attacked. I wouldn't have made it to my parents without you."

His expression darkened; the furrowing of his brow turned his model good looks into something a little more intense, like the hot bad guy who was planning on taking over the world. "Those recruits of Laous' should not have gotten that close to you." He didn't waste time denying he was there, and I appreciated his honesty. "I lost track of you when you left the party. It took me longer than it should have to find your energy again."

He paused for a moment, shifting around to face me. "How did you know I was there? I wasn't that close to you."

Hmm, should I be as truthful as he was? I owed him that much. "From the moment I saw you at Mitchell's party, there was this energy in my body ... like sparks of adrenalin and confusion. I recognized that same sensation when we were in the alley."

That was the watered-down version. No need to tell him it was taking actual restraint to stop myself from touching him. His body went very still, and I was afraid of what he would say, so I hurriedly asked, "How exactly did you find me?"

His lips tilted up, and I decided then that his smile was one of the nicest things I'd ever seen. His lips were full and kissable, and there was the slightest of dimples in his right cheek. "Once I learned your name, it didn't take me long to figure out where you lived. Then, when I got the feel for your energy, I talked to the trees. You don't have many in your town, which is why I lost you a few times, but nature creeps into unexpected places. It's hard to hide completely."

"You talk to trees?" I deadpanned ... because I had no idea what sort of emotion I was supposed to be feeling right now.

His grin spread a little further. "On Earth we communicate in images mostly – it's easier, less open to interpretation."

I stared at him, trying to understand what he was saying. "How?" I stuttered out. How could that work? Trees didn't have brains, right? They couldn't send images to people. They were alive, of course, but in a different way to sentient beings. Still ... there was no denying that they got out of Chase's way when he needed more room. Which meant they had to understand what he wanted, to some extent.

Chase straightened and held out a hand to me. I stared at it for a longer-than-comfortable amount of time, and eventually placed my palm against his. I was expecting the jolt, so it didn't take me as much by surprise. But there was still no stopping the swirling and clashing of energy inside of me.

"I'll show you," he said, wrapping long masculine fingers around my hand. He might have said something more, but I was too focused on the sensation of his skin against mine. It wasn't the first time I'd held hands with a guy. I'd had multiple boyfriends and had been almost all the way to a homerun. I'd done everything before sex – something always held me back from the final deed. Maybe it was that even the most erotic of acts was almost negligible when compared to the simple feeling of holding Chase's hand. If I'd experienced even a small sliver of this with any of the guys I dated, I had no doubt there would have been no reticence on my part to give up my v-card.

"You feel it too, right?" The words were out before I could stop them. I'd cut him off before he could say it earlier, but I *needed* to know. Heat started to rise in my cheeks, but I stood my ground.

"I feel it," he said. "I'm not sure what we're supposed to do about it, especially right now, but from the first moment I heard your name, I knew you were going to be trouble."

Now, normally that phrasing would annoy me. Boys used it back home all the time, in an overtly discriminatory way. Like women who were strong and sure and confident were automatically "trouble." When, in reality, strong women were too much for those boys to handle.

But Chase didn't say it like that. He said it in a way that made me think that he knew I was going to disrupt his life, his emotions, the calm aura he possessed. I was going to shake up his peaceful existence, and that wasn't something he knew how to handle. But there was no indication that he wanted me to be anything less than what I was.

"Let's just deal with it one day at a time," I suggested. "We have some real life and death stuff going on. Not the best time to try and unravel whatever connection exists between the four secret keepers and the four overlords of the houses."

He shot me a half smile. "They told you about that?"

I shook my head. "Not in so many words, but I could deduce it from Emma and Lexen, and Callie and Daniel. Kind of made sense, especially with the ... pull ... I feel whenever you're around."

"Both couples had an immediate bond," Chase confirmed for me. "But when the others described it to me, I think it sounded less intense than ours. At least at the start. It grew stronger the longer they were together. Ours—"

"Is really hard to ignore," I finished for him.

He nodded. "Right from the first moment."

This. Was. Insane. But I needed to follow my advice – take it one day at a time.

At some point, Chase remembered the tree thing and started to walk again, only stopping long enough for me to pull my shoes on. He led me through a clearing and into a section of densely-packed trees. When we were surrounded by dark tree trunks, the cabin still visible in the distance, he stopped. "I'm going to need you to trust me," he said, releasing my hand.

Forcing myself not to mourn the loss of contact, I folded my arms across my chest, tucking my hands in under my armpits. "Think it might be a little early to throw the t-word around, especially considering you're not..."

I trailed off, wondering if I was about to make some sort of rude, derogatory statement.

"Human..." he said. "You're right, I'm not human, but our species are fairly compatible."

"I see that," I murmured.

Secret keeper one and two were making that very obvious.

"Am I completely human?" It was insane that I felt comfortable enough to ask Chase that when I hadn't been able to bring it up to my parents. "I mean, being born in your waters and on Overworld..."

Shadows washed over his face, only a few rays of light able to penetrate the canopy here. The trees were particularly dense in the part he'd taken me to.

"You're mostly human," he told me. "You have human DNA, but you're right, being born in the legreto of House of Leights, you inherited some of the energy of my land. The energy of the Galinta."

"What's a Galinta?" I asked, not sure if I was ready for the answer.

It's better to know. It had to be better to know.

"The Galinta are an ancient species of tree gods. They fill my house, making it very limited on any open land. They're sentient, and if they want, mobile. It's the power from them which allows me to merge into another form at times."

Tree gods? Merging into another form? Was he serious? "So … Lexen is a weredragon, and you're a weretree?"

I mean … why not, right?

Chase's eyes were laughing at me, even though his lips didn't smile. "I assume you're speaking of your werewolf lore, and if that is the case, then you're on the right track."

This was too much. I waited for the freak-out to hit me again, the need to run, but … it never came. I remained there, in the dark, with Chase.

"So, if I carry some of this energy from the Galinta, does that mean I will change into a tree?"

What would that even look like? All I could picture were those old Halloween costumes with the tree trunk you pulled down over your body, arms stuck out through holes in the side, legs through holes in the bottom, face through a cutout section of the trunk.

I almost laughed out loud at the mental image.

"You won't turn into a tree." Chase brought my attention back to him. "But you will have some advancements on regular humans. You'll have the same longevity as Daelighters. You can be killed by normal means – you're not resistant to bullets or anything. But if you don't suffer a life-ending injury or get one of the few diseases that can hurt us, you will live for many years longer than humans."

What. The. Frack?

Was he for real? "That's terrible!" I almost shouted. 'I'm

going to outlive all of my friends and family. I didn't sign up for that!"

Chase's hand came down onto my arm, and again he soothed the crazed emotions inside of me. "I understand. But you should know that there are certain foods from our world you can give to your family to lengthen their lives considerably – increase their good health."

His eyes bored into mine, and in those green-glass depths I found my calm again.

"If there have been secret keepers for over a hundred years, and we don't die, what happened to the ones before us? Or the ones before them."

I had so many questions. It felt like the moment I learned one thing, it only opened the door for a million more thoughts.

"There was only one set of keepers before you," Chase told me. "One of them – Callie's father, actually – was killed in an accident. The moment the line of four is broken, another four have to be brought in."

Right, made sense. Because one of us led to the next one. "Poor Callie," I said, my eyes drifting toward the porch, even though she was no longer there. "She said her mom was a horrible person, and her dad died."

Chase nodded. "Both secret keepers had it rough, in different ways. Emma's parents were killed by Laous in a fire."

Sounded like I'd been lucky to have the life I did. My parents were getting a huge hug when I went back inside. "I'm glad they've finally found happiness," I told him. Now we just had to make sure Laous didn't screw it all up for everyone.

Turning back to look into the forest, I asked: "What did you want to show me? The thing I need to trust you for?"

He reached forward and put his hand on a nearby tree

trunk. "Touch it," he said, inclining his head toward the rough bark.

I took a moment to observe the spot I was about to drop my hand. You know, just in case there was a spider, or ant, or thorny plant. Nature might be beautiful, but it was also deadly as hell. Just ask that girl who died last month from a parasite going into her brain after she ate some tropical fruit. The story had been all over the news. For a while there, I gave up fruit completely.

"You need to relax your mind." Chase's voice interrupted my thoughts, and with real effort, I managed to focus on the feel of the roughness under my hand. "Let nature take away the human stresses and allow you a sense of peace."

It should have been an impossible task. My mind had never been this full and confused in my life, but somehow, with his last instruction, I felt the tension drain from me. Tingles ran under my hand, tickling the palm, sending all the hairs on my arms up to attention. A part of me wanted to immediately wrench my hand away, because this was bordering on the weird again, but the stronger part was determined to learn everything I could. I needed to be prepared. Laous could have shown up on my doorstep a week ago and I would've had no idea what I was up against. That was not okay.

"Can you feel the energy?" Chase's smooth voice sent more goosebumps across my skin. "To me it feels familiar, but also ancient and beyond my understanding."

He nailed the description perfectly. I sensed, in a small sliver, the true enormity of nature. It had been here long before humans and would be here long after we'd all but destroyed this world. It had seen the rise and fall of every civilization, and it was still standing.

I felt completely insignificant. Like a speck of nothing.

"It's incredible," I breathed, unable to stop the tears from springing to my eyes. I'd never seen this beauty, and it had always been around me. How had I been so blind? I'd missed so much.

A warm weight pressed against my cheek, but I didn't open my eyes. I just let Chase rub his thumb across the planes of my face, dispelling the tears there, while I continued to *feel* everything.

"The trees on Earth are not like the Galinta," he said, voice low. "They long ago lost the ability to move and speak with words, but they can still communicate. They send messages to each other all day long. It's Earth's very own version of a network. And it's essential to the survival of your world."

"The same way your network is essential to your world?" I breathed.

"Yes..."

While I continued to explore this new connection with the world, he told me as much as he could about our two worlds. The reason for the treaty, how Overworld needed a permanent transporter, and how Earth had been having a lot of very serious weather activities, which calmed down once the stone was buried somewhere near the equator.

"Will I see this transporter?" I asked, finally opening my eyes.

The tears were long gone, and I felt at peace. "Yes," he confirmed. "It's how we'll all get back to Overworld when we move on from here."

We walked back to the cabin. I personally wanted to stay with the trees, feel that epic vastness a little longer, but people were going to notice us missing soon and start to worry. Each step away from the forest tugged at my heart, and I imagined not having to leave, being able to sleep amongst the gentle giants of the forest.

I never thought I'd want that ... but it was the truth. I was starting to see the trees in an entirely new light, and I definitely had Chase to thank for that.

9

———

My father was pacing near the doorway, and the moment I stepped inside he wrapped his arms around me. "What part of stay near the house did you misunderstand?" he said as he pulled away. He didn't sound angry, more like a combination of joking and upset.

"Sorry." I screwed my nose up as I shrugged. "Chase was trying to explain his tree thing to me, and we sort of needed to be among the trees for that to happen."

He didn't get a chance to reply, because I had a bone to pick with him. "When were you planning on telling me that I'm going to live for like a million years?" I was going to guess this was what that exchange of looks between my father and Chase had been in the car, after the overlord told us of Daelighters' longevity.

The conversation that had been going on in the background stopped, and then Brad was at my side in half a second, his long legs eating up the space between us.

"What did you just say?" he asked, somewhat breathlessly. His brown hair was even messier than usual, like he'd been running his hands through it a lot. I wondered if he'd been worried when I was outside.

"I - I..." I trailed off, not sure how to tell him that the plans we made as five year olds of being best friends for a thousand years might become an actual reality.

"The secret keepers receive energy from the houses they're born in," Emma piped up. She was on the single-seater couch, Callie squished in beside her. "Which means we'll live much longer than humans. Maybe even as long as the aliens in this room."

Lexen snorted but didn't comment. He just leveled a wolfish – *dragonish?* – sort of smile on Emma.

Brad's face went very solemn. "But ... Maya can't live forever if I don't. We made a pact when we were five." I wanted to laugh because we'd read each other's minds. Again.

Swallowing hard, I reached out and took his hands. "Chase says there are some special foods you can eat that will also extend your life."

"None of us know for sure how long the humans will live," Chase added, "but the previous secret keepers look no older than you all. And they're well over a hundred years."

Callie made a face from her spot on the couch. "I just can't believe my dad was sooo old. In the photos he looks twenty, at the most. It's hard to wrap my head around it. I wonder if he had kids and a life before he met Mom. I have so many unanswered questions."

Emma's eyes widened as she turned to her friend. "Oh my God, I never even thought of that. It's like Wonder Woman. Having to keep creating new identities to cover up the fact they don't age."

"That's what our government does," my dad said. "We

facilitate Daelighters integrating into our community. We help with identifying documents and the like."

After eighteen years of secrets, I finally understood their jobs. And they were so much cooler than I could have ever imagined. The theme song to *Men in Black* ran through my mind, and despite the fact that I had a target on my head, I still – mostly – loved this new reality.

"So ... this food?" Brad was single-minded when he wanted to be.

"We'll get you all started when we travel across to Overworld," Lexen told him. "Emma's guardians have been taking it with no issue, and they're already seeing some cell repair and rejuvenation."

Emma laughed. "You should see how excited Sara and Michael are. The grays are disappearing from their hair."

"Hard to believe that only forty-eight hours ago I believed humans were the top of the food chain." Brad shook his head. "Should have known ... those Roswell shows were very convincing."

Star, who had been quiet up until now, rose gracefully, crossing to us. She moved in close enough to nudge Brad, and he winked at her. *Okay, then.* Those two must have gotten to know each other while I was outside. Typical, he never could resist a pretty – stunningly pretty – face.

"Roswell and Area 51 is all smoke and mirrors," Star added. "We like to throw out some distractions so that you're all looking for little green men. That way, no one looks right under their nose."

"No one questions the weird and wonderful that exists right around them," my father confirmed.

I certainly never had. So, whatever they were doing worked.

Conversation died off then; everyone dispersed, back to what they'd been doing before we arrived. I was shown to a room with two twin beds. I would share with Brad because there weren't enough rooms to go around.

"Are you comfortable with this?" Chase asked, filling the doorway.

Brad raised an eyebrow at me but didn't comment. He wasn't one of those men who had to throw their dominance around all the time.

I smiled. Chase hadn't asked in a rude way. "Yep, it's no worries. Brad and I have been best friends since we were little."

My mom, who had just stepped out of the room next door, was now visible under Chase's arm. "They've had hundreds of sleepovers through the years," she confirmed. "We trust Brad."

I pouted. "You don't trust me?"

My mom just shook her head at me, that gentle smile tilting up her lips. "You, my little one, definitely need to be watched."

She had a point.

Chase still didn't look particularly happy, but he didn't say anything except, "There are some clothing and bathroom essentials in there." He pointed at the chesterfield closet. "We didn't know what you would have or need, but if you're missing anything, just let someone know and we'll get it for you."

Before I could even say thank you, he was gone. My mom took his place in the doorway, looking even tinier after Chase's large frame had taken up so much space. "It's only temporary." She wrung her hands, as she did when she was stressed. "I really am sorry you had to be thrown in like this." She shook her head with a rueful smile. "Would you believe I never knew a thing until I married Sam. They're forbidden from telling anyone, bar immediate family."

"Bet that came as a nice wedding surprise," I guessed, chuckling.

She let out a low laugh as well. "Yes, it was very difficult for me to understand. At first. But then I grew to love the Daelighters, their unique energy. The way they bring another element to our world. They truly add to it, rather than taking away."

"You've always had such a beautiful way of looking at the world, Konami," Brad said. He'd always called my parents by their first names. I did the same with his. "I'm really, definitely, a hundred percent this time going to try meditation one of these days."

She just smiled, knowing that Brad and I could not seem to stop long enough to even breathe deeply, no matter how many times she told us we needed to center ourselves.

Crossing to one of the beds, I sank down, completely exhausted. "Shower and then sleep," my mom told me. "I'll wake you if anything happens."

Her suggestion sounded like absolute bliss. I dragged my butt back up and walked to the closet. It was an antique, two-door monstrosity. Heavy wood frame, intricate filigree detailing, and so much excessive stuff going on. I was not a fan of antiques. Give me modern, sleek, and Hamptons any day.

There were two piles of clothes on a shelf inside, plus half a dozen shirts hanging up. One side was clearly for Brad – it was close to his pretty boy, Abercrombie style. The other was definitely more me. There was some brand-new underwear. Short denim skirts, high-waisted black shorts, a few cropped shirts, and some tanks.

Perfect.

I grabbed some underwear, what looked like a set of sleep shorts, and a matching tank. A bag of toiletries, which actually contained some makeup and everything, was on another shelf. Brad had one too, with a shaving kit and deodorant.

"They are thorough," I said as I emerged with my hands full. "Remind me to thank them."

Brad stepped in after me, going through his haul.

Moving out of the room, I leaned down and kissed my mom's cheek, and then entered the large bathroom across the hall. This was the one we would share with my parents, which was a pain, but at least everyone else had their own bathrooms. It could be worse.

It was older but very well maintained. A clawfoot tub dominated half the room, but I didn't have time or energy for a bath, so shower it was. Placing my new clothes on the bench next to the sink, I shucked off what I was wearing and padded across to the glass stall.

The water was hot, the pressure was good, and I spent at least fifteen minutes in there trying to clean the last twenty-four hours off me, finally emerging with clean hair, teeth, and skin – old makeup is so gross. I got dressed in the comfortable sleep clothes and was barely able to keep my eyes open as I stumbled into the bedroom. I'm not sure what happened after that, but I think I managed to dump my stuff in the corner before face-planting on the bed. Brad ruffled my hair – the ass – once or twice, as he left to shower.

Everything after that was blank.

I WAS PRETTY sure I didn't move a single muscle for the entire night. When I woke the next morning, there was dried drool on my face and my right fingers were numb from me lying on them. With a groan, I wiped my face and pulled myself up to sit. As more of my brain came online, yesterday's events hit me in a screaming rush. *Aliens. Secret Keepers. Starslight stones.*

And Chase.

Sweet alien babies, Chase was absolutely everything I both feared and craved.

For some reason, I hadn't expected the craving I felt for him to be as strong today, like maybe a full night of sleep would dull those hyped-up emotions. But, if anything, they felt stronger. Just knowing he was under the same roof as me ... in bed somewhere...

Give me strength. Resisting him was going to take a lot more effort than I was used to with guys.

"Dude, did yesterday actually happen?"

I swung toward the husky voice; Brad was half sitting as well, the sheets draped across his toned chest.

As our eyes locked, I shook my head, my face scrunched up. "I don't even know what to think about it all. I mean ... aliens. There are freaking aliens walking around Earth like they own the place."

Really, really hot aliens.

"I told you that dude in our science class wasn't human," Brad joked, swinging his legs off the side of the bed. "I'd like my apology now for the way you called me an asshole."

I shrugged, before rolling toward the side of the bed. When my feet hit the floor, I expected an icy chill, but the wood was warm. "You were an asshole. Hating on him because all the girls fell over themselves to talk to him. The alien thing was just an excuse for the frailty of your male ego."

Jesse Jameson had been really gorgeous and charismatic. *Maybe he was an alien after all.*

Brad snorted. "My ego is robust. A champion among champions."

I managed not to roll my eyes at him, and he laughed loudly.

"You want first shower?" He changed the subject.

I already knew he was starving, breakfast was the meal he carbo loaded at. And protein loaded. Not to mention grain, fat, and dairy. Basically, he could eat the ass end of a cow at breakfast and it barely even touched the sides. "You go first, I'm sure you're dying for food, and I always take longer than you."

He bounced out of bed, not denying the "dying for food" part. As he passed me, he dropped a kiss on my head, before grabbing his clothes and toiletries. When he was out of the room, I stretched out all of my limbs, and then headed to check out the clothing situation.

For some stupid reason, I wanted to look my best today.

By the time Brad was back in the room, his hair damp and spiked up in attractive disarray, I had decided on a denim skirt, black fitted long-sleeved shirt, and knee-high black socks. It was warm in the house, so unless we had to go outside, I wouldn't need a coat.

"See you downstairs," Brad said as he left for the second time. I gave him a wave, before making my way into the bathroom.

My shower was fast, and I was relieved to find a hair dryer in one of the vanity drawers. Once my long hair was dry and shining, I applied light makeup, focusing mainly on covering the dark circles under my eyes. Apparently not even eighteen hours or so of sleep was enough to recover from an almost kidnapping.

When I was done, I dropped my sleep clothes and makeup bag back in the room and made my way downstairs. My stomach was doing somersaults as I walked; when I reached the stairs, I actually paused at the top to try and get my shit together. Seriously. Why was I so nervous?

After a few calming breaths, I continued; I really did want to see everyone again. The *team* thing was starting to grow on me. When I made it to the main floor, I found everyone seated around a large, round dining table. It was just off the kitchen, in a nook I hadn't noticed yesterday. There were four banks of windows, surrounding it on all sides, and the sun streamed in giving the entire scene a very "picture perfect" look.

"You're awake!" Emma exclaimed, jumping to her feet. "How are you feeling today?"

"Much better, thank you," I said. "The sleep did wonders."

Her smile grew, and my nerves lessened as I hurried forward; the warmth of her greeting was exactly what I needed. What we all needed apparently, because conversations broke out, and everyone started reaching for the food that was piled in the center of the table.

As I took a seat next to Emma –Lexen was on her other side – I scanned the table. Star and Brad were sitting close to one set of windows, arguing about who could eat the most – Star seemed pretty sure she could eat him under the table. Callie and Daniel were filling their plates, their arms and hands grazing across each other as they moved. My parents were sipping coffee, smiling as they watched all of us, and Chase ... Chase was leaning back in his chair, broad shoulders spilling over either side of the backrest, his eyes firmly locked on me.

"Good morning," he said when our eyes met.

I swallowed roughly, because ... his voice was still the most seductive thing I'd ever heard.

"Morning," I mumbled, before clearing my throat. "How did you sleep?"

We were talking across the table, surrounded by people, but it almost felt like we were in our own little bubble. Whenever I looked at Chase, the rest of the world faded away.

"Chase insisted on taking guard duty last night," Lexen cut in. "Even though he didn't get any sleep the night before."

Concern for him pushed through all other emotions. He hadn't slept the night before because he'd been rescuing me. He must be exhausted.

"You should go and rest now," I insisted, half rising in my chair.

Chase leaned forward, moving in my direction. "I'm okay, I don't need a lot of sleep, and protecting ... the secret keepers is something I'm taking very seriously."

He'd hesitated over the words "secret keepers" and for a second I wondered if he'd been about to say something else.

"You should eat, Maya." Chase leaned onto his forearms, the fitted white shirt he wore, stretching across his biceps. "You need to build up your energy again after the events of last night."

Resisting the urge to fan my face, because it felt really hot in here all of a sudden, I leaned forward as well, and managed to look away from Chase long enough to examine the food-filled platter. It was piled with bread, cheese, and dips. Fruit of all colors were sliced and beautifully displayed. There was also a range of granola and pastries.

Not a piece of meat in sight, though, which would probably annoy Brad to no end. Except, for once, his focus was not on food. Star, the football tamer, had all of his attention.

I filled my plate, and as I bit into my first strawberry, followed by another, and then more of the fruit, I wondered if maybe this was alien food. Because it tasted so good. Like my senses were firing, and I was enjoying this meal more than any I'd had in a long time.

"So, are we planning on leaving today for Overworld?" Callie asked, having finished her breakfast already. "I think we should try to find the last secret keeper as soon as possible. Laous is going to be coming after Maya; he probably already knows where she is."

Daniel reached out, draping his arm across the back of her chair, pulling her closer. "We're waiting for the council to get back to us. Last time we talked to them, they advised us to stay put for another day. They think they have a lead on Laous again."

Emma snorted, before shaking her head. "The last lead went nowhere. Actually, it almost got us all killed, and it..." She broke off, before clearing her throat. "It did get Marsil killed. I don't think the council has our best interests at heart."

Lexen's face shuttered then; his brother's death was clearly too raw for him to even think about. But he did take the time to comfort his mate, holding her close to his chest, letting her bury her face against him. From the corner of my eye, I noticed Brad reach out and take Star's hand. He gave it a quick squeeze before letting go, and I actually thought that a little of the despair lining Star's features lessened. Her eyes were still drowning in sadness, though.

"We'll leave at first light tomorrow," Daniel decided. "The council has that long to deal with their sources. Not a moment more."

No one else argued, and I was relieved to think that we'd be moving on to the next part of the plan tomorrow. Even if it did mean I would soon be taking a trip to another world.

The rest of the day was way more relaxing than I would

have expected from a group being pursued by a homicidal maniac. For most of it, Emma was on the porch daybed, multiple novels spread out around her. After breakfast, I spent a few hours talking fantasy worlds with her. Callie joined in as well, and we switched it up to include favorite television shows and movies. Turned out all of us were into romance and fantasy – we had quite a lot in common.

After lunch, Emma started helping Callie with her reading, and because I didn't want to be a distraction, I decided to do a little exploring. I wasn't supposed to go far, but I felt an urge to step off the porch and move toward a pocket of trees close by. When no one called out to stop me, I grew braver, moving under the heavy canopy.

My eyes adjusted almost immediately, and this time, as I stepped between the giants, I let my hands brush across the rough bark and foliage. For once there was no fear of bugs. The normal discomfort I felt in nature was being eclipsed by a soul-deep peace.

When I was completely surrounded by wide trunks, my stomach started to flip and twirl. I slowed, only my head moving as I turned to find Chase.

"Up here."

His low voice drifted through the trees, and I tilted my head to find him sprawled across on a thick branch, his back against the truck. "Whoa," I murmured, blinking at how high up he was. He was like thirty feet in the air. "How are you going to get down from there?"

Without warning, he straightened and pushed off from the tree. A scream got caught in my throat as he dropped, my pulse pounding like a jackhammer in my veins. Chase landed with ease, barely making a sound as he straightened. "Not human, remember," he said with a wink.

I pressed a hand to my chest, trying to calm myself down. "I thought you were going to break your neck."

Chase laughed, throwing his head back just slightly, giving me a glimpse of the dark skin at the base of his throat. My fingers twitched then, like they were going to just reach out and touch him. *No!* My damn body had a mind of its own at the moment.

Chase took a step closer to me, his laughter dying off to be replaced by an intense look, those green eyes mesmerizing. "Why did you come into the forest?" he asked, still watching me closely. "Yesterday you seemed almost ... afraid of the trees."

It was hard to put into words why I was in here, mostly because I didn't really understand it myself. "I ... don't really know," I said. "Ever since you showed me the essence of nature, I've been drawn here. It feels right."

Just like standing with him did.

"It's getting harder to fight," I whispered, unsure if I was talking about the trees or Chase this time. Both, really.

He opened his mouth to say something, but before he could speak, a shout rang loudly through the trees. "Maya!"

Startled, I stumbled forward, tripping over an exposed root just in front of my shoes. Chase caught me with ease, holding on for an extended moment before righting me again. The moment our bare skins touched, ripples of energy crossed my skin, bringing all of the hairs to attention on my arms.

Another shout distracted us both. "Maya Anne Lewis, where are you?"

My father seriously had the worst timing known to human and alien.

"I better go to him before he brings in the full force of the

American government to search for me," I murmured, wishing I could just stay in the darkness with Chase.

I forced myself to turn away then, stomping my way back through the trees. I hadn't realized how far in we were, and by the time I reached the porch where my dad waited, most of my annoyance at his interruption had died off.

"Sorry," I said immediately, cutting him off. "I didn't realize I was so far away."

He just shook his head at me, before folding an arm around me. "Come on, your mom has prepared some food for everyone. Then it's straight to bed. We have an early start in the morning."

"Before dawn," Lexen confirmed as he came around the side of the cabin. "I'm not taking any chances of a Laous ambush."

Avoiding a Laous ambush was very high on my list of priorities, too.

That night, I ended up eating dinner with just Brad and my parents. The others were patrolling and packing. It was a quiet sort of meal, all of us wondering what tomorrow would bring. I went straight to bed after that, and despite the early hour, I fell asleep in an instant. With dreams of trees and the beautiful gods that walked among them keeping me company.

10

———

When I awoke, the room was still dark. My brain came online almost instantly, and even though I sensed it was too early for our departure, I knew there was no way I was going back to sleep. Not knowing we were heading to Overworld today. Soft breathing from the other bed told me that Brad was still sound asleep, and not wanting to wake him, I slid out of the bed and tiptoed across to the door. I pulled it back and waited for the creak – this was an old cabin, there had to be a creak, right? – but it swung in silently.

I closed it behind me and walked more freely along the hall. As I moved down the spiraling staircase, I wasn't sure what my plan was, but maybe a glass of water would help.

The light in the kitchen had been left on, and the clock on the wall read ... 3:56 A.M. Which meant it actually was pretty close to departure time. At that thought, I realized I was starving– it felt like a really bad idea to run for your life on an empty stomach.

The fridge was a huge, white, two-doored piece. Modern and sleek, it didn't really go with the dark wood kitchen, but it was one of my favorite pieces in here. Although the old wood burning oven, with freestanding legs, was a pretty cool second.

Opening up the fridge, cold air washed over me. There was fruit, some pre-made Greek salads, and a tray of sandwiches inside. I grabbed a salad sandwich and a bottle of water. I didn't have a plate, because there was no way I was opening cupboards to search for one, so I ate over the bench to catch any crumbs, sipping on my water in between bites. Just when I was about to shove the last piece in, a shuffling noise drew my attention. I froze, only my eyes moving as I stared toward one of the large bay windows near the front door. Curtains were across them, but as I continued to watch I could have sworn that a shadow darted across in front of it.

Just a flash of movement, then nothing else happened, but my unease did not disappear, my heart beating fast enough that I could hear the thundering in my ears. Swallowing, I slowly straightened, trying to decide if I would investigate or run back to my room to hide. *Come on, Maya, you can't let everyone be murdered.*

If there was something bad or dangerous out there, I needed to warn the people in this cabin. It was a no-brainer. Stepping forward, I ducked down and took an indirect route across the open floor, in case someone was peering through the curtain gaps. When there were only a few feet to go, I crawled, pressing myself to the wall below the front window.

Pausing for another mental pep talk, I prepared to stand, not even close to being ready for what I might see on the other side. Eventually, I convinced myself that if something was out there, sitting on the floor was not going to get rid of it. I eased up slowly, using the frame to stabilize myself. When I was standing right on the edge of the window, I flicked the side of the curtain an inch. Before it fell back into place, darkness was the only thing I saw. So I did it again.

Nothing...

Frustration pawed at me, so I sucked in a deep breath for courage, gave myself one final mental pep-talk, and then wrenched the curtain completely aside. I should have known better than to try to see into the darkness outside, especially with the backlight from the kitchen. The first thing I saw was my own reflection and I just managed to hold a scream back. Laughter bubbled up inside of me. My own reflection had almost caused me to pee myself.

That laughter died off as my night vision adjusted and I saw the second set of eyes ... and a face that was masculine, and scary, and creepy. He smiled, and even through the glass I heard the word "Gotcha." This time, there was no holding back my screams, and it felt like three seconds later I was surrounded by half-naked men. In any other circumstance I would be thanking my lucky stars and searching for dollar bills to shove into their shorts...

This wasn't the time for that, though.

"What happened, Maya?" Lexen had me by the shoulders, spinning me around and pulling me from the window. I was out of his hands in seconds, and I knew exactly who held me now.

Chase. My stomach was flipping all over the place. "There's a man outside," I gasped out. My body felt cold as shock kicked in.

Lexen and Daniel were out of the cabin in a flash. Chase didn't leave me. Shivers were rocking through me, and they weren't all about fear. I tried not to think about the way his arms were wrapped around me ... bare skin pressing against mine ... tingles racing across my skin.

Crazy guy. Creepy window peeper.

Those words should have been a distraction, along with the icy wind sweeping in through the now-open front door. But all I could see and smell and feel was Chase.

"What happened?" Emma's frantic voice was enough to bring me back to the reality of our situation.

With more reluctance than I would like to admit to, I pulled away from Chase and turned to the two pajama-clad females standing across from me. Emma's hair was wild, curls and frizz springing out in a million directions. Her eyes were only half-open despite the clarity and fear in her tone, and I knew she'd been pulled right from a dead sleep.

Callie, on the other hand, looked very put together, hair straight and brushed, eyes alert, expression hard.

"I came down for a snack, and while I was eating a shadow moved across the window," I said in a rush. "I couldn't let you all be murdered in your sleep, so I crept over and peeked out." His face flashed across my mind and I almost let out a small whimper. "It was the creepiest face, just standing on the other side, peering in. He ... he said 'gotcha' when he saw me."

Chase's expression turned stormy as he crossed his arms, and I tried really hard not to notice all of the muscles standing out. He wore a pair of shorts only, and the cold didn't seem to be bothering him. Meanwhile I was covered in goosebumps – which had a little to do with the chill and a lot to do with him.

I mean ... how did someone that tall build so much muscle? Brad would be jealous as anything. It took serious effort and dedication for him to keep his muscle mass up, and he wasn't even as tall as Chase.

The fact that Laous was probably outside preparing to kidnap and kill us all, and I was in here obsessing over muscles, was a little worrying. Maybe it was the shock.

Yeah, that made sense.

Emma moved close to me, face drawn. "You were so brave! Thanks for giving us the heads-up. It has to be Laous ... or one of his minions."

"This was why I was so worried yesterday. I knew he'd find us fast," Callie bit out. She looked pretty relaxed and casual, but I noticed her clenched fists. She was not as calm as she was portraying.

"What does Laous look like?" I asked.

"He's built like a barrel, round middle, scrawny arms and legs," Emma said with a snort of laughter.

Callie added some more description. "Creepy dark eyes and slicked-back dark hair. Has the same marks on his head as Daniel, but his are fake, of course."

There had been a flash of red I'd seen on his head. I was pretty sure. *Ah, crapfuckshit.*

"I think it was him." Real fear crept into my voice. "He found me in less than twenty-four hours. With that stone, he's going to be able to find me no matter where I go. I can't put you all in danger. I need to separate from you."

"No!" Emma gasped, holding onto my forearm. "We're a team, we'll figure this out together. It's not just you he wants, it's all of us. He seems to think that we might still be needed for something in the end, something required to find or unlock the stone."

Callie shook her head as well. "You don't have to deal with this alone. Just because you're next in line doesn't mean this is your problem. Emma is right, we're a team."

I could feel Chase's gaze on me. I wanted so badly to turn to him, but I didn't. When the girls said we were a team, they meant the three of us. They might have their soul mates, but as of right now I did not.

"It feels as if I've known you two forever," I said, my usual filters gone. "This entire situation is insane, but I believe what you're saying. We're a team. I feel a bond to you both, stronger than any I've ever had, even with friends I've known my entire life."

Except for Brad.

"If you think about it, we've known each other since before we were born." Callie's eyes were very shiny. "I've never had a family, but from the moment I saw Emma ... and now you, Maya, I've felt like I was home. I'm not letting go of it for anything."

Emma nodded, her eyes also sprinkled with tears. "Sisters from another mister. The four of us are bonded. It's a simple fact."

Sometimes the simplest of facts are the ones that can change a life.

Lexen and Daniel returned to their very worried girl-friends, both of them looking windswept and pissed off. "Nothing," Lexen growled. "He managed to give us the slip, but there was definitely an energy trail."

Daniel nodded. "House of Imperial is easy for me to pick up, but then it just cut off. Like he managed to disappear into thin air."

A sound broke through the early morning silence then, a weird whomping noise, and as it moved closer it grew more familiar. It wasn't until my father rushed down the stairs, dressing gown flapping open over his sleep clothes, shouting: "Helicopter!" that I realized what it was.

Really should have clued in quicker, since we'd flown in one recently.

The Daelighter men and my dad all moved toward the front door. Emma and Callie pressed close to Lexen and

Daniel. I hung back. Chase stayed near my side, but we didn't touch.

"How the fuck did he get a helicopter?" Daniel was growling, his arms winding protectively around Callie.

"Your council said some members of our government are compromised," my dad bit out. "Which means he'll have access to all sorts of our technology. The breach is not in my immediate division, or it doesn't seem to be. But there's no doubt that branches of Daelighter relations have gone rogue."

"He's working with humans?" Emma snorted. "His entire aim was to separate Daelighters from the 'grubbers,' wasn't it?"

Grubbers. Got to love a good old-fashioned insult.

"He'll use any means to ensure he finds the damn stone," Daniel said darkly. "My uncle is desperate, and deadly when cornered. He wants the power of the stone, and he'll stop at nothing to get it. He's already killed my father to put his entire plan into motion."

No doubt I was gaping at him, at least for a beat before I managed to pull myself together. Laous was his uncle and he'd killed his father? The guy was a freaking lunatic. Poor Daniel.

"We have to move now," Lexen said. He was out on the porch, face turned toward the fading thrum of a helicopter. "Take only what you need. The rest we'll figure out when we get back home. It's time to get back to House of Darken and see if we can find this fourth secret keeper before Laous. We have to make sure that stone is moved, and she's hidden where no one will ever find her."

No one argued. We all hurried back inside. As we moved toward the stairs, my father wrapped one arm around me. I could feel his worry in the extra tight squeeze. "I will fix this for you," he promised me. "Now, go and wake Brad. You know he could sleep through an earthquake. I'll get your mother."

He went up the stairs, taking them two at a time. I was about to follow when my stomach did some flip-flops. I spun to find Chase standing at the base of the stairs.

"Are you okay?" His low, accented words sent trills of energy over my body. I was a puppet to this alien. It was like he held every string I possessed and could move me to his will.

Nope. All the nopes. I refused to puppet myself for a man. I needed to get this under control.

Crossing my arms, I took a step back. Chase's eyes followed me, but he didn't move, allowing me to keep my newfound need for personal space. "I'm ... I have no idea. I'm definitely not fine, but I've had about forty-eight hours to adjust to this life. In that time I've been chased, almost kidnapped, took an elevator to a secret government agency, found out my parents work with aliens, found out that there were aliens period, flown in a helicopter..." I trailed off breathlessly.

The intensity in his glittery green gaze was too much. I wanted to squeeze my eyes closed, but instead I settled for dropping my gaze.

"You don't have to pretend," Chase said, and my head swung up, because for a second, I thought he was talking about me "faking" my disinterest. "It's okay to say that you need a minute to wrap your head around it." Okay, phew, he wasn't talking about *that*. "Lexen and Daniel, they're my best friends – have been since we were young – but if you let them, they will bulldoze you over. They push when it's not always needed."

There was a snort of amusement from behind us, and I turned to find Lexen in the doorway, bag slung over his shoulder. "We all have our strengths and weaknesses." He raised an eyebrow. "Chase keeps too much inside. He's not the easiest of Daelighters to read, but he's solid. He will always have your back, and it's impossible to bulldoze him over. So don't let him talk shit like we've ever been able to force him into anything."

I didn't need Lexen to tell me that. There was something innately strong about Chase, as immovable as nature itself. Just like the trees, he would remain long after everything else was gone. I felt safer with him than I had with anyone in my life, and considering the short time I'd known him, that had to be magic.

"I'm really glad you're all on my side in this war," I told them both. "I'm looking forward to seeing the four of you together ... whenever the last one shows up."

I'd learned there were four of these muscled, gorgeous, overbearing overlords. The fourth, from House of Royale, was going to meet us in Overworld.

"Xander is like Chase," Lexen said with a smirk. "You think they're the laidback ones in the group, and for the most part they are, but if you rile them up, their wrath is the thing of legends."

I was torn between wanting to see that and knowing it would probably scare the crap out of me. "Well, I better go and grab my things," I finally said, reluctant to leave.

I forced myself not to look back as I walked up the stairs. Even though I could feel eyes burning a hole in my back. At the top of the landing I practically ran to the room I'd shared with Brad, slamming the door open. It hit the wall with a bang, but Brad just snored a few times, rolling over. I threw myself onto his bed, body-slamming him as hard as I could.

"Seriously, how could you sleep through that?" I asked, half across him, which was not always the best thing to do to a guy first thing in the morning. I quickly scurried off before he woke up fully.

"Piss off, Maiz," he mumbled, throwing a pillow at me.

Standing beside his bed, I reached down and shook him. "Get your lazy ass up right now, we have a situation. The psycho Daelighter who's trying to end the treaty was outside. I was face to face with him, so now we have to bail."

To his credit, he managed to pull himself half up in the bed, blankets pooling around his lap. "What? He was here?" A few more rapid blinks and the dots connected in his brain. His gaze grew more focused. "Are you okay?"

With a nod, I moved to open the closet. There were two large canvas bags on the floor, probably what they brought our stuff in to begin with. I grabbed one and shoved in the spare clothes. I left out one set to wear, grabbing the bag of toiletries and dashing into the bathroom. It was empty, thankfully; I could hear my parents across the hall packing. There was no time for a shower, so I quickly got dressed in jeans and a black pullover sweater, brushed my teeth, and applied light makeup: mascara, bit of concealer, and some blush. I needed the armor today.

By the time I was back in our room, Brad had started to pack as well.

"I'll meet you downstairs," I said, dropping my PJs and the toiletries in my bag before hauling it over my shoulder.

He nodded. "Yep, I'll be right down. Just got to brush my teeth."

He was wearing the same basic outfit as me. His hoodie was gray, and he looked good for someone who'd been yanked out of bed in the early hours of the morning. I envied men and their ability to run fingers through their hair and give it a disheveled charm.

They didn't know how lucky they were.

When I was almost out the door, he said, "You need to be more careful."

I spun, not sure what he meant by that statement. Was this about Chase again? Lifting one eyebrow in his direction, I waited for him to continue.

"The deeper you get into this world, the harder it is going to be to get out. I can't lose you. It's team Brad and Maiz forever. You made a promise."

He had a smile on his face, but there was an undercurrent of seriousness as well. I took an extra second to think about what I was going to say, mostly because my immediate reaction was anger. Teams supported each other, they didn't hold one another back because they were scared. But I did understand where he was coming from. The friend he knew and loved was no longer the same. I had changed, my history had changed, and he could feel me slipping away.

I stepped closer to him, softening my expression. "Of course we're a team, Brad. There will never be a friend in my life like you. But we've always known our paths would divert away from each other. Like if we went to different colleges. The key is to make sure we always find our way back." I also felt it was time for us to bring a few new members into our team. But I didn't mention that.

I left before he could say anything more. He no doubt was going to point out that living on different worlds was a far cry from different colleges, and right now, I wasn't ready to hear that. By the time I got downstairs, almost everyone was waiting in the living area, including my parents. I gave my mom a hug before joining the main group. They all had the exact same bags as me over their shoulders, and the only one talking was Callie.

"Coffee. Me. Now." A note of crazy entered her tone. "You can't make me leave without it."

Daniel smiled – all women needed to get themselves a

man who smiled at them like that. He reached across to a small shelf in the kitchen and pulled down a travel mug. With a wink, he handed it to her. "Just how you like it."

Callie screeched and leapt for it, her focus on the cup.

Emma let out a relieved, exaggerated sigh. "For a second there I thought they were going to make us travel with an uncaffeinated Callie."

"Better to take our chances with Laous," Lexen agreed.

Both of them laughed when Callie flipped them off. She then took a long sip of her coffee. Her expression turned dreamy and she cradled the mug with both hands like it was precious. "I'd respond, but I'm busy right now with something far more important," she said smugly.

"It's nice that you all haven't let the stress kill your humor." I snorted out a laugh. "Most people wouldn't even be able to tell that we're running for our lives."

Emma shrugged and waved her hand toward me. "It's laugh or cry, and Lexen says his dragon will disown him if he cries."

"Dragon," I murmured. "Not sure I'll ever get used to that one."

Brad was down the stairs now, and I was surprised to see Star cross from the door to greet him. The pair exchanged some words I couldn't hear, and I had to blink a few times as she patted his arm. What was going on there? Seriously though, he better not break her heart, because something told me Lexen would break his entire body if he did. Or Star would. She seemed like she could take care of herself.

Lexen, Daniel, and Chase – who I was sort of avoiding, but also keeping an eye on because I couldn't help myself – all moved toward the front door. Dad kept one arm wrapped tightly around Mom's shoulders as he followed.

"We're going to move out now," Lexen told us. "I've had my father arrange transport and some decoy cars. We're going to have to split up: the secret keepers are going to be in one car with the overlords, the second vehicle is for everyone else. We'll be moving fast without delay, so as soon as I open these doors, you get your shoes on, and then you move. Do not speak until you're in the car. Understood?"

Everyone nodded, and I caught an unhappy look on my father's and Brad's faces. My mom just untangled herself and moved in her gentle way toward me. "Stay safe, my little one." She hugged me close, and I breathed in her familiar scent. She liked to wear rosewater.

"You too." I sniffed. "Stay safe and I love you."

My dad waited for a hug, stepping in after my mom pulled away. We exchanged words of love, as I did with Brad, and then it was time to go. Emma held a hand out to me and I hurried across to her. The heavy weight of my bag lifted off my shoulder and I spun to find Chase with it in his hands. "You'll move faster without it," he said simply, sliding it on the same arm as his bag.

I didn't protest because there was no time, and he was right. Lexen also had Emma's bag, but Callie still had her own. "I have control issues," she said when she noticed me looking. "Daniel had no idea what he was getting himself into when he tied our souls together."

Um, I'm sorry, what? She'd said that she was tied to Daniel and his land, but I never thought it was an actual, literal thing.

She waved at me, her eyes creasing with humor at my no doubt stunned expression. "Another story for another day. For now, all you need to know is that I *have* to be around him and House of Imperial for a certain amount of time, or my soul fades away. Too much time apart and I'll die."

"I own her soul," Daniel added with a smirk, and she swatted him.

Emma leaned in close to me, her hand still holding mine. "They're the real-life Hades and Persephone." She let out a dreamy sigh, and a happy sort of feeling flipped in my chest.

I always had been a sucker for romance and a happily ever after. I just felt like life should follow the same path as the movies. You can go through lots of shit, bad times, grief, but eventually you got your happy ending. It was only fair.

Lexen opened the door then, distracting us all. *Go time.*

I almost broke his rule and laughed when I got out onto the porch. Because there were three pairs of black Converse sitting there, and it took us a minute to figure out which belonged to who. Luckily, all of us had different size feet. Callie had the biggest at size nine. Emma's were eight, and mine were seven. Cascading, just like our heights.

The three overlords led the group; my father and Brad brought up the rear. I was just wondering where the cars were when four appeared in the distance. They cruised in through the trees, taking the same path – or lack thereof – that Chase had.

When they were about ten feet from us, they stopped and the drivers of the first two jumped out and opened the doors. Callie, Emma, and I were ushered into the wide back seat of the first car. Daniel took the driver's seat, Chase the passenger, and Lexen got in the back. I turned to see my parents filing into the second black, unmarked, SUV. Once they were inside, the tint was so dark that I couldn't tell who was sitting where.

No time was wasted, all four cars took off, somehow not hitting any trees, and then we were moving far too quickly for my liking. Chase turned: "Don't worry, my father is in the second vehicle, making sure the trees get out of our way."

For some strange reason, I wished I had seen his dad. It would have been nice to glimpse the Daelighter who raised Chase.

"Your dad might be chatting with Chase's dad," Emma whispered in my ear, giving me a wink.

I just stared back at her, because she was probably right. It felt weird, but at the same time it was my dad's job to liaise with Daelighters. He should be fine. I also felt better knowing there was a powerful overlord in with them, protecting them.

The moment we were out of the trees and back on the main dirt road, I strained to hear a helicopter. Knowing Laous might be above somewhere, with a massive machine gun, ready to blow us all away, was giving me heart palpitations.

"Do you guys have weapons?" I asked. "Like guns or grenades or ... anything?"

"Nope," Daniel said from the driver's seat. "Daelighters don't use human weapons. We're more inclined to use our own energy, the network, and the specific powers of our house to fight."

Which was great, except right now Laous *was* using human technology, and I felt like we should as well if we wanted to stand a chance against him.

"Don't worry about Laous," Lexen added. "He won't risk hurting the secret keepers. Not until he gets what he wants from you. That's why I requested vehicles with the darkest tint. He won't know for sure who's in which car, and we need him to be confused enough that he hesitates."

My hands were clenched tightly, which I didn't even realize until Emma reached out to grab one, and Callie grabbed the other. The three of us clung to each other while Daniel practiced some racecar driving maneuvers.

"Don't worry," Callie said, trying to sound cheerful. "Dan

can take a Lambo around a corner at eighty miles an hour. He'll get us there in one piece."

I really wasn't reassured by that, but at least I knew it wasn't his first time driving a car. At these speeds over dirt roads, our odds of surviving felt like they were on shaky grounds.

And now, more than ever, I really wanted to live. I was about to go to an alien world. That was not something I could miss.

11

———————

*W*e made it through the first section of the trees without an issue. I didn't relax in all that time though; I wouldn't relax at all until we were a hundred percent safe. There was too much at stake here, and the thought that something was going to jump out at us from nowhere had me on edge.

Daniel was living up to Callie's confidence in him, barely braking as he swung around corners, spraying up dirt and rocks in his wake. I spent my time stressing, sweating, and turning to check my parents' car was right behind us. The final two cars, which must have been filled with Daelighters, were bringing up the rear.

I was just turning to face the front when Chase barked out: "Brace yourself." It was so unlike his normal cool and collected tone that my fear spiked immediately, and I leaned forward to try and see what we were bracing for. The road looked empty; we were on a straight, with trees on either side.

Chase hit the button to lower his window, leaning out. When he was half out of the car, I had to stop myself from reaching out and pulling him back in. What he was doing looked like a good way to get himself killed.

Leaning forward further, I kept one eye on him, and one on the road. Something caught my eye through the front windshield ... like a heat haze hovering over the road. But it was cold here, so that couldn't be right.

"What is that?" Emma asked, her voice higher pitched than normal.

Lexen leaned over the seat, staring forward. "He's set up a transport barrier," he snarled. "That asshole is trying to take us out using the barrier."

"What happens if we hit it?" I asked, not sure I really wanted to know the answer.

I was already picturing us crashing into it and ending up squished into a small box of metal.

"It will transport everything that hits it to another location," Daniel told us, hands firm on the wheel as we continued to fly toward the barrier. "Same technology as our transporter between Earth and Overworld, but less permanent. It will disappear as soon as we go through it."

"Shouldn't we stop?" Callie asked then, her tone suggesting we were idiots for still driving.

"If we stop, he's going to have someone waiting to take us out," Lexen said shortly. "This is going to be one of those double-sided traps."

"There are fifty Daelighters in the forest," Chase confirmed, his voice faint because he was still out the window. "The trees are telling me."

I loved trees. Seriously. How had I been living my life without them?

"You got the barrier, Chase?" Lexen sounded relaxed, which felt wrong in this sort of situation. What the hell could

Chase do from the car? Unless he was getting the trees to do something.

"Trees on Earth can't move, right?" Emma looked between the front and back. "Just communicate in a limited way?"

That's right, he'd told me that.

"The trees can't move, but Chase can," Daniel said, which seemed to satisfy Emma. But I still had no idea what that meant.

Both of my legs were bouncing so hard now that it almost felt like my chair was shaking. That might also be because Emma and Callie were jumping around as much as me. My eyes remained locked on the broad back hanging out the window. *What was Chase doing?*

I was watching him so closely that I noticed the moment his shoulders broadened out, filling almost every spare space in the window, and ... was he getting taller? It felt like even more of him than usual was hanging out of the car, while the same amount was still inside.

Something brown flicked across the front of the wind-shield, drawing my attention briefly. It flicked back and forth a few times before I figured out what I was seeing. *Vines?* Where did the vines come from? The trees here weren't exactly the viney sort. Mostly they were tall redwoods, their foliage high in the sky. The vines whipped in front of our car again, disappearing when they dropped below the window level. When they reappeared, they were wrapped around and carrying a large tree trunk.

"What in the world?" I breathed, trying to understand. Was this Chase? Was he commanding those vines somehow? The log flung forward with force and speed, smashing against the barrier. The moment it hit, the barrier shimmered and the log disappeared.

That's when everything clicked into place for me. Chase was not commanding those vines ... he *was* them. Somehow he was shooting the long tendrils from his body – something I couldn't actually see to confirm because of his positioning out the window. *Unbelievable.*

We sped through the section of road where the barrier had been and dozens of beings poured in from the trees. But we were moving too fast for any of them to do more than be flung off around us. Chase remained out the window, his vines cracking Daelighters in the head as we passed them. When the coast was clear, he finally returned to his seat and I let out a deep breath. By the time he was seated, his body had returned to its normal, perfect shape. Any resemblance to a tree was gone.

"We have company on the way," he told us, turning around. "They're closing in on us." His gaze lingered on my face for a moment. "Are you okay?" His voice was low, thrumming in the energy between us.

I nodded a few times, swallowing hard. "Yes, thanks to you." I was spilling all my feels, uncaring that we were in the middle of a group. "You saved us." He had saved me again.

His eyes ran across my face, like he was trying to determine if I was freaking out because of what he'd just done. I smiled. There was nothing Chase could do that would make him unattractive to me, certainly nothing to do with his abilities. If he was an asshole, that would be a deal breaker, but he wasn't. None of them were. I mean, I knew there were bad Daelighters – cough, Laous, cough, cough – but the ones in this car were keepers. If humans knew these sorts of "aliens" walked among us, there would be fewer movies with little green men and more with hot gods that everyone wanted to be bonded with.

The sounds of engines revving distracted me, and Chase's

gaze shifted up and over my head, looking out the back window. I turned then too, to check on my family. *Shit.* Behind the three SUVs, a bunch of motorbikes had appeared.

"Get down low," Lexen growled, before he turned to face the back window.

Dark clouds washed across the previously very blue sky in a rush, and I realized that Lexen didn't need an open window; he was fine just where he was. The rumble of thunder started competing with the roar of motorcycles, pretty much deafening all around. Callie put her hand on the back of my head then, forcing me to lean forward with them. "I thought Lexen had a dragon power," I whispered, my chin resting on my knees. Luckily I was flexible from cheer.

"Lexen has multiple skills," Emma murmured back, pride very evident in her tone. "He has the normal House of Darken powers, which include electrical storms, weather manipulations, and cool shit like that. And he also does the dragon thing."

"Six more coming through the right," Chase noted, his voice faint enough that I knew he was back out the window again.

"This is ridiculous," Emma griped. "If we're going to be stuck in this world, dealing with this sort of power and such, we should have been given some ourselves." She let out a huff of air. "Well, I suppose Callie did get some, but the rest of us..."

I shifted my head around the other way to meet Callie's eyes. "What power did you get?"

She gave a strained grin. "When Daniel tied our souls together, the bonding shared his power with me. I can shoot out a burst of flame ... like the heat of a volcano."

Unbelievable. No doubt I was going to say that a few more times before this day was over.

"So, all Daelighters have these skills, right? Differing between the houses they're born in?"

I heard multiple noes from the car.

"All Daelighters have a very small level of power," Emma explained. "But only those born in the overlords' bloodlines have the strong gifts. Mostly because they're more closely connected to the network. Able to use more of its power."

"Yep," Callie confirmed. "On Earth, ninety percent of Daelighters are almost as useless as humans. We're just lucky to be in this car with some of the most powerful dudes in both worlds."

Daniel chuckled, even though it sounded a little strained. "I love your way with words, Cal."

She shrugged, which he couldn't see. "Call it like I see it."

Our car lurched, skidding across the dirt, and I had to lift my head to check on my parents. Emma and Callie followed my movements, and I wondered if they instantly regretted it as much as I did. We were surrounded on all sides by dark-helmeted, leather-clad, motorbike riding people. There were at least twenty, and that didn't include the ones already taken out by strikes of lightning, tree branches, and bursts of fire.

The fire was sporadic, because Daniel was focusing on evasive driving, but as soon as Callie got a view of those trying to attack us, she let out a low rumble of anger and lowered her window. She took in a few deep breaths, and then the air around her started to heat. If there hadn't been a breeze of cool air coming in from hers and Daniel's open windows, I would have been sweating up a storm.

Flames flew from her hands. They missed the riders close by, crashing into some of the trees. Fire engulfed those trunks and branches, which startled at least three riders enough that they lost control and crashed. My heart tightened at the sight of the trees burning, and I sensed a new tension in Chase that hadn't been there until now. He had felt it, too. The trees should not have to burn because of humans with an inability to understand that everything wasn't theirs for the taking.

"You can hit them, Callie," Lexen growled, turning back to focus on his storm in the dark sky above. Lightning was zapping Daelighters. "They're trying to kill and kidnap you."

She shook her head, words bursting from her. "I can't take another life, not unless there is no other choice. I'm ... I'm sorry, I just can't."

"We understand," Emma soothed. "Don't we, Lexen?" That was muttered through gritted teeth. He didn't say anything, but he did reach forward and pat Callie on the shoulder.

My parents' car was rocketing along behind us, but it looked like there was only one black vehicle behind it. Had we lost the other one somewhere along the way? "Do you think Laous is on one of the motorbikes?" Callie yelled as she blasted another patch of trees.

"Are you guys going to start a huge forest fire?" I cut in before anyone could answer her. I just couldn't handle the trees suffering any longer.

Chase swung around then, his gaze so intense that I couldn't breathe. I wasn't sure what that look meant, but whatever it was, the emotion was strong. "I won't let the fire spread," he told me, and I acknowledged that with a nod.

Callie had her hands back in the car now, staring down at them. "I don't want to kill people, but I should have realized, after being in House of Leights, that trees are as important as people."

"Aim for their bikes," I suggested. "Light them up enough that they have time to jump off before it blows up."

She tilted her head in my direction, her eyes a stormier

gray than I had ever seen them. "I think I better just keep my power to myself until I can figure out what my hard lines are. Hesitating in these situations can get us all killed, and right now, I'm unsure of everything."

She sounded so devastated; I really felt for her. These were not the sort of decisions we should be making at eighteen, or ever, but here we were, in a life-or-death situation.

Three motorbikes swerved into the path a few yards ahead of us. Two of them revved up their engines and let their bikes fly forward toward our cars. At the last minute, they bailed, which left us in the path of two riderless bikes.

Vines whipped out of nowhere and slammed against the out of control bikes, knocking them off to the side. "There are too many of them," Emma cried as more bikes appeared beside us. "No matter how many times the guys knock them down, they're back again with the same numbers."

As if to prove her right, something hit the car with force, sending it skidding to the side. This was followed by multiple bangs as our tires popped. We flew out of control and I let out a low gasp, planting my legs and bracing myself as the car started to flip, over and over, at least five times, finally stopping on the edge of the tree line, on its side.

I let out a groan, pressing the numb strip across my chest where the seatbelt was cutting into me. I quickly moved my arms and legs, satisfied that I wasn't seriously injured.

"Everyone okay?" I called out. Callie, Emma, and I had been wearing seatbelts, but I was pretty sure none of the guys were. Especially not after they started using their gifts.

"I'm fine, just a few bruises," Emma said.

"Same," Callie added.

"I'm fine," came from Daniel.

I held my breath, only releasing it when Chase said, "I'm fine, no injuries."

"Lexen...?" Emma called, fear in her voice.

"Don't worry about me, baby girl." His reply was immediate. And he sounded perfectly fine.

A low familiar whomping sound echoed around the cabin of the car, and the moment it registered all of us scrambled to free ourselves. I tried to get the seatbelt off, which was hard because all of my weight was pressing it down, making it almost impossible to unclick.

I struggled for about eight seconds before Chase was there. He leaned in, using one arm to lift me while the other unbuckled my belt. Lexen did the same for Emma. Callie managed to free herself on her own, and she climbed forward to help Daniel with the front windshield.

As I collapsed against Chase, he wrapped his palm around my face, thumb brushing along my cheek. A sting followed its wake, and when he pulled back I saw the blood. I blinked, lifting a hand to press to the cut. "I didn't realize I got hurt," I said. "Is it bad?"

He shook his head. "It's not bad, just a small scrape." The hand still wrapped around my face tightened minutely before he gentled it again. His eyes were darker than usual, almost gray.

"Is there something else?" I asked, unsure.

He shook his head. "I just don't like seeing you hurt. It's testing my control. And I'm usually very good at remaining calm in crisis situations."

A low rumble shook him, and I had a firsthand view of his gift when he spun around and pushed both of his hands forward. I sucked in deeply as the very hands that had just held me started to lengthen, shooting out as vines.

The glass shattered when the vines hit the front wind-shield, which I knew took a hell of a lot of force to do. Daniel kicked out the remaining glass, and then we crawled through one by one. The black-clad motorbiking assholes were surrounding us, of course, and the sound of the helicopter was extra loud now, wind whipping through the trees and grass to hit us.

"My parents?" I asked, looking around for them.

Lexen, who was maneuvering himself in front of Emma, said, "They kept going. Chila, Chase's father, will get them to safety."

He would have been as worried about them as I was. His baby sister had been in that car; no wonder he'd continued to stare out the back window. He'd already lost one brother to this war. No doubt he was going to do everything in his power to make sure there were no other casualties.

I was going to do the same. My family had to remain safe. I would not entertain any other options.

12

———

"If you send the three humans across, no one else will get hurt." The muffled threat came from a helmeted asshole nearby. Yep, it was time for the big curse words to come out. I was pissed.

"Screw you, dickbag, I would rather eat shit and die than go anywhere with you."

Emma snorted quietly to my right.

"I get sweary when I'm mad," I told her back.

Heat washed down my spine; it was such a sudden burst of warmth that I immediately stepped away, afraid my butt was about to catch on fire or something. Swiveling toward it, I let out a whimpering sound. It wasn't my butt on fire, it was Callie and Daniel. Literally ... literally on freaking fire.

"That's normal, right?" My voice was still whimpering.

Chase took a step closer to me, angling his body across mine. "They're fine. This is their power." He started to change then, growing larger. "You three need to get out of here before Laous arrives. He's always two steps ahead of us, knowing

139

exactly what powers to use to counter ours. We can't risk him getting his hands on you."

"It has to be the starslight stone," Lexen added. "It's a huge asset for him."

"All those years I carried the necklace," Emma groaned. "Why did I never get awesome powers? I could have saved my family. Stupid ability to never get hurt enough to bleed on it."

Lexen, who was keeping a close eye on the men surrounding us, let out a rumble. "The fact you never got hurt is a very good thing, Em. I'm eternally grateful for that."

Her eyes went soft and dreamy, but before she could say anything, Lexen continued, "I can get the girls out of here," he said. "But I'm going to need a little space." His voice was deep ... graveled. All the guys were rocking a husky voice at the moment, and that could only mean one thing. They were about to throw down.

Emma held out her hand to me, and with reluctance, I turned away from Chase. Staring at her for the first time since we left the car, I blinked at the blood running down the side of her face. "Are you okay?" I gasped.

She nodded, patting at her cheek. "I hit my head when we rolled, but I'm fine."

No wonder Lexen sounded like he was ten shades of pissed. Seeing Emma like that was making me angry enough to want to start throwing punches.

Laous' guys around us were pushing forward while still leaving us with a decent amount of space. Like they were waiting for Laous.

We had to get out of here.

A shimmer washed over Lexen and I gave him my full attention. He dropped his head back and lifted both arms to either side of him.

"This is his draygone form," Emma murmured.

I found myself pressing back, instinctively searching for Chase. A quick glance over my shoulder told me that he hadn't changed forms fully yet. He still looked the same, just larger, with a slight wood texture to his skin. As I touched him, I expected him to move, but he remained a solid wall against my spine. The warmth of his body cut through the chilly air, and that tingle of energy between us was in full effect.

His long arm wrapped around the front of me, pressing against my hip as he held me in place. I would have closed my eyes – the sensations were that good – but there was no way I was missing seeing Lexen's final form. He was covered in white light, like someone had him in a spotlight, and a combination of ice and heat flowed over him. In a blink, wings sprouted from his back, huge and black, spanning out ten feet on either side. His skin darkened and took on a scaly texture. His body grew bigger, until he was almost twice his normal size; somehow, his clothes stretched with him. The white light running across him slowly died off at that point.

Holy mother of all that is holy...

Chase was pretty much holding me up now. That arm he'd wrapped around to rest at my hip kept my legs from collapsing under me. "He just ... where ... what?"

This was not something my human brain could comprehend. There were realities in this world, laws – things followed certain cosmic truths – and right now, Lexen was breaking all of those.

"You know my form changes like his, right?" Chase sounded slightly worried, and I realized how rude I was being. Daelighters were different to me, and different was okay. I needed to embrace it.

Spinning in Chase's arms, I faced him. We were so close

that the front of our bodies almost touched. I tilted my head back to see his face clearly. "I know you change, and it doesn't bother me at all. It's just shocking, because I've never seen anything like this before. But I don't fear you." My voice grew stronger. "I am not disgusted or upset. I actually think Daelighters are amazing, and I'm a little jealous that I only have my regular old human abilities." I lifted my hand and placed it on his chest. I needed to touch him. "I'm ready to see your other form, whenever you're ready to show me."

He cupped my face again, brushing his thumb over my cheek in gentle sweeps. "I was not prepared for you," he murmured. "I thought I was. I watched my brothers go through it with Emma and Callie ... but I didn't think it would be the same for me. In Leights, the Galinta choose our mates. But something far greater is at work here."

I wanted to ask what he meant about the trees choosing, but there was no more time. Lexen was flapping his wings hard, sending up plumes of dirt and debris into the eyes of the guards around us. The helicopter, visible just over the tree line, was closing in fast. Laous had been holding back, waiting for his goons to take us down.

"You need to go," Chase pushed me toward Lexen. "He's going to get you to safety. Trust me."

"What?" I half shouted, as a strong band-like grip went around my waist. In a split second I was jerked off the ground and my scream was lost in the wind. We were flying, but I didn't struggle, because by the time I found my voice, we were already at a height that would kill me if I fell. The noise of the helicopter was almost deafening up here.

"Hold tight," Lexen muttered in his deep voice. "I'm going to stir up some cover for us."

I turned my head to find I was being held in one of his

arms, a no-longer-on-fire Callie was in the other, and Emma was sort of in the middle, pressed against both of us, her arms wrapped around Lexen's neck. Callie was holding onto her, so I did the same with my free arm, which allowed her to relax her grip on Lexen a tad.

Dark clouds were still thick across the sky, and we were flying right in the midst of them. "Laous is following in the helicopter?" Emma squeaked.

"He's following," Lexen confirmed. "Don't worry, he's not draygone, he's not going to catch me." I liked his confidence, and despite our combined weight, Lexen didn't sound even slightly fatigued. Dude was Superman.

"We left the others behind," I bit out, not happy about being yanked out of Chase's arms. And what he'd been saying ... I needed to know more. I needed to hear everything. "What if Laous doubles back and captures them?" I'd turn myself over in a heartbeat. I would not leave Chase to die at Laous' hands.

Emma sent a wonky smile in my direction. Our faces were close enough that I could see the glassiness of her blue eyes. "They'll be okay. Not only are they formidable opponents that Laous will not want to take on, it seems that the helicopter is focused on following us. The boys will get away. I know it."

That had better be true, because I needed to know what Chase meant about the trees choosing their mates, and ... everything else. I needed to know it all. I refused to think that was the last time I'd feel my stomach jump when he was close by, the last time I drew comfort from his calm presence. I wanted more moments with him. Trees and all.

No one back home would believe this was me. After all of these years being an indoors, dirt-a-phobe chick, I was embracing nature, embracing everything that felt right.

This felt righter than anything else in my life ever had.

Lexen continued to power along, the darkness of his clouds covering us. "Are you sure you're faster than a helicopter, Lexen Darken?" Callie asked bluntly. "Because I do not want to be eviscerated by some rotors."

A low deep chuckle was his reply. He sounded confident, though, so that was something. "The hardest part will be making sure no humans see us," he rumbled. "There are some things the human mind just cannot process. Which means I have to concentrate on keeping this cloud cover around us."

We all shut up then, letting him focus. He was swift at first, but the longer we flew, the more he slowed. No doubt it was a huge burden for him, carrying all of us and expending energy to keep the clouds around us. At least the helicopter noises didn't appear to be getting any closer. It was still behind us, though. Which for me was comforting. It meant that Chase was not in Laous' hands right now.

"We're over Astoria," Lexen said, speaking for the first time in a while.

"This town is not going to think anything of dark clouds, at least," Emma chuckled before sobering up. "Bloody place rains six days out of every seven."

I couldn't see the town; there was nothing but black mist under us, but I thought I caught a glimpse of the ocean. Lexen started to drop lower, and as he did the helicopter noise lessened and lessened. Each time we dropped another few feet, we seemed to drift further from those pursuing us. Eventually, the darkness around us eased up, and I could see a street below. "He's turning around," Emma cheered, her voice loud. "Because we're over Daelight Crescent, right?"

Lexen heaved in a deep breath, nodding. "Yes," he wheezed

lightly. "Laous knows we're stronger here, in our territory. Closer to the transporter."

Daelight Crescent. I paid closer attention to the street that belonged to the Daelighters. It was pretty. There was no other way to describe it. It looked a lot like the gated street I grew up in – well-maintained rose bushes, perfect roads, mansions ... whoa, hold the phone. They were not your average McMansions. More like castles. Lexen was almost on the road now, and I noted the thick white line that ran right down the center of it. As he dropped to a final stop, I released Emma, my arms aching from holding her for so long. Luckily, I'd been sharing the strain with Callie. Poor Lexen, though. He'd had no help.

Turning around, I paused when I saw the side of the road opposite the castles.

"What are they for?" I asked. Everyone turned to see what I was talking about. "They don't really seem to, uh, fit in with this area." Understatement of the year. These dwellings were about as far from the mansion side as it was possible to get. Maybe they were like ... houses for their staff. Groundskeepers and such.

Emma cleared her throat, turning narrowed eyes on Lexen. He ran a hand across his face, and I noted that he had already changed back to his human form. "Part of the treaty is that humans and Daelighters must integrate," Emma explained, eyeballing her mate. "They built the 'poor side' of Daelight Crescent so that humans would be part of their world, but also not cross over to this side. Apparently, poor people are used to obeying rules blindly."

"For their own safety," Lexen protested, only looking mildly contrite. "You all know firsthand the dangers in our world."

She wrinkled her nose at him. "I know you believe that,

but there's a reason you call us *grubbers*. You think you're better than us."

"Never," he said fiercely. I took a step back because a fierce Lexen was a scary Lexen. "I might have been resentful toward my life here at first, but I have never thought humans were inferior. Just different." He took her hand and she swallowed hard, her throat visibly moving. "I think humans are amazing, for the most part. I know I'm the lucky one to be part of your life."

The anger faded from Emma's face, and her eyes were shiny pools of blue as she blinked up at him. "You just seemed to hate us so much ... it's always worried me."

Lexen wrapped his arms around her, holding Emma tightly to his chest. Her feet were no longer on the ground, and her eyes were closed as she let out a sigh. He continued to talk to her, his voice too low for me to hear.

Seeing them like that, it only reminded me that Chase was not here.

Callie met my gaze. "They're going to be okay," she said, nodding decisively. I wasn't sure if she was trying to convince me or herself. Personally, I needed to see with my own eyes that Chase was okay. Daniel as well, of course. I didn't want anything bad to happen to him. But Chase was at the forefront of my mind.

I hesitated just for a moment before patting Callie's arm. She wasn't as tactile as Emma, but I wanted her to know that I understood, and that she wasn't alone. She sniffled for a second, then pressed her lips tightly together, trying to smile.

Emma and Lexen rejoined us then, their bodies close, holding hands.

"Do you know if my parents' car got here safely?" I asked

as my eyes ran along the street, stopping at a large gate at the end. A very imposing sort of gate.

"They got here," Lexen said, pointing toward one of the castles. Just on the other side of the fence I saw the familiar black SUV. "They'll be in Overworld already, and we should be on our way, too."

Emma shifted forward with him, but I crossed my arms and shook my head. "Nope. No way am I going without Chase. What if he's in trouble? We need to make sure they get here safely. No one is a sacrifice in this situation."

"What Maya said..." Callie's face held a very stubborn expression. "In reference to Daniel."

Lexen's eyes were so dark now that I could not distinguish between pupil and iris, which was freaky. Thankfully, there was still some white around the very outside; otherwise, he'd be repping a hot, scary-ass demon from *Supernatural.* "This is not a game. Four secret keepers are all that stand between the end of two worlds." I became his sole focus. "Especially you, Maya. Laous needs you to find the fourth keeper. Once he finds her, he finds the stone. Do you understand?"

Anger flared inside of me. It was a guttural kind of thing, unstable, and much deeper than I usually felt emotions. "I'm not an idiot," I bit out through gritted teeth. "I understand the larger concept of what is happening here, but sorry, I've never been big on 'sacrifice one to save many,' so you need to figure out another plan, one which doesn't involve leaving without Chase or Daniel."

Lexen moved preternaturally fast, wrapping an arm around me and yanking me off the ground for the second time in an hour. I was over his shoulder before my mind fully registered what he had just done, and then we were walking. I blinked down at Emma, who was by my side. Callie was keeping up too, even though she lagged a few steps behind.

"I'm going to give you until the count of three," I seethed, anger and astonishment warring inside of me, "to put me down. This is kidnapping. You're supposed to be the good guys."

Emma's worried expression briefly morphed into something resembling amusement. "Lexen lives in a gray area when it comes to good and bad. It's relative, depending on which side of the war you're on. Plus, he's got a history with kidnapping."

"I like to refer to it as *abduction*," Callie added. "Kidnapping is for children. Abduction is for aliens."

I screamed as loud as I could, bringing both fists down and pounding on his back. "Let me go! You should never use your strength to force my compliance. That's the best way to lose any trust I had in your people."

Emma stopped walking, and that was probably the only thing in the worlds that would stop Lexen. He turned to her, and I ended up staring out into the street. "She's right," I heard Emma say. "Maya is a grown woman. She needs to do what she feels is right – the same way Callie and I did. We're going to be a team, the eight of us. I can feel it with every fiber of my being. But for that to happen, there needs to be cohesiveness. A breach of trust will damage our dynamic severely."

My body lifted as Lexen exhaled loudly. For a brief moment, I thought he was going to ignore her argument, but in the end his love and respect for Emma won. As my feet hit the ground, I took a step away from him. My instinct was to run, because I didn't feel safe with Lexen at the moment. He had already demonstrated that he would do whatever it took for my compliance, in a bid to control the situation. Emma had stopped him this time, but maybe next time she would agree. Then we'd all be screwed.

"I'm sorry." Those words took me by surprise, because I got the feeling he wasn't an apologizer. "But you have to understand, I have thousands ... no, hundreds of thousands of lives in my hands. Overlords put their people first. Their safety. Part of me wants to gather you three up and fly to the end of Overworld with you, out of the land of Daelighters and off to another of the sectors where I know Laous will never follow." A blast of icy air hit me ... disappearing as Lexen got himself under control again. "But I also trust in what Em is saying. The team thing. I ... promise I will never force your compliance."

He reached out and Emma went willingly into his arms. "Emma is always worried about losing her free will," he said, staring down at her, before he turned back to me. "It was wrong of me to use my strength against you. For that, I am truly sorry."

I relaxed and felt much more comfortable remaining near him. "Apology accepted. As long as you remember that I am a person, not a doll to throw around, then we should be all good."

He opened his mouth but paused before he said anything. I waited a moment, thinking he might have forgotten what he was about to say, before realizing he was focused behind me. Spinning around, I saw that the huge main gate was opening. We all stared as it swung wide, and on the other side were two familiar figures. Chase and Daniel.

Without a word spoken, Callie and I both took off. My brain was too fuzzy for logical thought. I just knew that I had to see Chase. My sanity depended on it.

13

———

I thought I heard Lexen shout something after us, but we were too far away at that point to hear him clearly. Probably he was annoyed that we hadn't waited for him, but it was Chase and Daniel. There was nothing to worry about.

The pair had stopped just inside the gate, waiting for us. The fact that I was running to him should have embarrassed me, but it didn't. Something had snapped inside of me when we left Chase behind. Whatever fear I had been harboring about fate arranging these connections between the secret keepers and overlords had dissipated with the thought that I might never see Chase again. It was a primal urge I had now, to explore this bond between us.

It was weird. I could admit that, but honestly, after everything that had happened over the last few days, weird was all starting to feel like a new normal.

"They look fine, right?" Callie's long legs were eating up the distance, and she didn't sound at all winded.

Meanwhile, I was dying trying to keep up with her. It was

basically a sprint pace I had to set. "I - I think so," I spluttered out. "Why aren't they moving though?"

I wasn't sure at what point I realized that this wasn't going to be the happy ending I envisioned. But I definitely knew it when I ran into Chase's arms. There was no stomach flip, no clenching of my chest and fizzing of energy in my blood.

Not Chase.

I shouted and started to struggle, but the fake Chase already had his arms wrapped around me. There was a burning pain across my biceps, but I didn't let that stop me. Callie let out a muffled scream next to me, then she started throwing punches, kicking out with long straight strikes.

The guy holding me cursed, distracting me from the awesome that was Callie. "Stop moving, you stupid grubber bitch."

Yeah, okay, whatever you say. I struggled harder, trying to recall what we'd learned in self-defense classes last year at school. With a larger attacker ... stomp foot, knee groin, palm up into throat or nose.

All of these needed to happen pretty much in the same instant, and that's exactly what I did. The crunch of his nose was satisfying, even though it kind of hurt my heart to see Chase's face bleeding and broken like that. He let out a roar and shoved me away, sending me flying back.

Gravel bit into my palms, and in that same moment heat burst from Callie – past her worry about killing assholes by the look of it. The guy who'd grabbed me took off, but Callie had her hands on the other one. Her hands were the only part of her body not on fire, but judging by his screams, they were still hot enough to burn into his skin as she held him. "Where are Daniel and Chase? What did you do with them?" she shouted into his face, shaking him despite his size.

I jumped to my feet, wincing at the new pains ricocheting across my body. I had no idea what to do. Getting closer to Callie seemed like a very bad idea. Her flames were flaring in an unstable pattern.

Luckily Lexen was here now.

"Callie!" That word was a bite of command. "You have to let him go. We can't find out what he knows if he's dead."

Emma was at my side then, running a hand across the grazes that decorated my skin. "Are you okay?" she asked, but I didn't answer, too busy trying to see what was about to happen.

Fireball Callie turned to Lexen, and it was the most insane thing I had ever seen. Her eyes were swirling red, like lava. "This is how they tricked me last time," she said, her voice shaking with rage. "The one impersonating my mom told me that they could grow skin from a single cell. Does it mean they have Daniel and Chase?"

Lexen took a step closer and Emma's hold on my arm tightened. She didn't like him getting that close. "No, it takes at least a week to grow a skin. Laous must have taken cells from all of us at one point or another." He paused. "Actually, we all had to go for a healer scan when the overlord minors were first sent to Astoria. The process was overseen by Laous." His lips pressed together. "No doubt another part of the reason he got us all sent here."

Callie must have almost burnt the guy's wrists to the bones at this point; he was just whimpering now, no longer fighting her. With a huge burst of exhaled air, her flames disappeared as she let him fall away. Lexen stepped forward, reaching down to feel for a pulse. "He's alive," he said as he turned to us. "Once we get him back to House of Darken, the healers can fix him up so that we can question him."

I still didn't want to leave, but I wouldn't fight Lexen again – no one could say that I didn't learn from my mistakes. I'd just have to hope and pray that Chase was not far behind us.

Lexen hauled the guy up off the ground and then turned around. "I'm going to have to check the guardhouse," he said, face grim. "There should have been security out here by now." His eyes met Emma's.

"Ace?" she said, sounding like she was going to cry.

"Just stay close," Lexen replied.

There was a small booth on the side of the gate, one which looked like it would seat two guards. There was no one visible through the glass window; Lexen continued around until he got to the door. A foul smell hit me just as Lexen stepped forward and blocked the view from the rest of us.

"Lex..." Emma reached out and touched his shoulder.

His head lowered as he stepped to the side. Emma's muffled cry was enough to tell us everything. The two guards were on the floor, half draped over each other, congealed blood pooled all around them. They were clearly dead, eyes staring unseeingly; the stench increased exponentially at that point.

One of the guards was young, African American. The other was older, with a gruff face, and wiry gray hair. "How long have they been dead?" Emma asked, her hand pressed to her chest.

"A few hours," Lexen replied, voice low. "Which means they were waiting here for us even before we left the cabin."

This Laous seemed to be a planner. The bastard.

Emma knelt down, her hand hovering just above the face of the younger man. "Ace was a really nice guy," she choked out. "Helped me when I first moved here. Got a message to Lexen's family so that my guardians were protected."

She broke off as she sobbed a few times, sucking in some deep breaths. I couldn't see her face because of the way she was crouching, but I could see Lexen's. He was doing that scary thing again. Dropping the Daelighter he held – pretty much on his head, because he was clearly way past giving a shit – he reached down and lifted Emma, holding her together as she sobbed.

"First my parents..." Her next words were lost in more sobs. "Then Marsil, and now Ace and this other poor security guard ... who is next, Lex? Who will he take from us?" She shuddered. "Thank God, Sara and Michael are away on business."

I felt my own eyes grow hot and damp. Seeing her devastation, her fears were my fears, but she'd already had those she loved taken from her. Callie stepped up and stood by my side, not saying anything, heat still shimmering in the air around her.

Lexen shook as a rumble of anger emerged. "No one else will die." His voice was low, controlled, and icy. "I'm going to kill Laous the next time I see him. He's dead. End of his story."

After another moment of Lexen stroking a hand up and down her spine, murmuring words I couldn't hear, Emma calmed herself. By the time he set her back on her feet and picked up the still unconscious and burned Daelighter, there was determination crossing Emma's tearstained face.

"We need to go now," she growled, mimicking her mate. "Let's get this asshole healed enough to hurt him some more."

Lexen hit a button to close the gates, then we all hurried through before it shut on us. "What are you going to do about the guards?" I asked, hurrying to keep up. Callie remained silent, her expression unreadable. I expected she was both worried about Daniel and trying to deal with the fact she'd hurt someone again.

"Most of the police are on our payroll." Lexen's words were clipped. "We'll let them know what happened. They'll take care of it."

"My father should be able to help," I added, realizing this was probably part of his job. Covering these things up. "Call his office or something. Once he gets back to Earth."

"Yes," Lexen agreed, falling silent.

The rest of the journey along Daelight Crescent was a subdued one. Emma marched ahead, her eyes shiny. Callie was silent and hot. Whatever flames existed inside of her, they were bubbling just under the surface. And I was having a mini-breakdown. I just really needed Chase to get here, so I could stop imagining him with his throat cut, bleeding his precious life back into the trees he came from.

My morbid thoughts cut off when we reached the end of the street and turned down a lane covered in roses and vines. They were dense on top, trailing down the sides to form a barrier.

"I'd kill for some coffee," Callie muttered randomly, breaking the tense silence.

I couldn't help but smile. "What's your favorite?" I asked. I wasn't a huge coffee drinker, but I enjoyed a macchiato at times.

"Café au lait from Café du Monde in my favorite city, New Orleans." Her voice was wistful.

My smile grew. "I went there on vacation once, with my family. They weren't around a lot, but we tried to do a family vacay once a year. We ate beignets in Café du Monde almost every day."

Some of the blankness left her face then. She turned toward me, and as her eyes ran down me, she jolted.

"What?" I asked.

"You do realize you're covered in blood, right?" she said, voice low.

Emma and Lexen stopped, looking me over as well. "I only got a bit scraped up," I muttered, even though the injury in my arm felt a bit more than "scraped."

I lifted the hand on my injured arm, surprised by the red on my palm. Pushing up the sleeves of my dark sweater, I felt a little faint at the sight of a thick line of red running down it. "That's more blood than I expected," I murmured.

"What happened to your arm?" Lexen asked.

I held it closer to me, feeling very protective because all of a sudden it felt really painful. "I don't know. The guy who grabbed me dug his nails in or something. My arm hurt right after he touched me."

I was probably going to get tetanus from that piece of crap.

Lexen reached out and I didn't flinch, which was an improvement from the last time he tried to touch me. I'd mostly forgiven him, especially since he had been correct about the dangers. Not that it gave him a right to grab me, but he'd apologized for that.

His hand skimmed across to the neckline of my sweater. He pushed it to the side just enough to see my shoulder.

"Not nails," he said. "You've been cut. It's deep."

Swallowing hard, it felt like the pain shot to another new height then. "Why would he cut me? Was he trying to injure me so I couldn't fight?"

Lexen and Emma exchanged a look. I clicked in a second later. "He took my blood for Laous, didn't he?" I was such an idiot. I'd basically handed it over to them without a thought.

"That's why he ran off so quickly and didn't try to help his friend."

Callie spun. "Should we go after him?"

Lexen shook his head. "No point. They were organized. He'll be long gone."

"I thought Laous wanted us?" Emma sounded weary, her anger fading away. "So why has he given up so easily?"

"Getting Maya's blood would be the priority for him. If they managed to capture her, or any of you as well, it would just be a bonus."

At least teaming up … bonding … whatever was happening with the secret keepers and four overlords, was making it harder for Laous to just scoop us up. Maybe fate *had* thought this plan through.

"We need to move again," Lexen said. "Maya is losing blood. She needs a healer."

My legs were a little wobbly at this point, but I was blaming it on adrenalin crash. The blood loss, though, probably didn't help. As we continued along the rose covered path, a light at the end caught my eye. It was hard to see exactly what it was at first, but as my eyes adjusted to the brightness, I … still had no idea what I was looking at.

"That's a transporter," Emma answered my unspoken slack-jawed question. "This is the permanent one which connects Earth and Overworld."

The transporter appeared to be made up of a million strings of light. Or something close to that number. They were intertwined with each other, moving constantly, with ends shooting off at random intervals.

"It's going to be difficult for me to take the three of you across," Lexen warned. "But I think it's worth the risk. Leaving any of you behind is not an option, not with Laous and his resistance members out there."

"What makes it difficult?" Callie asked. "What could happen?"

Lexen adjusted the guy over his shoulder. "The path between Earth and Overworld is not that easy to navigate. If you lose contact with me, you might be lost forever. I know the transporter looks like a straight line, but that's only because I've connected to Overworld. If I let that go, we'd be adrift in a place with an infinite amount of destinations."

Emma let out a sound of alarm. "How could you not tell me that? I could have accidentally let go of you, and then I'd be stuck wandering in space forever?"

Lexen shook his head, one side of his lips quirking up. "Not forever. You'd die of hunger long before that."

She smacked him on the arm, and I was happy to see some color returning to her face. She'd been so pale and quiet since we found the dead guards.

"Are you sure it's worth the risk?" she asked, more serious.

I didn't like the fact he hesitated first, before nodding. "I believe this is the better of the two choices, but there's no guarantee."

Emma turned to me and Callie. "I trust Lexen. But I think we should put it to a vote. Are you two okay with taking the risk and all three of us holding on to Lexen as we cross?"

Being lost in space until I starved didn't sound like a fun time, but I also didn't want to stay here on my own until Lexen came back for me. What if there was something dangerous going on in Overworld? He might never come back for me. What if Chase was somehow already in Overworld?

"I'm in," I told her. "I should have listened to Lexen before when he warned me it was too dangerous to stay here. This time let's go with his instincts."

Callie also agreed, so the three of us stepped closer. Lexen took Emma's hand with his right, Callie then took Emma's other hand, and I grabbed Callie's. We were a chain, and before I could ask what happened next, Lexen reached out with his free hand, latching on to one of the strings of lights.

With a jerk, I was pulled off my feet and the world disappeared. I was hurtling into a long tunnel of darkness and light. At first I freaked out, my mind all like "What the hell is happening here?" – especially since it appeared we were racing along the tunnel without having to walk or move our feet. My stomach was in knots, but after a few moments, I started to enjoy the experience. It was like one of those carnival rides where you pretend you're spacewalking, using a harness to jump your way along a dark tunnel.

Only this time there was no harness. And it was real spacewalking.

Okay, so nothing really like a carnival ride, but if I kept my thoughts on an experience that was familiar, I didn't freak out as bad. It was silent in the transporter, although there was the faintest white noise in my ears. I couldn't see what was at the end, because it was just very bright, but my body felt eager to get there. Like I was being called ... pulled.

Could it be House of Leights? Was I remembering the place I was born? Were the trees calling me? At some point I forgot that it was important not to let go of Callie. When she squeezed my hand, I jerked, and in slow-motion turned to her. Her face was painted in shock and horror. "What?" I tried to speak but ended up mouthing the words because there was no sound.

Her eyes darted down to our hands, and I focused there as well. *No! Oh crap.*

Only the very tips of our fingers were still joined. In my fascination with whatever called me at the end of this tunnel, I'd started to slip away from her. The bright light at the end was close, thankfully, so I just had to hold on for a few more seconds.

I slipped again, and only my index finger remained linked with hers. I tried to reach out for more leverage, but I couldn't get any more grip. We were literally being pulled apart, like suction was on either end. Another little slip and silent screams ripped from me.

One final slip, and then I was hurtling away into the endless darkness.

14

———

*P*anic took longer than it should have to crash into me. At first I was spiraling. Then there was some disorientation. Then there was panic. As the out-of-control spinning stopped, the world around me stabilized. My head cleared as I began to drift along in darkness. After some time, the darkness didn't seem quite as ... eternal. There were these tiny pinpricks of light, which appeared to be very far away, and somehow at the same time seemed like I could reach out and touch them. Nothing made sense in this place, not distance, or time, or emotion.

You're going to die.

This voice of reason woke me up to the serious nature of my predicament. *I was going to die.* I would literally float along in this darkness until my body ceased to function. It was so unfair. I'd just found out the world was bigger than I ever expected, and I hadn't explored more than a tiny percentage. I hadn't seen the land of my birth. I hadn't ... I hadn't kissed Chase. That hurt more than anything.

House of Leights had been so close...

One of the lights in the distance burned a little brighter, catching my eye. By instinct, I reached for it, but the light faded before I could touch it, and I was again just floating along in the nothingness. Despite logic telling me otherwise, I refused to give up this quickly, so I started to experiment, figure out what I could do while I drifted. Obviously doorways could be opened from here, because Lexen had said there were infinite possibilities of travelling to other places. So how did I get one to open?

Instinct was telling me it was the tiny pinpricks around me. Those lights were the only thing to differentiate the emptiness, and the transporter itself had been made of light. We'd literally used a light beam to get from Earth to Overworld. Focusing lessened my fear, so I put every ounce of effort into that. I reached for lights, over and over, and after some time I figured out a way to swing my body closer to them. Eventually I actually brushed against one, and as shock rocked down my arms and across my chest, I immediately let go, unsure if I'd just done something really bad, breathing deeply until the tingles subsided.

With renewed determination, I tried again.

This time it was relatively easy to reach the speck, easier even to wrap my hand around it. The shock took me less by surprise, but that didn't mean it still wasn't uncomfortable. From this point, though, I had no idea what I was supposed to do. I'd connected to something, locking in, but utilizing the connection was not going to be as easy, apparently.

It was very bright being this close to the speck – which wasn't really a speck any longer since it filled my entire palm. The tingles increased the longer I held on, until eventually I had to release the light. My body started to move through the darkness again – those specks of light were anchors, holding me in place.

The panic I had been suppressing was starting to swirl within me again, not the best when trying to focus, so I drew on teachings from my mom, her methods of achieving inner peace. The first image that came to my mind's eye was Chase; I connected peace with him. He was my feeling of safety ... something that had been there from the first moment I caught sight of him at the party. Chase, the overlord of House of Leights...

One of the lights shone brightly again, startling me, and without thought, I reached for it, swinging myself out like I'd been practicing. The connection was easy, but unlike last time there was no shock. Warmth washed over me, and my stomach did a swirling thing. A very familiar swirling thing.

Chase... I couldn't call out loud, but I mentally screamed, *Are you there?*

There was no reply, because Chase was clearly not here. But the light had gotten brighter when I thought of him. What had I thought of the first time the light beamed at me? Kissing Chase and ... *House of Leights.*

Maybe that was where I needed to focus. On House of Leights? The land of my birth. The Daelighters kept saying we had a connection to it, that the water I'd been born in had filled me with energy and life, infusing into my essence.

With a speck of light in my hand, I remembered how I felt with Chase in the trees around the cabin. The peace, warmth, acceptance...

Take me home.

An infusion of heat rushed through my body. I gasped, and my arms started trembling, but I didn't let go. Not even when the light burst out from my hand, forming a long tunnel.

This time I would not let go. Not for anything.

Lexen had made it look pretty effortless, the way he'd dragged us along the stream of light. I, on the other hand, had to fight and work for every step forward, because it seemed this connection worked in two directions, and I was drawn back at the same time as being pulled forward.

Eventually, I reached the brightest part and prayed with everything inside of me that I was close to my destination, then closed my eyes and pushed onward. Whatever had been pulling me snapped, and I tumbled forward, just managing to get my arms out in time to stop my face from smashing into the ground. My face ended up being the only part of me that didn't hit the ground.

My groans were lost in the shouts around me, the noise so sudden after the silence that fear crippled me. I curled in on myself, mind frozen in terror. Hands touched me and I flinched. What if I had made a mistake? What if this was not Overworld? It was actually this thought that sent enough adrenalin coursing through me to clear my mind.

I pushed myself up, head already tilted back, so I could take it all in.

"Maya!" Emma's face came into view and the loud clanging in my brain subsided, allowing me to finally recognize that it wasn't noise around me, it was the voices of my friends and family.

Mom and Dad were standing there, faces tear-streaked, arms locked together. I got to my feet without any help and the three of us stared at each other. My mom's shoulders were slumped forward, which is what she did only when she was exhausted or grieving. Dad cradled her protectively. It had always been the thing I adored most about them as a couple ...

love didn't care about race or height or personality. It didn't discriminate, and it had chosen well for them.

"Maya," my mom choked out. The paralysis faded, and I was finally free to run into their arms.

"We thought we'd lost you." My father's voice was very hoarse. I was pretty sure this was the first time I'd ever seen him cry.

I went to explain what had happened and apologize for scaring them like that, but before I could say a word, a huge bang rocked the metal platform we stood on. By the time I'd spun around, my father had already pushed my mom and me behind him. Another bang, and I realized this time that it had come from a land of gigantic trees, just in front of us.

This was my first time observing Overworld. The sky was green, the platform we stood on had a lot of symbols carved into it, and there were three very distinct and unique lands surrounding us. It was completely mind-blowing to think I was in another world. *Another world!* But there was no time to really comprehend this, because something was happening in House of Leights.

The moment the name crossed my mind, my body strained to move toward it. I needed to step foot into the world of golden trunks and ancient trees.

"Did Chase and Daniel show up?" I murmured.

"Yes," my mom confirmed in a whisper. "Right after Lexen and the girls." Her next pause was extended, and then she added: "Chase did not take the news well."

I stilled. "What news?"

Her kind brown eyes softened, and I barely managed not to hug her again. I'd almost lost the chance to see my mom again. This moment was a blessing.

"When he found out that you were ... still in the transporter." Her voice broke, and I had to swallow down the sudden pain in my throat.

I had to ask. "What happened after he got back? Where did he go?" I looked around realizing there was one person I was missing. "And where is Brad?" I would have thought my best friend would have been waiting here all freaked out and ragey, doing that football player stance that he pulled out when he was worried. Panic hit me. "Nothing happened to him, right?"

My dad answered: "Brad is fine. He's gone to House of Darken with Star. They're trying to track you through the network there. He was as angry as Chase, just with fewer powers."

That made me smile a little, relief at knowing that Brad was okay replacing the panic.

Dad continued: "Daniel took Callie to House of Imperial, so she could recharge her energy, and Chase ... you're hearing the aftermath of his rage." A wiry smile lifted one corner of his mouth. "Anything you want to tell us, little one?"

Breathing deeply, I ignored the urge to tell them to mind their own business. The absolute last thing I wanted was to talk to my parents about whatever was going on with me and Chase. Mostly because they were my parents, and also because I really didn't have any idea. But this wasn't a normal teenage crush. This was more. I knew with everything inside my body that Chase and I were *meant* to be. Callie's words had never left me. I didn't care what brought Chase to me. All I cared was that something had.

Another crash, the platform rocking again. My stomach flipped and my heart clenched – he was close. Stepping around my parents, moving toward the House of Leights, I said, "Chase and I ... nothing has happened, and at the same time ... he's changed my entire life. I don't know what it was like for you and mom, but for me … it's like I've known him forever … as if he is as essential to my survival as oxygen. I … need him."

It was as simple and complicated as that. I didn't know him very well, that was true. And I definitely wasn't ready to get married or anything. I'd like to get to know him before we did anything too crazy. But I couldn't deny my need – and want – any longer.

"You should go to him," my mom said as she turned me toward the trees. "He's hurting and you're the only one who can help him heal."

My mom was so wise. I couldn't imagine living without her sage advice. My father looked less convinced, but he didn't object as I started toward House of Leights. No one stopped me. Emma briefly hugged me as I moved past them, before she moved back to stand against Lexen. He wrapped his arms around her.

"I'm sorry you were lost," Lexen told me. "But you have proven your connection to Overworld by finding your way through the transporter." I sensed his pride, which kind of made me want to blush, because I hadn't really done much.

Nodding, I started to walk again, only stopping when he added. "Bring him back, Maya. We need to go to House of Darken and track the fourth secret keeper."

"We'll be back as soon as possible," I promised. I was determined to make sure Laous didn't destroy this world, because I was already in love with it.

Home.

"Be careful," Emma called after me. "Trust the trees. They're good."

Those words barely registered with me, because I was completely focused on my land. Well, on the trees. I stood right at the edge of the metal platform. The tree trunks were thick, close together, and I could see no clear path to enter. Not sure what I was supposed to do, I reached out to touch the nearest one. Hopefully at minimum I'd feel that same sense of peace like last time. Its trunk was an unusual gold, with barky flakes giving it an aged and roughened appearance. The moment my hand connected, I jolted. It felt like someone had attached a rope to my center and then tied the other end to the tree ... like I was tethered to it. There was no other way to describe it.

A rush of whispers entered my mind, an unnatural noise. At first I could not differentiate anything, but the longer I remained with my hand against the trees, the clearer it was starting to become.

Daughter.

They called me *daughter*, over and over, a million voices speaking at the same time, until it was almost deafening. I felt much more than peace. I felt everything. I wanted to stay there forever, but I needed to get Chase. Though, I'd be back for the trees.

Closing my eyes, I brought forth a mental image of Chase. Those beautiful green eyes. The marks etched into the short hair on his head. The perfect planes of his face.

Can you take me to him?

The ground started to shake, rocking me back so that the connection between me and the trees broke. Within five seconds the shaking had subsided, and the trees parted. Like ... actually shifted out of the way to form a path through their branches. Peering over the edge, through the gap between the platform and the first branches, I could see no ground at all in sight, just long trunks below. I drew back, blinking and breathing to calm myself. Heights were not my favorite thing, and if there was ground below, it was much further down than I could see.

It was only the knowledge that Chase was close by, and that he was hurting, that calmed my racing heart. I stepped in under the dark canopy. My feet were surer against the branch path than I expected, and each step forward felt a little easier. After a few moments I continued without worry, the only sound a rustling behind me as the trees closed the path.

The tether in my stomach remained as it was when I first touched the tree. It didn't stretch or strain, but I could feel it there like a physical connection. For the first time in my life, I walked among nature and did not stop for one moment to freak out about bugs. And that wasn't because there were none, because as my ears adjusted to the "quiet," it became apparent that this world was filled with small noises, different creatures rustling through the branches, some tiny, others larger and more unique. I particularly liked ones that looked like a cross between an owl and ... maybe a koala, those Australian animals. It was fluffy and bear-like, but with large feathered wings. It perched on the branches in the same manner as an owl.

One in particular, almost completely midnight black, barring one splash of terracotta across its chest, started to follow close behind me. I'd turn my head and there it would be, moving through the branches, and after some time I started to feel like I'd made a friend. I even chatted to it as I moved.

"You're very beautiful," I cooed, my hand lifting almost involuntarily to touch it. Large yellow eyes darted toward my hand, and I hesitated, not wanting to scare it away. "Thanks for taking this journey with me," I continued on, lowering my hand. "I'm searching for Chase. Do you know him?"

A small chirp of noise; I took that as an affirmative. This creature did indeed know Chase. "Will you help me find him?"

There was a soft whooshing sound, and then those stunning wings spread out on either side of it, somehow finding the space within the tightly packed trees. Before I could blink again, a heavy weight landed on my shoulder, and while at first the urge to freak out was strong, I took a moment to calm my mind. After a few deep breaths, I accepted my new friend.

We were going to find Chase.

15

———

The further I ventured into this House of Leights, the lighter I felt. I truly believed it was my soul that was growing ... healing ... soaring. Whatever essence made me Maya Anne Lewis was bursting free from the confines my life on Earth had placed on it. The bear-owl squeaked on my shoulder, a soft, gentle sound that I took as an agreement even though I hadn't spoken my thoughts out loud.

The trees within Leights were consistent: huge, ancient, tightly-packed. I assumed there were villages somewhere in this land, hidden away, but so far, I'd not stumbled across anything more than a few animals.

I also heard no more crashes, and I wondered if maybe Chase had left or calmed down. Still, I continued to follow the path laid out for me by the trees.

Galinta...

The whisper of the name flittered across my mind, and I remembered Chase telling me about them. They were all around me, these ancient, godlike beings. It was overwhelming, trying to take it all in. Stepping cautiously, the path seemed a little darker than before. I ducked my head under a few low-lying branches. My skin felt sensitive and tight as I moved, cool air brushing across it, the feeling similar to the time I'd gone to the pyramids in Egypt with Gracie – like I was stepping through ancient air, filled with history and magic and energy, so much that it was literally seeping into my blood.

My stomach jumped. Strong. The tether in my center started to tug me forward. *Chase.* I ran. Not something I would advise when you only had branches to jump across and often-times the gap between was large enough to get your foot stuck and break an ankle. At that moment, though, I didn't care. I had two ankles. Chase was more important.

I heard my name, like a whisper on the wind, so much pain in that one word that I misstepped. My new friend let out a low sound of alarm, taking flight just as I tumbled down. Rough bark bit into the skin on my hands, tearing more of my skin. My foot was screaming at me, because I had managed to wedge it in a hole, and it was being held at a crazy angle. I tried to roll over, hoping to dislodge myself.

I groaned as a sharp stabbing pain shot up from my ankle and through my shins. "Crap, ouch." The discomfort increased the longer I was wedged in. I wanted to turn over so I could see what damage I'd done, but for the life of me, I couldn't get my foot free. And I wasn't quite brave enough to just yank it out, because it was killing me already.

There was a whisper from the trees around me, and my body tensed a heartbeat before warm hands wrapped around my biceps. My head jerked up to find Chase right before me. His eyes were wide and wild, the green dark.

"Maya..."

He breathed my name like it was a prayer, and I had never seen any human guy look at a girl the way Chase was looking at me. It sent my heart fluttering. He ran his hands up my arms until he was cupping my face. "I thought I'd lost you," he murmured. "How did you make it out of the transporter?"

I had to swallow and clear my throat to be able to talk. It was overwhelming being with him like this. Just ... so much of everything. I almost couldn't handle the intensity.

"My connection to House of Leights," I finally got out. "To this land and ... to you. I managed to find a beam of light which took me back home."

Home. There had never been a greater truth than that one. This was my home. In the trees. His face moved closer, and my heart was thundering so hard that I was at a very real risk of a heart attack. He adjusted my weight forward, taking the strain so he could lift me up. I heard him whisper words – not English – and my foot was suddenly free. Chase lowered himself down to rest against a nearby trunk, holding me close to his chest.

"Are you too hurt to move?" he asked me.

I shook my head, my face brushing his shirt. He stood then, carrying me with him. He walked along the branches more gracefully than I could walk on solid land.

"The Galinta tell me you were running, that's how you got hurt." He sounded upset.

I grimaced. "I needed to find you ... tell you I was okay. The others said you didn't take it well."

Chase chuckled darkly. "Understatement, but sure, let's just say I did not take it well. I sent you ahead to keep you safe, then Lexen tells me that you were attacked, hurt, and lost in a transporter." I tilted my head back, resting it against his arm so I could see the play of muscles in the dark skin at the base of his neck. "I should have followed my instincts and kept you with me."

His eyes met mine, and I was relieved to see that the shimmering light green had returned. He slowed, and my breath caught in my chest, the air almost visibly strumming between us, him looking all Tarzan and me looking like I'd been hit by a car. But in that moment, all that mattered was this feeling and how we could capture it.

His lips brushed against mine, but before I could kiss him back, that tether in my stomach sprang to life. There was an almost audible sound as the end which had been attached to the tree dislodged and slammed into Chase, tethering me to the overlord minor. As the two ends settled, it felt much more permanent than it had when I was tied to the Galinta.

"What ... what just happened between us?" I asked, my voice barely a whisper. "Did you just feel that...?"

"Bond," he finished for me.

"Bond," I choked out. "We're bonded?"

I knew he wasn't lying. Firstly, why would he? Secondly, I could feel it. It was real, tangible.

"The Galinta have not blessed a union like this in a long time," he said, voice low, eyes locked on mine. He started to walk again, apparently not needing to look where he was going.

"I don't understand," I said honestly.

He ducked down, stepping under the low-lying branches, ending up in a round clearing. We were still in the trees, but instead of tightly-knit branches, there was a large space. It had a floor of leaves and branches, and it felt like we could move about more freely.

Chase gently sat me down in the center. "Wait here," he said. "I'll grab something to help your foot."

He made sure I was comfortable before taking off. I let my eyes linger on those broad shoulders until they completely disappeared. I wanted to touch him, wrap my arms around him, hold him close.

Bonded. I suppose I should be able to touch him, right? There had to be a perk to being bonded without my permission.

Do you not want this union? The whisper of those words in my mind had me jerking upright and looking around. Was that the ... Galinta? Speaking to me in those ancient whispering winds. Were they giving me a choice? Would they break the bond if I said I didn't want the union?

My immediate reaction was one of complete and total horror. The thought of losing Chase to another, of not having that twirling sensation in my chest and body again, of losing the feeling of completion, of home ... I could never say I didn't want it. It was a force greater than anything I'd felt before.

"I choose him," I said out loud and mentally. "I choose Chase."

Fire burned in my belly, matching the throbbing pain in my ankle. I cried out, because it felt like I was being branded, flames across my skin. Scrambling to pull up my shirt, I stared down at my bellybutton. Just above it now was a dark green mark about the size of two quarters. I stared at it for an extended amount of time, trying to figure out what the hell had just happened. The mark was a lot like the symbols the overlords had tattooed onto their heads, swirls and lines intersecting in what looked like tribal patterns.

Footsteps padded lightly across the leaves, and I lifted my head. "What. Is. That?" I pointed at my stomach.

Chase stopped a few feet from me, then lifted the bottom of his shirt up. My eyes just about fell out of my head as I traced the lines of his abs, and the mark that matched mine across them. "What the hell ... you have one, too?" I half lurched to my feet, groaning as my ankle protested.

Chase caught me, taking my weight as I pressed my hands to his chest for balance. I was touching bare skin at the neckline of his shirt. It felt so warm and silky, hard and soft at the same time, I wanted so badly to continue moving my hands under his shirt. I wanted to touch him, press my lips down and see how he tasted.

Mark. You have a damn mark.

That reminder was enough for me to gain some composure and pull myself back from him.

He didn't seem upset. "What happened while I was gone, Maya?"

"I ... think the Galinta gave me the option to break our bonding, and I told them I choose you. Always. Then my stomach started to burn." I'd done this, there was no other explanation. I jerked my head up to meet his gaze. "I'm so sorry. I think I might have taken the choice away from you."

He cut off my babbling by kissing me. Unlike last time, this was no brief gentle brush of our lips. This was open-mouthed, tongues tangling, lips moving across each other. This was desperate, and perfect, and ... I could not feel my legs or body any longer. My head spun, and the taste of Chase was everything I imagined, plus more. He shifted me around and picked me up so I could wrap my legs around him. I thought briefly of my sore ankle, but at this point I really didn't care. Chase was the best kind of pain reliever.

My eyes had closed initially, but I needed to see him in this moment. Our first kiss. As my lashes fluttered up, so did his, like he had known I was about to look. Our mouths stilled, and I tried not to get lost in the multifaceted color of his eyes.

His breathing was slightly accelerated when he said, "You

didn't take my choice away – I chose you long ago. The moment I heard your name, I knew that I had to find you. I had to save you." I was mesmerized by him, unable to look away. "I followed your energy, believing that my purpose – the reason I felt such a draw – was because I was supposed to keep you safe ... and then I saw you at the party, dancing. You threw your head back as you laughed with such joy. That was when I knew that there was nothing I wouldn't do to protect you, that there was no other for me in either world."

"Were you worried I wouldn't feel the same connection?" I whispered, my voice hoarse.

His eyes twinkled then as a slight grin lifted the corner of his mouth. "Not too worried. I figured I'd eventually convince you we were meant for each other. I had an eternity to try."

An eternity. That was a freaking long time. But I decided not to worry about that for now. Now I would just enjoy Chase, try not to get killed or kidnapped by Laous, and save the world. Dropping my head against his chest, I let out a sigh. "As much as I hate to say this, because I want to stay in our tree bubble so badly, we have to head back to help the others. We have to try to find the fourth girl before Laous, since he has my blood now."

Chase's hands flexed against my thighs and his chest rumbled under me. "Lexen only told me a little about Laous' attack. I'd like to hear the full story from you ... now that I'm in a more reasonable state of mind."

I wiggled for him to let me down. If I was going to tell this story, we might as well both be comfortable. With reluctance, he lowered me down near a tree trunk, which I leaned back against. He then took a few steps away, returning with a deep bowl – which must have been what he fetched before. My shoe and sock were removed gently, and now that I wasn't wrapped around Chase, the pain was kicking in again.

"It's getting very swollen," I said mournfully, staring down at my puffy foot. "That's going to slow us down through the trees."

With great care, and a gentleness that should have been difficult from such a huge guy, he lifted my foot and lowered it into the warm water. It wrapped around me, thick and gel-like, and the relief was immediate. "This will help with the pain and inflammation," he told me. "Just give it a few minutes to work."

He then took some of the liquid into his hand, lightly pushed the neckline of my sweater aside, letting the gel slide down the cut in my shoulder.

"How did you know I was hurt there?" I asked, astonished.

He shrugged. "You've been favoring the other arm, and Lexen told me they cut you. It wasn't hard to figure out."

The relief in my ankle and shoulder allowed me to relax finally. "Thank you," I sighed. "I don't know what this is ... and if it's something gross, please don't tell me ... but whatever it is, it's working."

Chase laughed, and it was nice to see a happier emotion on his face. "It's just water, legreto. This sort is extra special. It comes from the Galinta and has their healing energy within it. The same water you were born in."

He lowered himself so he was sitting next to me, our arms and bodies pressed together down my left side. I leaned into him, not because I needed to, but because I wanted to. The mark on my stomach responded to our touch. I could feel the bond wrapping around me like the most comfortable blanket in the world.

Chase lifted his arm and I shifted forward so he could slide it behind me, then we fell back together again, not an ounce of unease between us. Our conversations started up easily enough. I told him about the events from the time Lexen landed with us in Daelight Crescent, to the fake Chase and Daniel, and getting lost in the darkness of the transporter. As I talked, our bodies continued to mesh together, until I was practically lying across Chase.

There was no guy in my entire life, outside of Brad, who I would have ever felt relaxed enough around to be like this with. Especially not one I hadn't known for years. It gave me that feeling of *home* again.

When I finished telling him everything, he was quiet, and I could feel the simmering emotions just under the surface waiting to burst free. "I'm okay," I finally said, reaching out and taking his free hand. He interlinked our fingers in the same instant, and that happy jump was back in my chest.

"Knowing you were hurt, could have died—" He broke off. "It riles me in a way that I'm not used to dealing with. In general, House of Leights are calm and tranquil. We do not involve ourselves in the drama of the other houses much. We remain neutral. But after what Laous has done, the way he has taken so much in his selfish quest to retrieve the starslight stone, neutral is no longer an option for us."

Twisting myself around, I hugged into his body, offering whatever comfort I could. He'd been there for me so much, this was the smallest thing I could do to try to return the favor. "I will support whatever decision you make," I murmured against his chest.

His lips pressed against my hair, and I tried not to cry at the perfect moment we were having. "That's good to know," he said, remaining close. "Because you're going to rule with me one day as overlord. I already know that you'll have the final say, because I can't deny you anything."

I jerked, having forgotten that very important and pertinent detail. Chase was an overlord minor. When his parents decided they were done ruling, that role was passed on to him.

Wiggling free, I tilted myself back to see him. "What if I make a mistake? I don't know anything about ruling people. I'm a freaking human ... what if they don't accept me?" There were literally a million what ifs. I mean ... I was the girl who couldn't even decide on a college – or an outfit half the time.

He twisted around, his free hand cupping my face. "You don't have to do anything but be the person I already know you to be. Kind. Compassionate. Incredibly smart. Ruling together means you don't ever have to worry about carrying the burden alone. As for the fact you're not a Daelighter..." His hand pressed against my stomach – which jumped like crazy – right where the symbol was. "You wear our language, the mark of a bonded overlord. You're one of us."

Just like that, at least ninety percent of my fears faded away. How in the hell did he do that? I guess it helped that most of the restlessness I'd felt in my life was gone now. This new path, the one with Chase and Overworld, felt right.

"Could I still go to school on Earth? If I want to finish up my education?" It didn't hurt to determine how all-encompassing this was. Like ... if I'd married a prince back home, I wouldn't get to have a career as well. Being a princess was your career ... life ... everything. Was it the same here?

Chase's arms tightened around me. "Maya Lewis, you can do whatever you need to for your future. I will support you, the same way you have vowed to support me. Being Overlord of House of Leights *is* a full-time job, but my parents plan on ruling for many more years. And even if they were to abdicate, you still have the freedom to make your own choices. I don't own you."

Perfect.

This was all my perfects. Now we just had to make sure Laous was stopped before he took them away.

16

———

By the time Chase was satisfied I had healed enough to leave, my ankle and shoulder felt a thousand times better. I had no idea what this *legreto* here was made of, but it was a hell of a lot better than the water we had on Earth.

"Where do you live?" I asked as he helped me to my feet. My foot felt slightly stiff inside my shoe, but otherwise I was fine to walk.

"We build homes inside the trunks of a special type of Galinta. They allow us to share their space, forming round rooms to keep us warm and dry. Most of my people live in their own communities. There are hundreds spread out across Leights."

"And you...?" I asked.

"The overlord families are nomadic. We travel and live with each of the communities, immersing ourselves in their world to hear of their lives and grievances. This is the best way to ensure we help all of our people."

Unlike most kings and queens back home, who sat in their castles and waited for the peasants to come to them...

"You're an only child, too?"

"Yes. Because Daelighters are so long-lived, our women are only fertile once or twice in an entire year. My parents have not been able to have any more children since me. My mother has mentioned more than once that she wishes the gods would bless her with another."

That was interesting. I definitely didn't take after their women, I had normal cycles. Something we would eventually have to discuss, because I was way too young, and not even remotely equipped to raise children. But I apparently had a long time to get around to that. I was going to enjoy being bonded first.

Chase called for a path back to the main platform. We waited as the trees moved themselves. We were just about to move through when a rustling of branches to our left had another path opening.

Chase paused, then let my hand go to maneuver himself in front of me. I was just starting to worry that we were about to be attacked when a man and woman stepped out of the pathway.

As soon as he saw them, Chase relaxed, and so did I.

"Chase, we have no news about your intended one," the woman said, hurrying forward, her voice low, smooth, and almost musical in nature. "We checked with the elders and the network..."

She trailed off when she saw me.

Chase carefully moved me to his side. "Mother, I'd like you to meet Maya. My bonded mate."

Mother. Oh man, I was so not ready – or dressed – to meet a queen. Nervously, I tried to smooth my hair back, all the while staring at the stunning woman before me. She reminded me of an African Queen, regal, dark skin, high cheekbones, and the same light green eyes as Chase. She had her long bronze-colored hair in braids, almost to her ankles, beads threaded through them that clinked together as she moved.

She was about a foot taller than me, with the lithe body of someone strong and flexible. On Earth I'd have guessed Pilates, but here it was no doubt all the running through the trees. She wore tight-fitting clothing, but they looked very simple and natural, not fancy like a queen, though she did have jewels woven into the crown of her head. I didn't recognize the gems, but they were in a range of colors similar to aquamarines, rubies, sapphires, and diamonds all blended together.

She took a step closer to me and I wondered if I was supposed to bow. I really should have asked Chase about royal protocol here.

"Maya," she trilled, and then she smiled. "It's an honor to meet you."

She didn't touch me, and I dropped my head in an awkward bow, returning her smile. "The honor is all mine."

Her smile was huge, and she was just breathtakingly beautiful. She turned to Chase. "You said bonded mate?"

He nodded, one arm still around me while the other lifted his own shirt to show her the mark. She let out a trill of delight, clapping her hands together. "Chila, get over here. You need to see this."

Chase's father, who had been standing a little back waiting his turn, strode forward. Chase might have had his mother's eyes, but in all other ways, he was just like his father. The same shorn hair, the same masculine planes across his face, and broad shoulders. The fact that the overlord majors did not look much older than us was a little disconcerting, but they carried themselves with wisdom that belied their youthful looks.

He was wearing just a pair of pants, fitted to his very muscled body – something I was trying hard not to notice, because it felt really weird to look at your father-in-law figure like that. He also held a long staff with a jewel on top; the base looked like it was made from the Galinta trees.

With his free hand, he reached out and clasped Chase's briefly. "I'm so pleased to hear of your bonding," he said, looking between me and his son. "Jasmin and I will organize a proper bonding ceremony as soon as we deal with Laous. Our people need to meet Maya."

Nerves rocked me and I tried to school my expression, even though the thought of standing in front of all House of Leights' people was enough to have me searching for the nearest bathroom. When I was nervous, I usually had to pee twenty times in about five minutes.

Chase cleared his throat, and from my angle it looked like he was sending warning glares at his parents. "Maya is very new to this world," he told them. "We should give her some time to adjust to our ways. There is no need to rush anything." He paused, his eyes searching out mine. The air practically shimmered between us, my stomach swirling. "The Galinta could not have chosen better for me," he said.

He turned away from me then and I struggled to get air into my lungs. That boy knocked all of my senses out.

Jasmin nodded decisively. "Yes, you are right, son. We have no need to rush. We are just so happy and excited for you both."

She reached out and placed her hand across my shoulders, long slender fingers wrapping around lightly. "Welcome to our family, Maya."

I was overwhelmed, and scared of saying the wrong thing, but I felt like I needed to be honest. "Thank you. Your kindness and acceptance mean a lot. I can't even tell you how much. I know I'm probably not the person you expected your son to end up with – being human and all – but I promise I will do my best to never let Chase down. The bonding … it's the best thing that's happened to me. Chase makes me feel … complete."

No more searching endlessly. I was finally home.

She nudged her son out of the way and wrapped her arms around me. "I always wanted a daughter," she said, her low accented voice soothing. "You are perfect. The Galinta would never choose someone unworthy."

My heart felt like it would burst, and I had to bite my lip not to cry when she pulled away. She stepped back to her husband's side, and Chase drew me closer to him. I could practically feel his happiness.

"You have done well, son," his father said. "Your mother is right, Maya is worthy."

Cue a raging blush from me and more emotions threatening to send tears down my cheeks.

"We need to go," Chase said, looking between his parents. "Lexen is waiting on us to try and find the fourth keeper. We have to get to her before Laous does."

Everything turned a little more serious then. Chila straightened and gave a low nod. "I am amassing our warriors. We will not stand on the sideline for this fight. Not any longer."

I wanted to freak out about the word "warriors," because it made me think of war, but Chase, grim-faced, just returned his father's nod. "Yes, this is a good idea. We might have to call on them quickly. I will be in touch as soon as we know something."

Jasmin looked upset but didn't say anything more. We exchanged farewells and they stepped back into the trees again, their path closing behind them.

I let out a long, deep breath. Between Chase and his parents, I'd barely been able to get my lungs to work.

"So," I said, swallowing hard, "your parents are so lovely ... and kind of intimidating."

Chase just laughed before he wrapped an arm around me. "You have nothing to worry about. They already adore you. I promise."

Maybe it was better I didn't have time to build the meeting up. The randomness of the last few minutes had meant it was an authentic first introduction, and it did feel like it went well.

"Ready to go now?" he asked, gesturing to the other path he'd opened. It was still there, waiting for us.

I nodded, and Chase kept his arm around me as we stepped out. I felt more than capable of walking on my own, but there was no way I was telling him that. He was touching me. I liked the touching.

"Do you and your father have short hair because of the overlord thing?" I asked him. The few other House of Leights members I'd seen all had long hair, which had me wondering.

Chase nodded. "Yes, overlord major and minor have their hair short to display our marks. Otherwise it's customary for our people to grow their hair long. It's a sign of age, which is a sign of wisdom."

I got the feeling wisdom was something *our* people respected a great deal.

"Tell me about your life," he said as he held a branch back

for me. He was so much taller that everything hit him first. "I want to know who you are, the life you've lived."

I paused, trying to think of something fun and interesting to say. After a few moments, I realized there was nothing. "I've been kind of lonely, really." Pathetic, but it was the truth. "My parents love me, don't get me wrong, but their jobs have dominated their time. So, I just drifted along. If it wasn't for Brad, I'm not sure if I'd be as well-adjusted as I am. His parents also work for the government, so we kept each other company."

"Brad..." He let the name trail off, and I worried we were about to have our first moment of jealousy and male dominance. I wouldn't give up Brad, not even for Chase, so I really hoped he wouldn't ask that of me.

"I'm very glad he was around." His words took me by surprise. "It's nice to see the bond you two have. It reminds me of my friendship with Lexen, Daniel, and Xander. The four of us have been through a lot together. We had to hide our friendship for many years because of bad blood between our houses, but we're connected on a level which I don't believe can be broken."

In some ways, I felt like Chase might have been as lonely as I was. Moving nomadically all the time would have been really tough. I doubted he would have seen his friends much, especially if they were hiding their bond.

"I'm really happy you had the other guys," I said, echoing his sentiment. "I believe humans ... and Daelighters, I would guess ... thrive in a close community. We need love and support. No person should be an island, you know."

We'd had to move apart as we got further into the trees, so I reached out and took his hand. He automatically laced our fingers together. I loved the way he did that. "You won't be lonely anymore," he said, his voice sounding a little rougher than usual. "You have me. Our bond is from the fates, and you have the other secret keepers and their mates. The eight of us ... it's soul deep."

He was philosophical. Never how I would have described myself, but I was starting to come around to his way of thinking. "Already marrying Xander and the last girl off," I teased, needing to lessen the emotion for a beat. "Don't you think he might want a say?"

Chase chuckled. "Xander is going to be the hardest to crack. He's adamant that he'll never settle down. He moves through women ... not disrespecting them, but always making sure they know he's not the serious kind. Not now. Maybe not ever."

"Do they normally have marriages, or bonds and mates in House of Royale?"

"The *caramina* – tailed folk – are much more isolated in nature than most of the other houses. They live in pods that move together beneath the legreto. Honestly, no one knows that much about their families and relationships, but from the little I have learned from Xander, I think it's possible that they do not have any traditional bonds. They tend to just switch and change partners whenever they get sick of each other. If a child results, that's no problem, because they are raised in a collective, pretty much."

"So, no one knows who the father is?" That kind of weirded me out. "Do they make sure not to get into relationships with someone younger? Just in case it's their kid?"

Chase nodded. "Yes, that is generally the rule. Also, most young are sent to other pods. Like exchanges. It would be very rare for that sort of situation to arise."

Still kind of creepy. I hadn't met Xander yet, but I had some mental images of him that weren't very flattering.

"You said tailed folk..." I blurted suddenly as I remembered that. "Like ... literally? They have tails and swim under the water?"

Mermaids. My mental image of Xander changed completely, and now he was a hot, buff mermaid. God I was shallow.

"They can choose to have tails or legs. Under the water, I believe they mostly have tails, for the speed."

"How long can they stay under water for?"

His smile grew and I had to shake my head to focus again. "Forever. They have a dual breathing system that allows them to filter the oxygen in the legreto. Again, they can choose which to utilize."

That was so unfairly cool. "I'd love to see their world. It's a bit annoying that I need oxygen out of water to breathe."

Chase laughed, the sort of full-on laugh that transformed his face – beautiful to breathtaking. How was it even remotely possible this man was bonded to me?

"There is a way you can visit," he told me, leaning down closer. I had no idea if he had been planning on kissing me, but I wasn't missing that opportunity. I launched myself forward, pressing our lips together. He wore an odd expression as I pulled back, and I was about to get all embarrassed and stuff because I was not one to usually take the initiative like that, but then he wrapped his free arm around me and pulled me closer. My feet left the branches so that he could reach my mouth easily.

The mark on my stomach tingled, sending trills of sensation down my body into all the other parts that really liked

Chase. "I wish Laous was dead," Chase growled as he pulled back. "The fact that I can't just keep kissing you right now makes me very unhappy."

"The world has picked a very inconvenient time to need saving," I agreed, my lips barely moving away from his.

His look was regretful as he lowered me back down, holding on until I was finally steady on my feet. "You'd better never die," I warned him. "If you make me addicted and then leave, I'm going to be super annoyed."

He didn't laugh as I expected he might. He lowered his head to drop a kiss against my forehead. "You're stuck with me, *sayana*, for now and always."

"Sayana?"

"There is no literal translation to English," he said, after seeming to think for a moment. "It's more of a feeling. Something akin to 'adore.'"

My tear ducts felt very sensitive all of a sudden, and I wondered why that one word suddenly felt like so much – like everything. It wasn't even the normal four-letter word that most people aspired to hear.

Adore.

This was so very new for us both, and I knew how strong my feelings already were, but in that moment, adore was perfect.

Further conversation was cut off by a loud rustling in the trees. I ducked low; the noise was close and it sounded like there was more than one creature coming at me.

My heart stopped racing when my new friend flew into sight, the bear-owl. "Oh my God!" I exclaimed. "You're okay. I wondered where you'd gotten to. I'm really glad you didn't get squished."

Chase wore a look of confusion, and when the bear-owl tried to fly closer, he stepped around me, blocking its path.

"What are you doing?" I asked, tapping him on the shoulder. "That's my friend, it helped me find you." Or at least tagged along for the ride.

The confusion he wore morphed into something like astonishment. "Maya," he started slowly. "This is an oliconda. They're one of the deadliest creatures in House of Leights. They're strong, vicious, and can rip a Daelighter apart with their claws. Claws that secrete a very lethal poison."

At first, I thought he was screwing with me, especially since he hadn't thought twice about stepping between me and the oliconda. "Are you sure?" I finally asked. "I carried it on my shoulder for quite a while."

He looked between me and the creature multiple times, then shook his head. Using this to my advantage, I slipped around him, and this time he let me. Holding out my arm to the oliconda, I smiled. It didn't hesitate, spreading those broad wings and soaring across to me again. As the heavy weight landed, I let out a relieved sigh. "Thanks for coming back to me, Oli. You don't mind if I call you Oli, right?" Oliconda was too much of a mouthful.

It squawked lightly, and then we both turned in Chase's direction as he let out a rumbling sound, shaking his head. "I cannot believe what I'm seeing. Not in all of our history has anyone tied themselves to an Oliconda. In fact, usually the ones to see them do not live to tell the tale. Luckily, they tend to remain hidden, in the shadows. Otherwise, we'd be down a lot of members of my house."

I shrugged. "This one seems okay. Maybe it's different to the others?"

You're different.

That voice in my head was not like the Galinta. It was a single feminine tone, and it took me more than a moment to realize it had come from Oli. It had to have; there was no one else it could be.

"You talked to me," I said out loud. "You can talk!"

Yes, and I don't mind if you call me Oli ... I will also answer to Flet. If you ever need me, just call and I will come.

With that, Flet's wings spread again, and then she took off.

Once it was gone, Chase wrapped his arms tightly around me, his breathing fast and ragged. "Don't ever do that to me again," he grumbled. "I was afraid to try and interfere, in case that upset the oliconda and it attacked. But allowing it that close to you went against every one of my protective instincts."

Patting his shoulder, I had to chuckle. "You definitely don't have to worry about that particular oli. She spoke in my mind, said her name was Flet, and that I could call on her if I ever needed."

He shook his head a few times. "I don't know what you are, Maya, but you seem to fit into this world better than most Daelighters. Your energy feels ancient ... like the original overlords. You were meant to call this world home."

He set me gently to my feet and I regarded him for a moment. "Why would that be?" I had a thought then. "Do you think the last secret keepers had the same sort of balance and energy with each other?" We already knew none of them bonded to overlords.

Chase lifted his broad shoulders in a shrug. "I have no idea. If we get a chance, it wouldn't hurt to speak with one of the three still alive. Maybe they'll have information for us. Something they have learned in the last hundred plus years."

That was a good idea, but I doubted we'd have the time to do that. Our pace picked up then for the rest of the journey, and I mentally thanked the Galinta more than once for their water. My ankle barely even smarted at all, and that was solely because of their healing. Still, by the time we reached the end of the trees, I was exhausted. It felt like a million years ago that we had set out from the house in the forest. Two million years since I first saw Chase at the party. How could so much have happened in such a short amount of time? How could I have changed to the point where I barely felt like the same person anymore? It was impossible, and yet here we were.

"You need food and water," Chase said, pressing his hands to the branches blocking our path. "You're tired."

He was observant; it made me feel cared about. "I'm ready to do whatever needs to be done," I replied, "but if I can get food before we start, that would be great."

As we stepped out onto the platform, we found everyone gathered and waiting. I ran straight to my best friend and he growled at me. "Can you please stop disappearing on me! Star and I did everything we could to find you. Thank God Lexen got a message through the network to her, because I was about to panic."

I hugged him as hard as I could, so happy to see he was okay. "Sorry," I said as I pulled back. "You weren't here when I got back, but my parents said you were okay, so I went after Chase."

I knew Chase was standing close to my back. That feeling in my tummy was almost permanent now, especially with the tethering between us.

"We're bonded," I told my parents and Brad, who were all looking at me. "It's something that was chosen for us by the Galinta, and ... fate." The three wore expressions that told me they didn't know if they were supposed to be happy or concerned. I let my happiness free, smiling broadly. "Chase fills that restless part of my soul which has always searched for its home."

"Maya is my home," Chase agreed.

Yeah, we were the cliché couple who had known each other for mere days and were already declaring our everlasting love for each other. But when you looked at it another way, there was nothing cliché or normal about us. We were born to greater things than just a regular life, and I was going to embrace every second of it.

Smiles broke out across my parents' faces. My dad stepped forward to shake Chase's hand, his welcome to the family. I expected Brad to make some sort of disparaging remark, but he just stared off into the main group of Daelighters and murmured, "I think I understand what you're saying."

I followed his line of sight to a flash of dark hair and laughter. *Star.* I knew I'd seen something between those two. I really hoped Brad wasn't setting himself up for heartache. For all we knew, Star was in love with someone else. Or at least betrothed.

I'd have to talk to him about it later. Maybe Chase would have some insider knowledge, so I could feel less concerned that my friend was about to suffer his first heartbreak. Not that he didn't deserve to know how it felt all the times he'd crushed women with his lack of caring, but he was my best friend. I didn't want him to hurt.

"Now that everyone is back, let's move out." Lexen's voice was loud enough to be heard by all. "If we get the tracking just right in the network, we should be able to find the fourth. I've also called in Jero, my brother, to assist us, because I'm not sure how easily we could lose control."

Turning to where he pointed, I found a somber, gorgeous, dark-haired male. He looked like Lexen, just a little shorter, with fuller lips and a faded scar on the side of his face. He gave us all a nod but didn't join in with any discussion. Emma crossed over and wrapped her arms around him, and Jero squeezed his eyes shut tightly for a moment while they hugged, before he pulled back and re-crossed his arms over his broad chest.

I wondered if he was naturally reticent, or if maybe he'd shut the world out since his brother's death. I knew all of the Darken siblings were suffering. I could see the pain in their eyes. But Jero looked broken.

"It's so unfair that they haven't had time to grieve," I whispered to Chase.

The skin around his eyes tightened, and while I had no idea what he was thinking, there was definitely something stormy brewing in those green depths. "Laous needs to suffer for that, more than anything else he's done. Marsil was a good guy. He didn't deserve what happened. His family is so close as well. This will devastate them forever."

"I heard their mom hasn't left her room since it happened," Callie murmured. She'd drifted closer. "I keep picturing the moment in my head ... when he died ... all of the blood. I can't bury the images..." She broke off in a rough sob, and Daniel enclosed her tightly in his arms.

She buried her face in his chest, taking a few moments to pull herself together. When she finally lifted her head, her eyes were red and her cheeks flushed, but she had stopped sobbing. I wanted to comfort her, but I didn't know what to do, so I just stood there like a moron, trying not to cry myself in sympathy.

Before it turned into a huge tear-fest, Lexen ushered us toward the transporter and I actually flinched as I realized I'd have to travel through it again. Chase noticed. "I will not let you go," he promised, taking my hand. "There's more than enough of us to get everyone to House of Darken safely."

I believed him, and I had faith that if I got lost, I'd find my way out again. So, with a few deep breaths for confidence, I placed my hand in his, and then we were stepping back into the world of darkness.

17

———

*H*ouse of Darken was so freaking pretty. Legit. Like Switzerland but slightly more rugged. It was natural, no obvious towns or cities. Similar to House of Leights, but with far less in the way of trees. Its landscape was mainly mountains and valleys. Snow and trickling streams flowed through passes. The Daelighters explained that they had very strict rules in Overworld about messing with nature. Earth's technologies, for the most part, were not allowed here. No cars. No cell phones. Daelighters communicated through the network, or via a postage system that was delivered to the platform between the lands.

Despite those small inconveniences, I really liked their way of living. It made me feel comfortable in my skin. Although, I would miss organic sheets. The transporter had taken us right into Lexen's home, a beautiful dwelling made of a marble-like stone. Even more crazy, his castle was inside of a cave that had been completely carved into a city. Yep. A freaking mountain city, everything chiseled from the rocks. We stopped long enough for sandwiches, which were filled with a creamy cheese-like spread, and then we were heading closer to the network.

A lot of locals watched us as we walked through the city, most of them half-bowing with their hands pressed to their heads when they saw the Darken siblings. Probably, that's what I should have done when I met Chase's parents.

The bowing was a huge reminder that I was now bonded and friends with royalty. Chase just winked at me, a crooked grin in place, and I felt better about it. It was all worth it to have someone like him in my life. Once we were through the city, we took a path out of the mountain and down into the valley below it.

"You know, you could have stayed behind and rested," I told my parents, who were marching right beside me.

My father just shot me the "look," the one he reserved for the times I broke the rules. "Maya, little one, you know that's not going to happen. We need to be here in case you run into any danger."

My mother gave a deep head nod, as always, on the same side as her husband. I learned about teamwork from my parents; they always supported each other.

With a sigh, I turned back to face the way we were walking – fairly important when trailing down a mountain path. There was nothing my parents could do to help in this situation; neither of them had magical powers. But I liked that they were here. Despite all of the ups and downs, I'd spent more continuous time with them over the last few days than I had in the last few months. Maybe this would bring us closer now that they could share this world with me.

"Will you guys continue to work for the government agency?" I asked, curious about how much might change for them now. Everything had changed for me, but maybe they'd go back to their normal lives.

In some ways they had been preparing me well to live without them, but I still wouldn't like it.

My parents exchanged a look before they both turned back to me. "We'll go wherever you are," my mom said in her gentle way. "If you stay here in Overworld, in House of Leights with Chase, then that is where we will stay as well."

That response actually stunned me. It showed me the real truth of what they'd been saying to me all along. They'd taken the government jobs as a means of keeping me safe. I was their first priority.

Turning to observe Chase's profile, I realized that I hadn't given much thought to where we would live. I mean ... I wasn't sure I was ready for the whole "move in together" thing yet. But at the same time, I didn't want to be separated from him.

"You're bonded, that's like marriage to the Daelighters," my father added, reading my expression. "It would be normal for you to stay with Chase now."

"I ... yes, you're right. It's just fast, you know."

Chase wrapped an arm around me and I calmed. "Maya is going to finish school, and then decide about college," he told them. "Because she has to be protected, she'll have to transfer to Daelighter territory. But she doesn't have to make any other life-changing decisions." He brushed a hand along my spine and heat trailed after it. "I have a home in Daelight Crescent. All of the overlord families do. You're welcome to use it any time you want."

My breathing was even, and when we stepped into the valley floor I threw my arms around him. "Thank you," I whispered. "Thank you for being patient with me."

He leaned down and kissed the top of my head. "I will

always wait for you to be ready. Being a team means considering all players."

"I would prefer to stay on Earth," my mom said, surprising me. "At least for another few years. So I'm glad that's an option."

Brad huffed. "I'm going to start looking for colleges in Oregon," he declared. "No way is everyone living over here having fun without me."

My dad gave him a solid back pat, which didn't seem to bother my beefed-up best friend. "I'll talk to your parents," he said to Brad. "They might be okay with you finishing up the school year with Maya in Astoria."

Brad and I locked eyes, excitement bubbling within me. That would be amazing. Surely they wouldn't care; they were barely home at all. Before we could celebrate the possibility of staying together, Lexen burst our bubble, bringing us all back to the reality of this situation.

"This is our last chance," he started. "If Laous gets to the starslight stone before us, he will be very powerful. He will destroy the treaty, and possibly both worlds. Failure is not an option."

There was a flapping sound, and all eyes turned toward the sky. All eyes except Lexen's, because apparently he didn't need to see a dragon lazily soaring through the air toward us.

Jesus, take the wheel. What was happening?

The creature was a brilliant white that almost hurt my eyes to stare directly at, and massive, like three elephants in length and width. Its head looked to be bigger than my entire body.

"What's Qenita doing here?" Emma asked, shielding her eyes so she could stare up at her. "Do we need her?"

Lexen turned, a smile pushing up his lips as he stared at the majestic beast in the sky. "She's bringing Xander. He's been dealing with some unrest in House of Royale. They're having trouble with his sister and her new partner, so he wasn't able to get away until now."

I was interested in finally meeting the last of the overlord quartet – and the possible mate of the fourth secret keeper. If he could ever stop playing the field long enough to fall for her, of course. After my experience with Chase, I was pretty sure fate was stronger and cleverer than this Xander. He had no hope.

I'd worry about the Royale overlord after he landed, though. Until then, I was all about the dragon. Because ... uh ... dragons. A creature, until this very moment, that had been reserved for television and movies.

Callie echoed my thoughts: "Did we just stumble into a fantasy world? Because I can see a dragon. Everyone else can as well ... right?"

"Right," was the return murmur from more than one person.

Lexen moved forward, heading toward a little clearing of green grass that must have been the dragon's landing ground. I didn't follow, because as fascinating as she was, she was also absolutely terrifying. Qenita could eat me in one bite. Whole.

Yeah, I was perfectly happy staring from back here.

Despite her huge size, she landed with so much grace that she barely even made a sound. Her wings tucked in behind her, and a tall blond man jumped off. Lexen and Xander did a quick guy-hug, pat-on-the-back-thing, before they both placed their hands on the dragon, speaking to her, and then her wings were out again and she was soaring back into the sky. By the time the two overlords made their way to us, Qenita was nothing more than a pinprick above.

Which was scary when one thought about trying to hide

from a possible dragon attack. They could be a tiny dot above, and seconds later would be right on your butt. Made me want to shuffle a little closer to Lexen, the dragon lord.

Xander greeted Daniel in the same way he had Lexen, then he crossed to Chase. After their hug and back pats, Chase reached for me, bringing me closer. "This is Maya, the third secret keeper. She wears a bonded mark, blessed by the Galinta."

Xander's eyes widened, then he let out a series of colorful curses. "You have got to be shitting me." I wasn't the only one staring wide-eyed at the Royale overlord. "I don't like this. It's bullshit that we're having our choices and freedoms stripped from us."

I didn't want to flinch, but tall, muscled, angry men hit all of my wary nerves. I'd never physically match someone like Xander, so I usually chose to retreat. Even though it was annoying that I had to.

Chase's arm tightened, stopping me from moving. "Calm down," he said to his friend, bite in his tone. "You're scaring Maya, and I'm about five seconds from teaching you some respect."

Xander's face was awash in fury, blue eyes darkening to something very stormy. "You've all been brainwashed," he declared. "Especially you, Chase. Seriously, you've always been content with your life. You turned down all of those possible matches when your parents suggested them between some of the other Leights. Now you're telling me you're just going to fall for the first pretty piece of ass—"

He was cut off by a fist to the face. Chase had released me, moving me back a few inches before he slammed his fist into Xander's jaw. The punch knocked the Royale overlord back a decent six feet. He straightened, shaking himself off.

Chase did not hit him again, but he moved in front of me, his body changing. He was at least six inches taller than usual, which meant I was basically staring at his butt.

Short girl problems, I tell ya.

I peeked around to see Xander glaring and rubbing his jaw. "You know I'm right." He sounded resigned. "Within a matter of months, the three of you have all bonded to a human. Doesn't that sound a little coincidental?"

Lexen and Daniel moved behind Xander so that he was now surrounded by his best friends. "Fate designed it this way," Daniel told him, turning so he could see Callie. "My life was shit before I met her. I would not give up my bond with Cal for anything in either world. I consider myself blessed."

"It's the same for me," Lexen added.

"And me," Chase finished. "I could search my entire life for a woman like Maya and I would never find one. Not even close. How do I know this? Because I have searched for fifty years already, and no one has stirred even one percent of the emotion inside of me that she did from the first second I heard her name."

Holy gods. I was going to cry, seriously. I stepped up and pressed myself to his back. His body was back to normal size now, so my face wasn't pressed into his butt. Was I disappointed or relieved about that? Hard to tell.

My skin was tight and flushed from all the energy and adrenalin, so I just breathed in the fresh, outdoorsy scent of Chase, and let myself calm down. His hands wrapped over mine.

Xander pushed his hair back in agitation. "I ... fuck – sorry for being an asshole. I've had a hell of a week, which I know is nothing compared to what everyone else is dealing with. I don't begrudge any of you this new happiness in your lives.

Just … don't expect the same from me. I'm never going to be the Daelighter for the fourth secret keeper. It's better that everyone knows it from the start."

No one argued with him, and I started to breathe easier as the palpable tension faded out of the group. "You've always been free to make your own choices," Lexen said. "You do what's right for you."

Sounded to me like Xander did that anyway, but again, who was I to judge? I didn't know what went on in his life. Maybe Xander was trying not to bring anyone into a mess of a world.

I'd give him the benefit of the doubt for now.

Lexen and Daniel went straight for their girls, needing to touch them. I understood that need. Xander's rant had left a sour taste in my mouth, tainting some of the happiness I had been feeling. But the moment Chase turned around, his arms scooping under me so he could hug me properly, the world felt right again.

"None of what he said is true, not for me," he told me, very seriously.

Using all of my strength, I pulled him closer to me. "I know, I've never doubted that for a second. What you said … that was beautiful. Thank you." He squeezed me extra tight, and then set me back on my feet.

We moved into the main group, and I did my best not to stand near Xander, because he was kind of on my shit list right now.

"Okay, so the council used the network to find Callie and Maya," Lexen explained. "But they don't believe it can be done with the fourth. There are securities that make it nearly impossible to find the fourth without the stone."

Okay, so why were we here, then?

"But they don't know what we do, that together the eight of us are a very strong, powerful unit," Daniel added. "A unit which is missing one part, and we believe that together our power will search for her."

Xander crossed his arms, staring out into the mountains beyond. Moody bastard.

"So what do we have to do?" Emma asked, her hands clasped in front of her; she looked nervous. "I get the concept of the network, but the thought of trying to connect to it ... I'm not sure I can do it."

"Same," Callie piped up.

Same, I mentally added.

"We'll show you the way we learned as children," Lexen told her. "Our parents take us in the first time, and then after that, the pathway becomes more instinctive and natural."

Star stepped forward from where she had been standing back with Jero, both of them silent bystanders. "I have this to help you out." She held something square in her hand, about the size of a large picture frame.

Once she handed it to Lexen, she returned to Jero's side. My parents and Brad gave me a wave, then moved closer to Star, leaving just the seven of us in a rough circle.

"We need to hold hands," Daniel said, and I shuffled around so that I was in between Chase and Callie. We reached for each other at the same time, and the moment my hands were in theirs, my stomach did a flip. It was like the "Chase feeling" – intense, but less ... sexual. Which was definitely a good thing. It wasn't that I had any problem with the poly life-style, but in this case, I was a one-man sort of woman.

Once the seven of us were joined, the energy running through my hands grew stronger. It felt like tingles that built up and then calmed down in waves. "The network exists beneath our feet," Chase explained. "It's a grid of energy; you can picture it as long lines of light, spanning Overworld, criss-crossing each other."

Lexen nodded. "Exactly. These lines connect all around our world. Even into Earth, somewhat. You can use the lights to find something or someone. If you know what you're looking for.

"We send coded messages to each other," Chase jumped in, "because we are familiar with the energy of our friends and family. Now we just have to find the light that leads to the last secret keeper."

Callie interrupted: "She's going to be on Earth, right? Lexen said the network stretches somewhat into Earth, but will it be far enough?"

There was a beat of silence, and then Daniel said, "It's not common knowledge, but since we set up the permanent trans-porter, our network crosses further into Earth's energy. We've kept it from the people because too much network use on Earth could throw the balance off. But ... desperate times."

The council must have taken the same risk with the balance, which clearly turned out okay.

"Jero, we need your help now," Lexen called out to his brother. The solemn male crossed over to our group, ducking under his brother and Emma's clasped hands. He shook his head, body visibly shivering as he straightened.

"The energy you're sharing right now is intense." He sounded surprised. "For a moment, I wasn't sure it was going to let me cross."

"Lucky we aren't intentionally trying to keep you out, isn't it?" Daniel said with a grin. "Then you'd probably be peeling yourself off the mountain." He inclined his head toward a nearby rock face.

Jero actually cracked a smile, and it changed his face so much. The difference was mesmerizing. He reached down and grabbed up the square frame that Star had brought with her, the thing that was supposed to help us connect. Jero held it up in front of Emma.

"Hey!" she exclaimed. "I loved these things when I was a kid."

Immediately I wanted to know what it was, but since I couldn't move I'd have to patiently wait until it was my turn.

"You need to let your eyes adjust, just like you did as a kid," Jero explained. "Once you see the lines, let them extend out of the image until they reach the ground. Follow them down. You'll understand once your mind is connected."

"I'll help you," Lexen added. "Guide you along the lines of energy."

Emma didn't say anything, she focused her attention on the square Jero held. The rest of us were left to deal with tingling hands while watching Emma's face go from interested to confused to frustrated, back to confused, before eventually landing on devastated.

"I can't see it," she wailed, tipping her head toward Lexen. "I tried everything I could to see the different image, but there's nothing there."

She sounded extremely upset; her eyes were watery. Lexen leaned down and kissed her on the lips, startling her, but also bringing a much happier expression to her face.

"You're pushing too hard," he said. "The key is to let your mind relax. Don't force it. Try to remember that you have been in the network before. It's the only way your secret keeper's abilities could work. The only way the four of you could be linked the way you are. When you were born, your souls touched the network. The imprinting from that remains within you."

Emma sucked in a loud breath. "I can do this," she murmured, to no one in particular. "I will not let Laous beat us."

I felt her statement deep in my soul. The truth of it. We could do this.

18

―――――

*I*t took Emma thirteen minutes to master the mystery picture. I was pretty excited for it to get around to me, but also nervous, because I had no idea what to expect. Callie was next, and while I had a side view of what looked like a dark blue pattern sprinkled through with lights, the image was angled away from me, limiting my vision of it.

Instead I watched Emma, who was now staring off to the side, unfocused. I wondered what she was seeing. Was she actually in the network? It seemed that the only way to know was to go there yourself, so I'd just have to work on my patience.

"This is insane," Callie snarled, breathing deeply, until eventually her face relaxed. "I just need to calm down, I just need to focus." She started murmuring to herself. "I can do this."

"You got this, Cal. Just follow the lights," Daniel said, lifting their joined hands up slightly. "I'll help you go the rest of the way."

It took fourteen minutes before her eyes took on the same

unfocused cast as Emma's, then apparently, she was in. Jero took two steps to the right and I tried to breathe through the absolute rapid pounding of my heart, feeling it in my throat and hearing it in my head.

"Your turn, Maya," he drawled. Chase swung his head toward him, like he was shocked by something.

"No nickname?" Chase asked him. I was confused, but I figured this was a "Jero" inside joke that I'd hopefully find out one day.

Jero's lip twitched a little. "I'm working on it," he replied, with a lopsided smile.

He lifted the frame higher, and for the first time I could see exactly what it was. Like Emma, I was familiar with it. It was one of those three-dimensional images hidden inside a two-dimensional pattern. You had to readjust your focus and you could see the hidden image inside. I was always terrible at it. Like ... horrendous.

The pattern was akin to a night sky filled with a million shooting stars, beams of lights crisscrossing each other. My eyes flicked across to Chase, who was watching me closely. As he inclined his head at me, the smile he wore never faded. *You got this*, that look said. And I nodded. So what if I sucked at this sort of thing when I was younger? People learned new skills every day.

Turning back to the image, I tried to calm my mind, blocking out the world around me.

Come on, Maya. No matter how hard I tried though, the damn picture still just looked like a night sky. It reminded me of when I'd been in the transporter, all of that darkness, with the pinpricks of light in the distance. Only these lights were closer and smudged into each other.

Maybe I needed to just focus on one light in particular and

try to see which smudge belonged to it. I searched around for one near the edge of the image. It had a tail that spun and flipped around, crossing back in on its self. I continued to follow, losing the path once or twice and having to backtrack, but I eventually got there. As I reached the tail it … moved. So I continued to follow its path … which continued to move.

That feeling of excitement inside of me brought the thrum of energy in my hands to greater heights.

"That's it, *sayana*," Chase murmured close to me. "Follow that light."

It extended off the page, and I kept my focus, scared if I lost sight of the line for even a second, I'd lose whatever ground I'd gained. It spiraled down the side of Jero's leg toward the ground. It was easy to follow now; there were no other lights to interfere. The moment the beam hit the green grass, it solidified.

Lifting my eyes, I stared at all the lights on the image, tracing some of their paths, and without any effort this time, all of them started to move. It took me ten minutes to have hundreds of bright lights anchored to the ground. They were vibrating, and I could hear noises, maybe even voices coming from within them.

One twanged loudly at me, and within it I felt Chase. I mentally reached for his light and it hit me in the chest. The energy I felt when I was near him filled me up, then it dragged me down into the ground. I didn't physically move, but my consciousness was going with that beam of light, and then I was "standing" … existing … in a world of darkness. Only it wasn't just darkness, there were beams of light everywhere, crossing in front of me and over each other.

There was a lot of noise here at first, but when I focused, most of the chatter died away. I could feel them all here:

Emma, Callie, Lexen, Daniel, Xander, and Chase. I couldn't see them, but I recognized the bright beams of light around me. The seven of us glowed, running almost parallel to each other.

Maya, you did it, I heard Emma's words in my head.

Be very careful what you say here, Lexen reminded us. *All conversations can be recorded and overheard in the network.*

We fell somewhat silent, and I wondered what we were supposed to do now.

Let's start with a little test, Daniel suggested. *Try to find Jero. His energy will be close to ours, because he's physically near us.*

I hadn't had much time to get to know Jero, but that didn't seem to matter. I only had to picture him in my mind, had to remember the sad, heavy emotions he carried around, and my light immediately shot toward a tattered-looking beam about ten yards away. It strummed at me, almost like a greeting.

We can feel if someone is searching for our energy, Chase told us. *Jero will know, but if he wanted to respond or communicate, he would have to enter the network.*

Callie's light went bright then and I felt like she was laughing. *This is just like virtual reality. Our bodies are where we left them, but our consciousness and vision is now in another world.*

That was true, and while there wasn't much going on in the way of world building here, I felt the vast endless opportunities that lay beyond us.

Okay, now that we have found Jero, let's try for someone on Earth, Emma suggested. *Maybe my guardians. For those who have met them and know their energy.*

That wasn't me, so I sat that one out.

Easy as, Emma finally exclaimed.

That was definitely a positive, but since none of us had met the last secret keeper, it was no doubt going to be more difficult. I hoped they had a good plan.

Lexen sounded serious. *We're going to have mere seconds to find her, because the moment we locate her rough proximity, we need to cut the connection. Otherwise she could be found by others.*

Daniel interrupted: *And if there is any instability with Earth's energy while we do this, we're also going to have to abort immediately.*

So how do we do this when we haven't met her? Callie asked.

The pause felt very long, but it was probably only a second before Xander answered: *Jero is going to prick each of the secret keepers' fingers ... if they are agreeable to this. We'll mix the three drops of blood together, and then he is going to send it down into the network.*

We all agreed, because there wasn't much choice. We had to find her.

You might feel a pinch, Chase added. *Don't let it pull you from the network. Keep your focus here.*

With those words, I locked myself onto his light and waited for the pain. My energy jolted when it came, but it was mild and over so quickly there was no danger of me disappearing. After another beat, a new beam of light entered in our midst, one that was not the bright white I'd grown accustomed to. This one had a tinge of red to it.

Our blood.

Hold on to that beam, Daniel said. *Use the secret keepers' connection.*

I felt more comfortable in the network now. It felt almost instinctive to reach out with my own energy and connect to that reddish beam. *Find the fourth. Find our fourth,* I chanted, urging the light forward, the same way I had when the beams spread off the paper. I needed that light to follow its path. All the way to the last girl.

The red started to vibrate, moving with such frequency

that it blurred. All I got were flashes of color in the darkness. But it wasn't extending, it seemed to be anchored to us, not interested at all in moving.

What are you three thinking? Xander asked with impatience. *You all have to give it the same goal, or it's going to just remain where it is.*

Find our fourth, I said.

Let's all go with that, Callie chimed in.

I focused everything again on that red line, that had slowed its vibrations, only to start up again as soon as I mentally pushed it to find the fourth. Just like before, though, it didn't move. Almost like it was caught on something.

You said that all seven of us were needed to find the eighth, Emma reminded the guys. *So ... maybe you all need to bleed a little, too.*

There was a pause, but no one disagreed. Then Daniel said, *Jero is on it.*

In the next moment, the red of the blood beam went blindingly bright. It splintered in almost the same instant, part of it shooting away from us. My focus latched on tightly, and I found myself zooming away with the beam. I could feel the others close by as well.

Focus, I heard Lexen shout.

Find our fourth. Find our fourth. Find our fourth.

The moment we crossed out of Overworld and into Earth was very obvious. It was like a jolt, and then a surge, and then a foreign feeling. We were in a place we weren't supposed to be in. The darkness even had a divide – a chasm – that we had to mentally leap over.

This is so weird...

Our lights were dimmer on the Earth side, even though the endless darkness around us remained. The red beam stayed on course, and when it started to slow down, I slowed with it. It spiraled toward a dull, bluish-looking light, which I threw myself toward, letting it guide me up to the surface.

How did I know how to do this? No freaking idea.

The moment my energy hit the surface, it was all sun and sand and waves. And since I had been there before, I knew exactly where we were.

Maya! Don't follow the light like that.

The shout startled me and I lost my focus. The sun faded away, and with a snap I was back in my body in House of Darken, my hands still held tightly in Chase and Callie's. I looked between them, and then the rest of the group, realizing I was the only one back. The others still wore that faraway gaze.

My parents, Brad, Star, and Jero rushed over to me. "Did you find her?" Star asked, her hands pressed tightly together in front of her. "You've been gone for about two minutes. I expected longer. Why are you the only one back?" Her questions picked up pace, rushing together as she wrung her hands.

I shook my head hard. "I think I might have done something wrong. I followed the light, and it led me to Lanai, in Hawaii. I lost focus and snapped back into my body. Wait a minute ... did you say two minutes?"

"Time moves differently in there," Jero said. "Usually we can get in and out in under thirty seconds when we need to utilize the network. Two minutes is actually quite a long time."

"How do you form a transporter?" I asked, realizing now that there was so much more I could do in there. No wonder the Daelighters didn't need Earth technology, they had the network. So much cooler.

Jero's lips curled up slightly. "You move along the network

until you find the place you want to travel. Then you take the lights there and spiral them. Spin and twirl them until they form a solid doorway. If you do it right, the transporter appears in the physical world as well as in the network."

"You have to be so careful, though," Star told me. "Anyone can track and follow you when you do that. To stay off the radar, it's better just to travel the human way."

That should be easy enough to do. Hawaii was just a plane ride away, after all. But it was definitely a lot slower than the transporter. My dad brushed strands of my hair off my face. "Are you okay?"

I nodded. "Yes, definitely. Mostly because I think it worked. The fourth secret keeper is in Hawaii. Remember that little island of Lanai that we went to for our 2013 holiday ... that's where the line stopped."

My dad exchanged a look with Mom, and she nodded, agreeing with what his eyes had been telling her. "What?" I demanded.

"One of the families was stationed near there," she said. "They were Astronomers, I think."

That had to be them. "We have to get there now before Laous finds her. From what I saw, she was fine. Her energy felt stable."

Chase shifted at my side, and I turned to him. "Are you okay?" he said immediately, releasing my hand and Xander's so he could turn to me.

I stepped into him, pressing my hands to his chest. "I'm fine. Sorry if I did something wrong back there. One minute I was rising up to the surface to see where the red and blue light stopped, and the next I was back here."

He regarded me without an ounce of judgment. "Did you see where she was?"

"Yeah." I nodded. "The cord stopped at Lanai, an island near Hawaii. I've been there before on holidays."

He snatched me up, hugging me tightly, before his lips crushed into mine. I had no idea what was happening around us after that. All I knew was Chase. The feel of his lips. The tether to him that rested in my center thrumming.

"Guys, seriously, can you all get a room? I don't want to see my best friend slash sister doing that..." Brad's complaint registered faintly, and with a disappointed huff I pulled back.

Mostly so I could flip him off.

"The number of chicks I have had to see you suck face with..." I trailed off at the panicked look in his eyes. As his gaze shifted to Star, I realized what he was worried about – that once she found out about his past, she might not like the person he was. Later I would remind him that there was no point hiding his past. He would just have to show Star that he was no longer that same guy.

Everyone was out of the network now, and there was a lot of confusion as they all spoke at once. I realized that no one thought I'd made it to the surface. When I told them I did, the mood lightened.

"We need to move, now," Lexen declared, his eyes glittering with white lights. It was freaky when he did that, because I knew the draygone soul he hid inside. He turned to my parents and Brad. "You three should stay here. I will have Star escort you to our home, where you can wait safely for our return."

My dad opened his mouth and I recognized that stubborn clenched jaw and pursed lips. He was going to argue about this and generally make life very difficult for everyone until he got his own way. Before he could, I reached out and wrapped my hand around his forearm. "You can't protect me from this,

Dad." That stopped him in his tracks, and when he slowly lowered his head to meet my eyes, the stubborn emotion had been replaced with sadness. "I know you blame yourself for choosing to involve me in this world ... but no matter how this works out, I want you to know that I have no regrets. I have found a place here, a future. I have found more members to add to our family."

"Hells yeah, you have," Emma chimed in, before slamming her mouth shut and slapping her hand across it.

Lexen laughed. "She will forever be listening in on your conversations. You might as well get used to it."

"Emma is right, though," Callie added. "I had no family at all, and now I feel like there are so many of you damn people I care about. And that scares me..." She trailed off for a moment. "But I believe that together we're the strongest team I've ever seen. There is nothing we can't accomplish. It's ... a true family. None of us will be left behind. Laous will not take any more from us."

Amen.

When I returned my gaze to my parents, my dad had glassy eyes. "Take care of my little one," he said, still looking at me while he spoke to the others. "And welcome to our family."

He leaned forward and kissed me on the forehead. My mom kissed me on both cheeks, holding my face in her hands, staring at me. When they turned away – and I was trying not to cry – Brad wrapped both of his arms around me and hoisted me up into his big body. His familiar smell brought back a million memories.

Brad would always be my best friend, but our lives were changing, expanding. We were finding new people to love and that was a good thing.

"Come back to me, you hear," he said as he pulled away,

dropping me down to my feet. "Best friends forever does not have an out clause. You're in for life."

I patted his chest, and he cleared his throat and turned away. Star didn't argue about having to stay behind, she just smiled and hugged her brothers and Emma before she joined my parents and Brad. The four of them then made their way back up to the mountain city.

I watched them until they disappeared from sight. "They'll be okay," Chase told me. "The overlord's home is protected by the draygones. This is the safest place for them."

"I know." I nodded. "As hard as it is to watch them walk away, I would prefer they were not out in the battlefield. Still, I have to wonder if I'll ever see them again."

There were no guarantees in life.

"You'll see them again, Maya," he said, somewhat fiercely. "I will not let anything happen to you."

Before I could answer, low laughter echoed down through the valley we stood in. Chase – and the other overlords – reacted in an instant, moving to surround us. That laughter had been loud and unnatural, and even though I could not see who it came from, there was no doubt…

We were not alone.

19

———

A man stepped out from the shadows. He was about twenty feet away, appearing from behind a nearby rocky outreach. He had dark hair slicked up in the center, olive skin, and a sharp but still handsome face. Tattoos ran across his neck and down into the black long-sleeved shirt he wore.

He looked familiar. Ish. But I couldn't recall how I knew him.

Daniel made a grumbling noise nearby and I turned toward him. "Fraizer," he said, sounding more than a little annoyed. "What the hell are you doing here?"

The boys closed in even further on Emma, Callie, and me. Jero included. He had lost every ounce of sadness now, wearing a mask of fury. He looked very fallen angel. Whoever this "Fraizer" was, he was not a popular guy in this group.

I realized then why he seemed familiar – he kind of looked like Daniel. Less rugged, more attitude, but there were similarities. I tilted my head up and mouthed "brother?" to Chase, and he nodded once.

"I'm here because I think we need to talk," Fraizer said,

crossing his arms over his chest. His stance was relaxed, legs slightly spread, boots firmly planted. But there was uneasiness in the way he held his shoulders, tension there that betrayed his confident persona.

Jero took a threatening step forward. "There is nothing you could say which we want to hear. So I guess you've come here to die."

Lexen reached out and grabbed his brother, but Jero threw that hand off with a violent jerk. "He was part of the group which killed Marsil," Jero said, followed by a string of hurled curse words. "He needs to die."

Daniel didn't say anything, and the look on his face was difficult to interpret. There was clearly no love between him and Fraizer, but he also didn't look ready to join the lynching squad.

"I didn't kill Marsil," Fraizer protested. "I was there to try and stop it all from happening. I hoped to let you all know beforehand, but as usual, no one was interested in what I had to say."

"You tried to contact me through the network," Daniel said out of nowhere. "On the day Marsil was killed."

When Fraizer turned to his brother, there was a crap-ton of anger in those narrowed eyes. "Even though you don't deserve it, I was trying to keep you from getting killed. For Mom."

Daniel's face shuttered, and I saw the look Callie threw in his direction. Their mom was definitely a sore point.

"Aren't you on Laous' side?" Lexen drawled, a hint of death in those words. "Now you expect us to believe you have switched sides ... that you were there on the day Marsil was murdered because you wanted to warn us?"

Fraizer let out a huff of air, his cheeks puffing out. "At first Laous offered me what I wanted, a chance to belong. He is family, after all, and I have always been sorely lacking in that department." Another side eye at Daniel. "But ... our goals are no longer the same. I don't want ... if we break the treaty everyone will suffer, and ... I don't think my parents would be proud of the way I acted, so I'm trying to make amends." He looked between all of us. "He's on the way now to find the last secret keeper, so I came to the only ones with the power to stop him."

The silence felt heavy. No one seemed to know what to say.

"Where is Laous going to try and find the final keeper?" Daniel finally asked him.

"Hawaii," Fraizer said without hesitation. "He's heading across with some of his trusted inner circle as we speak."

Daniel's question had been a test, to see if Fraizer was actually speaking any truth at all. He'd passed the first step, confirming the location I'd gotten in the network.

"How did you even know we were in House of Darken?" Chase asked.

"Laous knows where you are," Fraizer replied quickly. "When he had Callie the second time, he took her to House of Imperial and planted a tracker just under her skin. Near her right ear."

"Are you fucking kidding me?" Callie stomped her foot hard, letting a ton of swearwords drop, and then she headed toward Fraizer. "Let me kill him. Seriously."

"It wasn't me!" Fraizer protested again. "Ever since Laous hooked up with the humans, he's gone even crazier. A lot of the technology he's using, private planes and all that, comes from this group called Gonzo."

I stilled, an instant feeling of revulsion washing over me. "I know that group," I told them; every face turned in my direction then. "My parents often talked about how they were an anti-government extremist group who want to ditch the current democratic way of running our country. They want to bring in rule by the people."

"They want anarchy?" Emma asked.

I nodded. "Yep, they believe that if they break down the entire way America is governed, raze it to the ground, then they can rebuild as something much stronger. Less corrupt."

"But in doing so, they're willing to sacrifice millions of innocent lives," Callie guessed.

I nodded again. "Yes, it must be a big deal because my parents were rarely ever able to speak about their jobs and lives. It was classified above top secret, because of ..." I shrugged. "The alien thing. But they did mention this group more than once. They wanted to warn me. Apparently they have people stationed everywhere, even in high schools."

"The human is right, they're bad news," Fraizer confirmed. "Connected. Rich. And ruthless. They're on the way to Hawaii with Laous to track this girl down. If they get to her before you all do, then it's game over."

Urgency thrummed through our group again. I wasn't sure about the rest of them, but I was ready for action. We needed to go now. "Give me a second to set up a temporary transporter back to Earth," Lexen said.

Before anyone could reply, his eyes were already doing that faraway stare thing as he went into the network. I focused on the ground as well, remembering how I followed the light down. The longer I stared, the more the grass and rocky ground faded away, before it flickered back and forth between darkness and reality. Ohhh, now I understood what they meant about the first time being the hardest. Because the path was easy to follow now, I just needed to ... switch my mind across.

Lexen's focus returned in about thirty seconds. Lights swirled up from the ground in front of him, slow and singular at first, but after another twenty seconds a full transporter was there. "Okay, I've informed the council and they're sending backup across to Hawaii," he told the group. "But that will take them a few hours to organize, so we're heading there first. This transporter will take us back to the main one in the platform."

"What are we going to do about Fraizer?" Daniel asked. He seemed to be avoiding looking at his brother, who in turn was avoiding looking at Daniel.

"This has got to end!" Callie threw her hands up in front of her, exasperation in her voice. "You two need to bury this bad blood between you. Have you both forgotten that you have another brother in Laous' hands, one who I don't believe is a bad guy? He just needs someone to give a damn about him."

Daniel's face was blank, but the corners of his lips were twitching, along with his eye. He was upset. I had no doubt about it at all.

Fraizer, on the other hand, wore a mask of confusion. "What brother?"

Daniel answered him. "Rao. He's our brother, not Laous' son."

I'd never seen color drain from a person's face so quickly. Fraizer took a step forward and threw a swing at Daniel. The Imperial overlord had a split-second to try to avoid the hit. He didn't though. He let his brother's fist connect.

As Daniel's head snapped back, Fraizer shouted, "This is all your fault. You let our goddamn family fall apart. You should be the one trapped in Laous' web of lies, not Rao."

Callie stepped forward, putting herself between the two of them. That was the first time Daniel had showed a strong emotion, his arms coming out to cage his mate as he pulled her away from Fraizer.

"You're right," Daniel admitted, fire in his eyes. "I have failed our family. I'm sorry I blamed you for what happened to Mom. I'm sorry that this all went to hell. But right now all the sorrys in the world don't mean shit. You don't trust me. I don't trust you. And none of us have time to try and deal with it."

"You're not going to Hawaii without me," Fraizer muttered. "Not now I know I have a brother to save. Rao is a good Daelighter who has had to do some really fucked-up things for Laous. And with his abilities, there's no way Laous will ever let him go."

"What can he do?" Emma asked, trying to sneak in under Lexen's arm to see better.

Daniel shrugged. "No idea."

Fraizer, who still had his fists clenched, chest heaving, snarled. "He's a soothsayer. He can see events before they happen. He has dreams. This has allowed Laous to be a step ahead of the rest of you morons. If you'd rescued Rao early on, you wouldn't be in this mess."

"We didn't know he was alive," Daniel retorted harshly, losing whatever control he had on his temper. "I only just found out."

That took some of the fire out of Fraizer. "Rao was the one who told him how to become Overlord by killing our father." His voice was quieter now. "He also told him how to find the first secret keeper. He saw it all before it happened."

After Fraizer said this, Emma stiffened, her face pale. Her parents had been killed by Laous.

"Did he really kill my mom?" Callie interrupted, sounding like she wasn't sure she actually wanted to know.

Fraizer hesitated. "It was a heart attack, I think. He burned her body after. To hide the evidence."

Callie's face didn't change; there was no grief in her expression, but she did seem to shrink in on herself.

Xander, who had barely spoken since we came out of the network, said, "I know this timing is not good, but the plane is ready. The pilot is waiting for us at the private airfield near Astoria."

"You guys have a private plane?" I blurted out. How rich were they?

"I have three," Lexen said with a shrug.

"Same," Xander added.

Daniel just smirked. "Imperial Exports has dozens, but I have three for my personal use."

Blinking slowly, I turned to look at Chase. "Please don't tell me you have three planes as well."

The other overlords laughed then, and I let out a low sigh of relief. I should have known that he wouldn't be like the others. He cared about nature and trees and things that stayed on the ground.

Chase's smile was a little crooked as he reached out and brushed his thumb against my cheek. "My family has hundreds of planes," he told me. "We own one of the largest commercial airlines in the world. You might have heard of Air Starleight, the one which runs almost completely without emissions. We put a lot of money back into the environment so technology doesn't completely destroy Earth."

"Hundreds..." I trailed off. "How much money do you four have?"

That might have been a rude question. I had no idea if they were secretive about money here like a lot of humans were.

Chase didn't hesitate to reply: "On Earth, our net worth is in the billions. Both individually and collectively. Our families own a lot of the major industries, companies, banking, and oil. We use the money to make sure that things run smoothly for Daelighters on Earth."

Before I could freak the hell out, Lexen added, "In Overworld, we don't use money, not in the same way humans do. The overlord families are supposed to provide for our people, and in return the people keep our communities running smoothly. There are some barter systems. The overlord families obviously have help to run their homes and such, but we are expected to keep our people safe, fed, and somewhat happy. That's how our world works."

If Earth focused more on keeping people happy rather than making money, I think things would be very different there. Meanwhile ... I'd just learned I was bonded to a billionaire who owned more private planes than I owned socks. When did this become my life?

"I'm still the same guy," Chase reminded me. My expression was not doing a good job of hiding my shock. A grin split his face. "I think you took it better when you found out about aliens."

A snort of laughter left me. Emma and Callie joined in. It almost felt cathartic after all of the tension. Fraizer even smiled, while still looking uncomfortable, standing off to the side of the main group. "I've never lacked for money," I said, still chuckling. "But it never occurred to me even once that you all would have so much ... Earth currency. I guess I should have realized. After all, you've entrenched your lives in our world deeply. The bigger picture is starting to come together."

Chase wrapped an arm around me and my body went willingly to him. As did my heart.

"You'll never want for anything that cold hard cash can buy," Chase said, low in my ear. "What's mine is yours. If you have any charities you want to donate to, just tell me. Properties you want to purchase for us to live in, I can do that."

I loved that he'd mentioned charities first. I went up on tiptoes and he lowered himself down so I could reach his lips. "Thank you," I said as I pulled back. "I have a ton of charities I love supporting, and ... I'd really love if we could set up a little center near where I used to live. There are so many kids and single moms there trying to escape domestic abuse. They're homeless, living in their cars. I talked to my parents about trying to do something, but there was never time."

Gracie, my nanny, had come from a domestic abuse situation. Luckily, she reached out to my father, an old friend of hers from school. He gave her a job and place to live. She said if it wasn't for us, she would have ended up on the streets. Her husband took everything from her. I had a special place in my heart for women and children who were in that situation.

"As soon as Laous becomes nothing more than a bad memory, we will set up your shelter," Chase promised.

Thank you, I mouthed to him, too overcome to speak out loud.

I pulled myself together then as Lexen started moving toward the transporter. Looked like it was time to go. Everyone followed, except for Fraizer, who didn't seem to know what to do. "Come on," Daniel told him, not sounding happy about it.

"Wait," Callie called from the back of the group. "What about the tracker? We need to get it out of me immediately. On the off chance that Laous doesn't know where the fourth is yet, we can't lead him to her."

I'd temporarily forgotten about that uncomfortable little fact. Callie clearly hadn't, and I could not blame her. The thought of someone putting something inside her body while she was unconscious ... the vulnerability of someone taking advantage of that ... made me really angry on her behalf.

Daniel reached out to her, his hand wrapping around her face as he probed behind her ear. It took him about a minute to find the device.

"Get it out," she said without hesitation. "Just cut the damn thing out, Dan."

His nostrils flared slightly, and I saw his hands flinch. "I don't think I can cut you. But I also don't trust anyone else to do it."

She reached forward and grabbed onto his face, pulling his head down to hers. "Daniel Imperial, you will cut this thing out of me immediately. I know you can do this, and I trust you with my life." She whispered, but I still heard her say, "You've saved my life already, more than once. You will not hurt me."

Daniel pressed his lips to hers once, hard, and then pulled back with a harsh breath. He released Callie's face and took a step back, reaching down to lift up the leg of his pants. He pulled a small blade from a sheath. It was dagger-shaped, looking razor sharp as it glinted in the light.

He glanced toward Lexen and Chase, who were closest. "Can you hold her still? If she flinches, I might cut deeper than I intend to."

The pair stepped up on either side of the blond girl, who remained calm, even though she was about to be operated on without any pain relief.

Daniel brushed her hair to the side. "I'm going to need you to tilt your head as far as you can." He demonstrated what he wanted, and when she immediately followed his instructions, he leaned closer.

"I will tell you when I'm about to cut." His voice was very graveled. "Try not to move."

From my angle, it looked like Callie rolled her eyes. "I've been cut before, Daniel. I'll be able to handle it, don't you worry."

Her assurance did not lessen the worry he wore. His hand remained steady, though, as he brought the deadly blade to her neck. "Cutting now," he said.

It seemed like he'd only lowered the knife for a split second before he was lifting it again, blood noticeable on the tip. Callie did not move, but she had closed her eyes. Daniel handed the dagger to Xander, before he ushered Emma and me forward.

"Are either of you okay with blood?" he asked.

I shrugged. "I've never had a noticeable problem with it, but I've also never performed surgery on someone."

Emma grimaced. "Honestly, I'm not great, but for Callie I'll do whatever."

"I've cut just over the top of the device," he explained. "But it's not coming out easily with the blade and I don't want to cut her any more. I need someone with long nails to lift it and then pull it out."

Emma waved her fingers at him. "My nails are always short. Long nails annoy me. So I can't help."

Her relief was very obvious. Meanwhile, I had a nicely manicured set of teal nails, so I did not have the same argument. Daniel pulled a small cloth from his pocket, which he used to dab at Callie's neck, and then gestured for me to step forward. I was too short to see, so Chase wrapped an arm around my center, lifting me up higher. Which, of course, had my concentration at about minus fifty, until I remembered that Callie could be bleeding to death.

The cut was about an inch long, and not very deep. Blood seeped slowly out of it; Daniel mopped it up every second or so. "Can you see the tip of the tracker there?" He pointed toward a glint of dark metal.

I nodded.

"Can you get your nail under it and flick it out?"

My initial response was no. I was totally not equipped to deal with this, but ... I knew I had to woman up. For Callie. And for the rest of us.

After giving myself a very quick pep talk, I tilted my head back to Chase. "You okay holding me a little longer?"

He just grinned, and I shook my head at him before turning back to Callie. This time I did not hesitate. "I'm going to get it out now, okay..." I told her. Daniel had stepped around to take Chase's place, holding her to make sure she didn't flinch. Pretending that this was not someone's neck, I gently slid my finger across her skin, and when I reached the cut, twisted my hand around so my nail was in a scooping position. It was difficult to get under the device without embedding it further into her skin. I dug deeper, knowing I was hurting her, because she made one low whimper.

Hurry up, Maya. Screwing around was making it worse, so I sucked in a huge breath, and then flicked my nail down and under in one movement, closing my thumb on top. She made another noise, but I was blocking most of that out, focused on using the two nails as tweezers, to pull out the small tracker.

It came with only a little resistance and I managed not to vomit on her, even though I sort of wanted to. As soon as it was out, Callie wilted, and Daniel supported her while he pressed the cloth to her neck.

"You're going to have to hold it on there," he said, eyes

locked on his mate with intensity. "The plane has a medical kit. I'll bandage you up once we're on board."

"I'm fine," she said, trying to laugh but failing. Her head turned to me. "Thanks, Maya."

I shrugged. "No problem, I've been dissecting my dolls for years. Plenty of experience."

Chase lowered me to the ground – I had completely forgotten he still held me. They were strong, these Daelighters. Lexen took the bloody device from me, incinerating it with a flame that appeared in his hand. I wiped my fingers on my already filthy and bloodstained jeans.

"Time to go," Lexen said. "Jero, can you wait for us back home? Make sure that everything stays in order while I'm gone."

The brothers exchanged an extended look, and I was betting there was a lot being "said" in that stare. Eventually though, Jero just nodded his head and turned to walk toward the mouth of the cave. Lexen continued watching him for an extra beat before he refocused on us and directed everyone toward the transporter.

One by one we stepped into the ball of light. We were on our way to the land of sand and sun. And possibly the end of the world.

20

———————

It turned out that Xander's plane had four bedrooms, a lounge and bar, plus three or four bathrooms. Basically, his plane was the size of most people's houses, or bigger, actually. It also turned out that flying private was much faster than commercial. On my last commercial flight, boarding had been delayed by twenty minutes, then we sat on the runway for two hours, and then they lost half the luggage.

Nothing like that for the billionaire boys. They got the red-carpet treatment. Chase and I buckled into two squishy armchairs, preparing for takeoff. My hands were clenched tightly on the side of the chair, because I might be in more comfortable seats, but that didn't mean I was any less scared of the process.

Chase, noticing my white knuckles, held his hand out to me, palm up. We were just taxiing down the runway, and I wasn't sure I could loosen my grip yet, but the thought of touching him was enough for me to try.

"Not a fan of planes?" he joked as I grabbed onto him with a death grip. "Want me to sell the family business?"

That part didn't sound like he was joking at all. "What?" I forgot for a moment what was happening, swinging my head toward him. "Definitely not. Your family is doing a good thing trying to provide aircraft that don't horribly pollute the air. Do they crash less as well? Because that would be doubly awesome."

It looked like he was trying not to laugh at me. "Planes rarely crash. You're safe. And even if, by some extremely rare occurrence, we have trouble with this one, then I will save you. We're hard to kill, and I have more than a few skills to keep us alive."

That did make me feel a little better. But my reflex reactions were still there, so the moment the plane surged forward I had to close my eyes and think happy thoughts. Usually if I was flying with my parents, I'd be dosed up on the Xanax my doctor prescribed me before vacations. Right now, though, I only had Chase.

Surprisingly enough, he worked almost as well, because by the time the seatbelts sign disappeared, I was barely even thinking about the fact that we were thousands of feet in the air. As everyone started to move around, Xander came by our seats. "It's about six hours to Hawaii with the headwind, so I suggest everyone gets some sleep while you can."

"Sounds good," Daniel told him.

Xander didn't sound angry anymore, just normal. He looked tired, though; fatigue lined his blue eyes. "Couples can take the bedrooms," he added, just before he left. "The rest of us will use the lounger beds."

He walked off and I had a moment of panic. This thing with Chase, I wanted it, badly. But I wasn't sure I was ready for us to share a bed yet. We were only just getting to know each other ... and, I'd never done that with anyone before. Except Brad, and he totally didn't count.

"You need rest." Chase was watching me closely. "I'll stay out here if it makes you feel more comfortable. But you should definitely grab one of the beds."

I shook my head. I was an idiot. We were only sleeping, nothing else. Chase would never push me, and possibly it would be me making the first move, because he was a total gentleman. I didn't have anything to worry about except my own stupid nerves.

I grabbed his hand. "Come on, we both need the sleep. It's been a long day."

He didn't argue, he just squeezed my hand and followed me through the plane. The first door was closed, so we went into the second. The room was small, fitting a king-sized bed and a single side table. There was a television on the wall, but neither of us turned it on. "I really need a shower," I said, staring down at the pristine white sheets.

Chase reached out and pulled the thick blanket back. "You can shower, but I don't think we have anything to change into. All of our bags were left at the car." When I hesitated again, he added, "Don't worry about making the sheets dirty, they'll change all of the bedding as soon as we leave the plane."

"I might just wash my face and hands," I decided.

Chase nodded, and I quietly left. I went to the closest bathroom, but it was occupied, so I walked on to the next one. There was a shower inside the small stall, but I ignored it. After I used the toilet, I quickly washed my hands and face. The soft white towel came away streaked with dirt and blood, and I ended up stripping half my clothes off in an attempt to get all the blood off me. My eyes lingered on the two-inch cut on my shoulder, surprised by how healed it already looked. It was half scabbed over. *Insane.*

Once I was eighty percent clean, I made my way back to the bedroom to find it empty. Chase must have gone to use the bathroom, too, which gave me a second to shuck off my shoes, jeans, sweater – despite Chase's assurances, they were way too gross to sleep in – and crawl in under the sheets. My eyes grew heavy almost instantly, and while I registered the door opening and closing again, I didn't move. As his warm weight settled in behind me, I instinctively turned toward him and he wrapped me up in his arms. Once my head was on his bare chest, everything inside of me calmed ... and grew excited at the same time.

"This is surreal," I whispered, my body molded to his. "I feel like I've known you my entire life."

Chase's lips brushed across my forehead and I just breathed him in, that mint and pine scent that was already so familiar. "I was there when you were born," he told me. "It was a special, sacred moment. We waited on the other side of the trees that held the legreto. When your mother was able, she wrapped you up and brought you over for us all to see."

I let the silence cloak us while I thought on what he'd said. "My entire life, I've felt out of place," I admitted. "Fitting in wasn't the problem. I was popular, a cheerleader, but always seeking more. Now ... that feeling is gone. It's clear to me that I was searching for you."

He tilted my head up and our lips met. Lying side by side, the difference in our heights didn't matter, and I had easy access to his mouth. My leg went up over his body because I needed to be closer to him. Everything inside of me was thrumming, and it was really difficult to remember that not only was I a virgin, I was on a plane filled with Daelighters who no doubt would have fantastic hearing.

Did I really care, though?

As my tongue brushed against his, a low breathy sound escaped and Chase's chest rumbled under me. After endless minutes – or days – of pure bliss, he pulled away, both of his hands cupping my face. "We should cool off," he breathed against my lips. "Because my control is shot right now."

He wasn't the only one.

"You need to sleep," he added, pulling me closer until I was half sprawled across him. "I'll keep you safe."

At this point I'd completely forgotten that I'd been nervous to sleep in the same bed as him. Tangled up in his arms was the most right my life had ever felt, and as I drifted off to sleep, I sent out a hope for many more nights like this.

I woke up with less than an hour to go in our flight. It was the first time I'd managed my fear of flying without medication, or a lot of emotional trauma. Chase remained asleep, holding me against his chest. The warm smoothness of his skin, along with his steady heartbeat, almost lulled me back to sleep, but my stomach was protesting too much about lack of food for me to actually doze off.

"I think I'd better feed you," Chase rumbled, his eyes opening. "Starving my mate on the first day we're bonded does not seem like a good way to start our lives."

Groaning, I buried my head into him, blocking out everything else. "Do we have to leave? The moment we get off this plane, we'll be back to tracking down Laous and trying not to die. I like it better in here."

In an instant I was flipped over onto my back, Chase perched above me. "What did I tell you before? You're not going to die. I won't let it happen."

His confidence was cute and amusing, and while it bordered on arrogant, I didn't mind. Chase was just doing Chase, and I happened to like exactly who he was.

"Neither of us will die," I agreed. "It's a deal."

Reaching up, I wrapped my arms around him, pulling his body down onto mine. I wanted to feel his weight while I wrapped my legs up around him and pressed my body to his. Chase did not fight me, and he was strong enough to resist if he wanted to.

"We still have an hour," I murmured, my lips pressing to his, while my body ached for his touch.

Chase let out a low groan. "We don't need to rush."

"We don't have to have sex," I reminded him, because he was right about the rushing. "Plenty of other fun things to do to kill time ... if you can be quiet."

I winked, even though it was no doubt going to be me screaming the plane down. Chase pushed himself back up, the muscles in his biceps standing out starkly as he stared down at me. I had no idea what he was looking for, so I just let all of my emotions and love for him rise to the surface.

I might not have said the words yet, but I definitely felt the emotion. In my old life I would have laughed at any girl who said she was in love after knowing the guy for less than a week, but as far as I was concerned, I'd known Chase my entire life. We were destined. He stirred feelings in me that went beyond the normal.

"You're my everything, Maya," Chase told me, still holding himself just away from me. "Beyond love. Beyond life. Beyond the worlds we are from. You are my first and only priority, and

I will strive every single day to never fail you, this I can promise."

I pulled him down again, and this time our kiss felt different. Hotter, more intense, and also more emotional. As he moved those full lips across mine, down my cheek, and along my neck, I threw my head back and bit my lip to stop from making noises. He stripped my shirt away, leaving me just in my black bra. I was thankful at this point that I'd taken the time to clean up last night. Not that Chase seemed to really care about a little dirt.

We wasted no time, touching, kissing, learning each other, and before I knew it there were only thirty minutes left in the flight. When I stepped out of the bedroom fully dressed – and wholly satisfied – I was still a virgin. But it felt like everything had changed.

I did agree with him, though. I wasn't quite ready for that step, and it would be nice for my first time not to be on a plane filled with other people. Although it certainly had felt romantic in our little bedroom. Our bubble.

"Come on," Chase said, leading me back to our original chairs. Mostly everyone else was seated. I waved to Emma and Callie as I passed them. They both looked more relaxed than before. Callie had white gauze visible behind her ear but didn't seem bothered by it.

I wondered if they'd enjoyed the use of the bedrooms as well. At least I didn't have to feel embarrassed to think I might have been loud. Over the noise of the plane, I hadn't heard anything. So hopefully they hadn't either.

"Do Daelighters have better hearing than humans?" I asked Chase as we buckled ourselves in.

His smile was knowing. "Yes, but not by that much. No one heard us."

Thank you, Jesus.

Just before taking their seats, a steward brought us a sandwich and bottle of water. We had twenty more minutes to descend, so there was time for me to get some food in my stomach. And hope I didn't throw it up as we came in to land. Chase held my hand the entire time, and even when the wheels touched down, bouncing a little – which normally was the point I'd freak out – he kept me from losing it. By the time all the checks were complete, and we'd waited for our turn to taxi into the main hub of buildings, I barely felt stressed at all. Someone needed to bottle these mate bonds; they were ten times better than Xanax.

"When we disembark," Daniel told us, "a car will be waiting. We have government contacts in this airport. They'll make sure we get through without any issue."

I freaked for a second, because I had completely forgotten I didn't have any identification on me. Really should have been something I thought about before this moment, but I guess no one had any on them, so it wasn't like they were going to leave me behind. As the stairs lowered for us to exit, there were two dark SUVs waiting a dozen feet away. Their engines were running, and the drivers – wearing slacks and casual shirts – got out and opened the doors for us. I slid in the back seat next to Chase. Xander took the passenger seat, while Emma and Lexen got in the very back. The others got in the second car.

"Straight to the house," Xander said, and the driver didn't waste a second spinning the car around and getting out of the airport. There were some security personnel on the gates as we exited, but none of them stopped us. Being rich opened doors ... or gates, apparently.

Once we were onto the road, I recognized where we were. Our plane had landed on a smaller airfield near Lanai Airport.

I could see the bigger airfield just off to my right. So we were about four miles from the city.

"Why did your family choose this island to holiday?" Chase asked, while both of us stared out at the sights.

"Mostly because it's quieter than the bigger islands," I replied. "And it's absolutely stunning here – sightseeing, swimming, day tours. We liked to stay active, but in between have really relaxed downtime, which was harder in the crowded areas. This was like ... being off the grid for a short time."

"There are no stoplights here," the driver said, joining the conversation. "A lot of the roads require a 4-wheel drive vehicle."

"Tommy is usually manning some of our businesses in Honolulu," Chase explained, "but he always raves about Lanai. I think it's his favorite."

Tommy didn't say anything, but if his grin was any indication, he was definitely a fan. As the car wove along the winding road, we ended up going past the main part of Lanai City toward some exclusive little alcoves where rich people built their beach houses.

Beach houses and private beaches.

"Who owns this property?" I asked.

Xander's hand went up. "It's mine. I have a house on each of the islands here. Surfing is kind of my thing."

For a merman, that made sense.

Xander's house was definitely not a house in any sense of the word. Okay, it did have walls and a roof. A lot of walls, if the size of the estate was any indication. It looked like a resort. We turned into the main drive and waited for the double fences to open. We were at the top of the land and had to wind our way down to the main residence. It was white, a sprawling square building. I caught a glimpse of multiple pools adjacent to a long stretch of stunning white-sand beach. You could swim in the pool and stare out into the ocean beyond.

Ah-Ma-Zing. "Could we maybe visit here another time? When we're not saving the world?" Emma asked from the back seat. "Because I wouldn't mind a few days swimming in that pool."

Dream come true for sure.

Xander's smile was crooked. "You're all welcome here whenever you want, of course. This is my personal property, so you won't run into any other Royales."

He was much more personable when he wasn't scowling and worrying about being forced into a romantic relationship. "Okay, let's make a deal right now," Emma piped up again. "Get rid of Laous quickly, no one else ... dies..." She choked on the last word before recovering. "And then we all finally get a chance to enjoy the beauty here, and in Overworld..."

"Deal," I said immediately.

The rest of the car, including Tommy, added their voices.

"Tommy, I'm going to need you to rustle up some clothing for everyone here," Xander said as the car pulled up. "We have to start our search, but we'll all need to clean up later and no one has a change of clothing."

Tommy nodded. "I'll just need your sizes and I can make that happen."

He got out of the car, hurrying around to let the rest of us out. Once we were all in front of the vehicle, we told him our sizes and then he crossed to the other car. As the second group joined us, I didn't miss the tension between Daniel and Fraizer. They stood as far apart as possible. It was only the withering looks Callie was shooting between them that connected the two at all.

"What's the plan now?" Xander asked, his back to the

magnificence that was his house. "Did you get any other details about her location, Maya?"

I thought for a moment of the glimpses of Lanai I'd seen when I surfaced. "I think she was near Hulopoe Bay – one of the main beaches. I also saw ... the underwater cathedrals, I think. I've dived a few times there with my parents. We're all big into water sports. Well, my dad is, my mom not so much. But the light streaming through the water reminded me of them."

Callie shuddered. "I'm not a very good swimmer, so underwater exploring will have to be done by someone else."

Xander rubbed a hand across his head, mussing the blond strands. "You all know that I can take anything underwater. I think she's just moving around a lot. That's why Maya saw more than one location."

It made sense, but it didn't help us figure out where to go.

Fraizer spoke up: "I know where Laous is stationed ... and since he doesn't know that I've jumped ship, do you want me to head there to see what he's learned?"

Everyone turned to Fraizer, and I knew I wasn't the only one with suspicions clouding my mind. Had this all been a setup? Pretending that he was switching sides? Helping us take Laous down? Had we stepped into another trap of Laous' making?

21

"I promise, this is no trap." Fraizer had his hands up in front of him, a pleading expression on his face. "I've already told you that I disagree with Laous, with the way he is going about this. He sucked me in initially because I believe that family sticks together, and I guess I wanted a way to punish Daniel. But he has gone too far."

He sounded sincere, and I was a pretty trusting person, so my instincts were to believe what he was saying. But this wasn't my call. I let the overlords do their thing.

"I'm inclined to believe him," Chase said.

Lexen shook his head. "If he goes to Laous, we're all going as well. That way we'll see for sure that he's telling the truth."

No one else had a better plan, and since the drivers had already taken off in one of the cars, we squished into the other. Emma and I ended up in the middle seats, Chase and Lexen on either side of us. The rest fit themselves where they could; Xander was driving. Once we were out of his estate, Fraizer told him to head toward the city.

The car was quiet, tension riding all of us. Closing my eyes,

I tried to reach out for the fourth girl, wanting to pinpoint her location now that we were closer. But there was no clear entry to the network on Earth, not really. I could feel the energy, but it was faint. We were going to have to find the fourth secret keeper the old-fashioned way.

Thankfully, Lanai City was less city and more sprawling village, so we shouldn't have to search for too long. I wasn't sure how many locals lived here, but it didn't seem like a lot. I personally loved the vibe. It was usually me who requested we come here for our yearly holidays. I'd never stayed in the town, though. We generally hired out a private rental on the beach.

Fraizer leaned forward in his seat. "He's on this side of town. It shouldn't be too hard to spot him. We tend to stick out on Earth."

I had no idea how the four overlords managed to pass for humans at all. They were so far beyond normal males that it was almost laughable.

"Laous has probably already found her. He might not even be here," Callie said, her words clipped. "This could all be a complete waste of time."

"At minimum I'm hoping we ferret out some more of the traitors," Xander said. "In particular, I'm looking for my father's best friend. He's been missing for a few weeks."

"Your father's the overlord?" I asked. It felt like this might be an obvious question, but maybe it was his uncle or something.

Xander shook his head. "My mother is the overlord. She was the one born to royal blood. My father rules with her, of course, but there's only one true overlord."

That was awesome. Good to see it wasn't only males wearing the title.

We continued weaving through the small town, locals

waving in their friendly way. For the most part. After about ten minutes, Fraizer leaned forward. "I'm not sure randomly driving is the right way to go," he said. "Do you have a phone? I'll just call him and tell him I'm here."

Xander flicked his head toward the center of the car. "There's an untraceable cell in there."

Fraizer found it quickly, powered it on and entered a number. I was surprised when Fraizer put it on speaker.

"Who the fuck is this?"

The unfamiliar voice was female, each word snapped out like bullets from a gun.

"Fraizer. I've acquired one part of the package. Laous needs to give me a drop-off location."

Chase tensed at my side, and I reached out and laced my fingers through his. Comfort for both of us. "There was a little trouble, but mostly, it all went to plan," Fraizer continued, and you could have cut the tension in the car with a blunt knife. "Send me the coordinates. My ETA is about ten minutes."

He hit the end button, and I was pretty sure it was taking every ounce of Chase's control not to reach out and punch him. "What's the package?" he bit out, not sounding at all like his normal chill self.

Fraizer dropped the phone into his lap, letting out a sigh. "The secret keepers are the package, of course. This is a double-cross, but Laous doesn't realize he's the one being crossed."

That sounded great in theory. But another part of me wondered if this was actually a triple cross, and we were about to be screwed.

"He won't believe I managed to grab more than one of you, which is why I mentioned only part of the package." The phone dinged then, and Fraizer lifted it. "He's stationed near the cat sanctuary. Apparently, your secret keeper girl works there."

I'd always wanted to go to the cat sanctuary. They had hundreds of cats that were kept there to ensure their safety, and the safety of the native wildlife of the island. I'd never managed to visit, but it looked like I was going to get my chance now.

Xander wasted no time swinging the car around, heading in the opposite direction. The sanctuary was back near the main airport, so we passed familiar sights as we headed that way.

"So, what's the plan, Fraizer?" Daniel asked from the back.

Fraizer hesitated, before he said: "If you let me go in with one of the secret keepers, Laous will be distracted. That's the perfect time for you to try and take him out. Or at least get the stone away from him. My suggestion is that when we get near the sanctuary, everyone hops out of the car, except for one of the girls. I don't care which one. I just need a distraction to give you all time to follow us."

No one jumped at that suggestion, but I kind of thought it wasn't a half-bad idea.

"He's not going to hurt the secret keepers," Fraizer reminded us. "He's convinced that he will need all four even once he has the final map. He has so many plans in place to snatch them up."

Chase, Lexen, and Daniel all growled simultaneously. Not even kidding, it was like the car was filled with angry lions. "If you think for one second I'm leaving Callie with you, you're insane," Daniel said bluntly.

"If Laous touches Emma again, I will not be able to stop myself from shifting and alerting the humans to the very real aliens in their midst," Lexen snarled.

Chase was equally as pissed. "Maya has no defense against a Daelighter. She cannot be the one."

They continued to throw around insults and curses. All the while Fraizer remained quiet. As did Xander, because he had no personal stake in this decision.

"It has to be me," Callie's voice rang out over the rest. Heat flared from someone, and I couldn't tell if it was Daniel or Callie losing control of their power. "I'm literally the only one who can defend herself."

"No," Daniel snapped. "Laous knows you have that ability. He will counter anything you throw at him. He almost stole your life from me last time. I won't let it happen again."

She lowered her voice, murmuring things to him I couldn't hear.

"The sanctuary is just around the corner," Xander said. "Decisions need to be made now." He stopped the car, because if we went around the next corner we'd be right where Laous was. "We might as well get out," he suggested. "Because not all of us will be going at him head-on. Even I know that's a bad plan."

He slid the car into neutral and we all climbed out. The arguing was circular; no one was willing to risk any of us. Callie was the only one volunteering, but Daniel flat-out refused to even consider that. I leaned myself back against the door of the car, letting them continue to argue back and forth. If it was decided I would be the bait, then I would accept the decision. But I didn't really have an opinion on the best way to do this.

As I dropped my head against the window, I felt the tiniest twinge in my neck. *Muscle spasm.* I used to get them on occasion during gymnastics. I tried to stretch my head around to ease the cramp – too much time spent on a plane and running for my life.

That shit was stressful. The pain continued for a few minutes, in which time I lost track completely of the conversation.

Lifting my hand, I rubbed the spot, kneading the muscles, pulling away. A splash of red caught my attention, and I stared at my fingers, wondering what the hell was on them. Using my other hand, I rubbed my neck again, pulling the hand away to find it was also slicked with red. Like ... blood.

Had I been hit? The twinge hadn't been that painful, but ... I was bleeding. I didn't want to interrupt the conversation, so I quietly opened the car door and crawled into the front seat to search for something to wipe my neck with. I also wanted to use the mirror behind the visor to see what hit me.

As soon as I climbed in, the door swung closed behind me. I hadn't remembered pulling it, so the wind must have caught it. My head spun. Leaning forward, I scraped at the latch to open the glovebox, but I couldn't seem to get any grip. Another door opened near me, and I figured it was Chase checking on me, so I didn't even turn my head.

"Think I hurt my neck," I mumbled, pretty much resting my head against the dash. "Can you ... see ... anythi—?"

What was wrong with me?

"You were just the first to break from the group," said a voice that was not Chase's. "I hit you with a little speck of stars-light stone. It should wear off soon."

Fraizer. Shit.

The car lurched forward, and since I wasn't belted in, I got bounced around, smashing my face into windows and the front of the car. I clawed at my neck, trying to remove the stone that was incapacitating me, but I couldn't keep myself steady enough to get it out.

Fraizer held his foot flat to the floor, and I let out a muffled scream when the car pitched strangely and almost flipped over onto its side. Somehow we didn't crash, but Fraizer immediately started to curse.

"Of course you would be bonded to the Leights able to turn his arms into vines."

The car lurched again; this time Fraizer swung it to the right. "Luckily..." he said, "he doesn't want to hurt you .... and he also has a limit of how far his reach is. I think we've just managed to get outside of that limit."

"Was ... thwis ... your pwan all awong?" I wasn't exactly making much sense. My tongue couldn't form the words, but Fraizer understood.

"Actually, no, it wasn't. I didn't lie. I do disagree with Laous and everything he represents. But ... I just learned I have another brother. He deserves to be freed from the life he's in, and to help him out, I'm going to need a ticket in. That happened to be you. I'm sorry."

My head hit the glass again, and this time I lost a few minutes of time. When I finally opened my eyes, the car was slowing. I could see the fenced section of what I assumed was the sanctuary. There wasn't anyone around who looked like they could save me from this situation, so I'd have to save myself. Which should be simple – I had so many survival skills, like ... uh...

Yeah, I was so dead.

Fraizer dragged me out of the car, and I tried to fight him, but just lifting my limbs felt like a mammoth task. He moved fast, dragging me as he started to run. He jumped over the fence, clearing the four feet with me in his arms no problem. The landscape flashed in black and white, my vision not working properly. Fraizer dragged me toward a group standing near their white kidnapper-special vans. And I recognized the guy at the center.

Laous.

Fraizer did not stop until he was standing right before the very man I had grown to both fear and hate. "This is an unexpected surprise," Laous said, grinning at us. "For some reason, nephew, I thought for sure you had betrayed me."

Fraizer sounded robotic. "I would never do that. They're after her. You need to get going immediately."

Laous moved toward me, but when he was about a foot away, Fraizer yanked me back and pressed a blade to my throat. *What in the...?*

"What are you doing?" Laous asked him, tilting his head in a curious manner.

"I want Rao first," Fraizer demanded. "I will swap her for him, otherwise I'm going to spill her precious blood right here. Maybe you don't need it to find the starslight stone, but what if you do?"

A very tall man stepped forward. I hadn't noticed him until then. He'd been hidden in the shadows. His face had some serious burns on it, the scars extending down under his shirt. "Why do you want me?" he asked slowly, sounding confused.

Fraizer snarled. "Because you're my brother. They've been lying to us from the very beginning. They told me you died!"

Rao's face took on a similar confused mask, before he twisted toward Laous. "What is he saying? You're Fraizer's father, too?"

"No," Fraizer screamed, but before he could say another thing, one of the men nearby took advantage of his distraction and shot him in the chest.

Fraizer jerked, the knife he held at my throat breaking the skin, but I managed to slip free before he could do too much damage. I landed at a heap near Laous' feet, and before I could fight or kick or scream – or turn to see if Fraizer was dead – dark material was pulled over my head, and I was tossed hard into what I guessed was the van.

The engine started and any sliver of hope I had of being rescued disappeared in an instant. Everything ached as I lay on the cold, hard floor, feeling the bond in my center stretch further and further as the distance between Chase and I extended.

If there was a worse feeling in the world, I hadn't experienced it yet.

Laous was loud, barking orders from his seat, which was way too close to mine for comfort.

"Stop!" he shouted. "She's close by. Get the girl up. Fresh blood will be the best."

The van screeched to a halt. I was hauled up off the floor, the bag ripped off my head. Laous' face was right before mine. "Didn't want you to communicate with your mate. I know some of you can see through the other's eyes."

I had no idea how he knew Chase was my mate, and it really didn't matter.

"Lucky for you," Laous added conversationally, "you're already cut, so I won't have to hurt you more. For now."

He lifted a long chain up from under his shirt. "Collect some blood," he ordered one of his followers.

They looked human to me, and I wondered if this was the military group. It would certainly explain their use of guns, which I'd never seen the Daelighters do. Rao was back to standing in the shadows, his features pinched. He was shooting some angry side-eyes at Laous. Fraizer's declaration had stirred something in the scarred Daelighter.

Maybe seeing his brother killed would be enough for Rao

to turn on Laous. That might be my shot. It wasn't hard for me to bring tears to my eyes, mostly because I was freaking the hell out. I winced as someone wiped a rough hand across my throat, collecting blood for Laous. I tried to fight them off, but my arms were being held tightly, and I had barely any strength left. At least it did feel like whatever Fraizer hit me with was wearing off.

Laous lifted the chain over his head and I stared at the starslight stone. This was what he'd been using to find the secret keepers. My blood was wiped across it, and then one of Laous' guys pulled out a map.

"You don't have to stress," Laous said, watching me closely, the stone held in his hands. "I'm not going to hurt you. I need you four. I know how humans and Daelighters work. There will be another obstacle that stands between me and the stone."

I glared as hard as I could. "You're going to destroy Earth and Overworld. You're completely insane."

Whatever calm he'd been possessing disappeared. He took a step closer to me, ignoring the map. "Let me tell you a little something about insanity. My father ... now he was insane. He kept me locked up from my first metamorphosis aging until I was in my last. I got fed once a day, beaten five times a day, and molested three. I had not an ounce of power. I was at his mercy day and night."

My stomach swirled at those mental images, and I just managed to stop myself from vomiting. Laous spoke matter-of-factly, but his demons were rising to the surface.

"The moment I found my strength, the moment I managed to break free of my cage, I killed my father. Turned out, I have a very special skill, forged under fire: when I kill a person, I can absorb their energy. It doesn't last long, but it lasted long enough for me to murder my complicit mother first and use her boost of power to rip my father to pieces." He got a satisfied look on his face. "I wasted no time then planning for my future. For a future which would mean I was never weak again. Ever. I've been biding my time for years, waiting until all the pieces fell into place. Now my time has come."

It sucked when the bad guy had layers, because I really wanted to just hate him. Hate him so hard that I could kill him if I had to. But right then, I saw that little boy tortured by his family. I saw and could not purge the image from my mind. He turned away, striding the few steps to the map, which he leaned over. Sucking in deep breaths, my pulse was racing, but I couldn't give up on my plan to escape.

While he was distracted, I looked around, hoping to find an escape route. We were reasonably close to the edge of a cliff. I didn't recognize the spot, but other than jumping into the rough ocean below, it was all open fields and long plains. I'd be taken out by a gun in a second. No coverage at all.

"She's right here somewhere," Laous bellowed. "Spread out, start searching everywhere." He waved a hand in my direction. "Throw her back in the van, cover her eyes, and tie her hands."

"No!" I screamed. "I won't go anywhere with you!"

I was short enough that I could easily punch tall guys in the balls. Which is exactly what I did to the first man who came at me. He let out a roar, swinging a fist in my direction. I'd been expecting it, though, and managed to duck in time.

My gait was still clumsy from Fraizer, but I didn't let that stop me from trying. Laous didn't move, preferring to let the others do his dirty work. Only problem was he'd sent most of his people off in search of the fourth secret keeper, which gave me a clear run.

The only one who could stop me was Rao. He reached out and snatched me up with far too much ease. I swung and kicked, my weak pathetic attempts glancing off him.

"Good save, son," Laous said, grinning at me with his disgusting face. "Throw her in the van."

Rao nodded, taking a step forward. Almost in slow motion, the huge man tripped and we both crashed into Laous. The three of us went down, and I felt a hand yank me back so I didn't get squished. Laous, on the other hand, wasn't so lucky. Rao slammed into him, knocking the stone out of his hand.

This was my chance; I knew it, and I was going to do the only thing I could. On my feet, I grabbed up the chain and started to run. It was about fifteen feet to the cliff. I heard shouts all around me. Just before I launched myself off the cliff, I slipped the chain over my head.

Then I screamed the entire way down.

22

———

Considering I hadn't looked before leaping, I was lucky not to smash into rocks. The coastline around these cliffs could be deadly, especially landing in some spots with strong tides.

I missed all the rocks, but as the cold water closed over my head, I knew I hadn't been as lucky with the tides. I tried to kick my way to the surface, dislodging my shoes as I went because they were dragging me down. But I got slammed against an underwater shelf before I managed to make it up for air. I had a decent lung capacity, but if I didn't get up in the next minute or so I was going to be in trouble.

I let the water carry me along, twisting my body to avoid more rocks. I couldn't avoid them all though, my arms scraping against the rough edges. I was bleeding. The sharks would be around soon; I had to get out of here. Something skimmed through the water and bit into my arm. I jerked, and more blood filled the water. *Bastards.* They were shooting at me. Apparently this necklace trumped my possible usefulness to Laous.

Managing to struggle to the surface, just near the cliffs, I took one breath, ducking right back down again. Damn the crystal-clear water, I was a sitting duck. As I went under, more bullets rained around me and I hid beneath a rock formation, trying not to panic.

A shimmer caught my eye, and I freaked out thinking it was the sun's reflection off a shark.

Only ... it wasn't a shark. It was a girl.

We stared at each other, me trying not to drown, her looking very comfortable. She had long white or gray hair that sparkled unnaturally. She wore only a bikini, her body very toned.

She seemed as surprised to see me as I was to see her. As more bullets rained around us, she shot a glare into the sky, and then zoomed through the water toward me.

I'd never seen anyone swim like that, so fast and agile, darting through the water like it was a pool and not an ocean of deadly currents. As she reached me, I found my hand in hers, and then she was speeding both of us along. She knew exactly where to go, moving with the tides. Just when I was about to pass out, she surfaced briefly and we both took in deep breaths. I opened my mouth to ask who she was, but we were back down under the water before I could.

This time we moved even faster and my head spun. Just when it seemed like the water started to calm, I passed out.

WHEN I REGAINED CONSCIOUSNESS, sprawled across the beach, sand all over me, my head was pounding. Pushing both hands under my body, I managed to lift myself up enough to brush the sand off my face. Everything hurt, like ... a lot. My back screamed at me, cut up by the underwater rocks. My hands were also bleeding quite freely, and the salt and sand only increased the pain.

When I finally got to my feet, I was surprised to see I was on the edge of the main tourist beach here, hidden behind some rocks. *Thank you, God.* I knew exactly how to get to Xander's from here. Despite my injuries, I managed to stay on my feet as I stumbled around to the main beach.

Half a dozen families were playing and sunbaking, and when I came into sight I heard shouting. An older man rushed up to me. "Are you okay? Were you caught in a rip?"

He went with the most logical explanation, but still sounded confused. Mostly because I was wearing jeans and a shirt, not a swimsuit.

"You should sit down," he advised, as I wobbled on my feet. "I'm an EMT, and I can tell you need to be seen by a medical professional. If you wait here, I'll get the local one for you."

I nodded, because I wanted him to leave me alone. I wasn't that far from the private beach of Xander's. I just needed to keep going. I pretended to sit, and the nice man ran up the beach, heading toward the lifeguard station. Meanwhile, I picked up the pace and started to stumble-run across the sand. Eyes followed me, but I ignored them, and eventually I moved beyond that main break.

I had no idea how I managed to stay upright until I made it back to Xander's place, but I somehow found the strength. I collapsed near the pool area and Tommy found me quite fast.

"What happened?" he asked, when he dragged me up to the pool house. "Where are the others?"

"Laous," I murmured. "Girl. Almost drowned."

That was the last of my words before I leaned over and vomited everywhere on the pristine white tiled floors. Tommy, to his credit, didn't freak out. He just lifted me from the mess, placed me on another long lounger, and ran a cool washcloth over my face.

He disappeared for a few minutes, reappearing with a phone in his hand.

"They're on their way back, and I've called in backup in case Gonzo retaliates."

"Are you human?" I asked, unsure if he was or not. He held himself like military, but there was also something other about him.

Tommy regarded me, wiping the cloth across my face and down over my neck. "I am human. I've known the Royales for a long time. Since I was a young boy. We lost touch when I joined the Air Force, but once I was done with my tours I retired, and Tristall, the overlord, offered me a position heading up his defense contracts here in Hawaii. I had nothing else to occupy my life, so over I came."

"And you stay with Xander when he's here?"

He nodded. "Yes, I look after Xander when he visits. Which has been a lot in the last year or so, but before that was very rare." He held out a cup to me. I almost dove on the glass of water. I greedily gulped it down, water spilling all over me. When the glass was empty, Tommy handed it off to one of the men nearby.

I hadn't noticed, but we were surrounded by armed men and women. At least a dozen or more were spanning out from the perimeter. One of them spoke into an earpiece; I heard them say "They're here," and I almost panicked until I felt the familiar flip of my stomach and twang of the bond at my center.

Chase stormed through and it almost looked as if dark clouds followed him. The trees that lined the pool area moved, crowding closer, as if offering their support. I was up and in his arms in a heartbeat, his face carved into lines of absolute fury, his skin swirling with gold, lighting the dark tone. I wanted to say something, but I had no idea what would help. Chase was so beyond human right then, almost god-like, and it was making me unsure.

He turned, holding me close, and strode toward the house. We passed Emma and Lexen – she gave me a wave, her face blotchy like she'd been crying. Inside, cool air washed over us.

Chase seemed to know where he was going, climbing up a set of stairs and entering a nearby bedroom. He didn't stop there, though, moving us into the bathroom, where he placed me gently on the bench near the sink. Then, with a ragged breath, he took a step back.

His eyes, when I finally met them, were the sea during a storm, dark green and gray, swirling and churning, jaw so rigid I could have probably cut myself on the edges if I touched them. Before I could say a word, he reached out and hit the lever to turn the water on in the sink, letting it run while he grabbed a fluffy white towel, which had been neatly folded in an open set of shelves.

He tested the water a few times, finally soaking one side of the towel in it, before reaching out and rubbing the warm end across my skin. He did this over and over, rinsing off the blood. It felt so good, and at the same time so painful, and I could see Chase cataloguing each wound as he came across it. This was making him even angrier, and I was starting to hate the silence between us.

"I'm okay," I finally said, stupidly.

His hand stilled, the one that had been washing sand off my arm. Straightening, he dropped the towel, brushing some of my hair back, pushing it behind my ear. "What happened?" His voice was hoarse. "I need to know everything."

My head was finally clear now. I had no trouble telling him as quickly as possible everything that had happened, finishing up with the girl in the water. I gasped then when I remembered something. With frantic movements, I scrambled to feel around my neck. In my dazed state, I'd completely forgotten that I got the stone from Laous.

As my fingers brushed across the metal I actually smiled, lifting it over my head. The stone that had been lodged between my breasts sprang free. Chase shot his attention to it.

"I got the starslight," I said with a huge grin. "You need to take it to Lexen or whoever, so they can see if they can find the girl."

Noise from the doorway had me realizing that everyone else had been waiting for me in the bedroom. "My necklace," Emma said, her eyes watery. "How did you get it back?"

Chase leveled hard eyes on Lexen, who shrugged. "This was the longest I could keep her away. She needed to make sure Maya was okay."

Emma wiggled her way forward, wrapping her arms around me. I shushed Chase's protests. He kept trying to tell her I was injured and to be careful. "I'm fine," I said. "It could have been so much worse if that girl with the shimmery hair didn't find me."

Xander, who was near the back of the group, stepped forward. "Shimmery how?" he asked, and I thought his intensity was kind of weird, until he turned on the shower in the stall nearby and dropped his blond hair under. My eyes went very wide as that same iridescent sheen moved through his hair.

It all made sense now. She was the fourth secret keeper. "Laous said she was nearby," I murmured. "She must have been in the water the entire time."

Xander nodded. "And clearly she got more than a little of the Royale energy when she was born. That hair thing is unique to my house."

She definitely got more than a little. "She's amazing in the water, too. Held her breath for, like, ever, and was strong enough to power both of us through the waves."

My mind kept flashing back to the girl. She was beautiful, and I had a feeling on dry land she would be breathtaking. Xander was in so much trouble.

Tommy appeared in the doorway. "We're surrounded by Gonzo troops. The helicopter is ready and waiting on the roof. We need to get to a safe house."

No one argued. They all fell into formation, like this was a normal event. "Why don't you just stay and defend your territory?" Callie asked. "If they're humans, they don't stand a chance against the power of four overlords."

Daniel swept an arm around her, trying to hurry her along. "We don't know what Laous might have set them up with, weapon-wise. I won't risk you. Any of you."

"He doesn't have the stone now, at least," I said, breathing a sigh of relief. "One good thing came from Fraizer and his stupid plan."

"Are you sure he's dead?" Daniel asked me. "There was no body when we got to the sanctuary."

Turning in his direction, I tried not to let my sympathy show. "I don't know for sure. I saw him get shot, and he fell, but then I was dragged away, so I don't actually know if he got back up." There was an extended pause, and I decided to add, "I think Rao saved me. He was definitely thrown off by Fraizer telling him that he was his brother, and then he tripped really obviously, which gave me a chance to escape."

Daniel's eyes, which were the lightest of browns with gold

rings, had so much sadness in them that I almost burst into tears. I felt the heat and pressure behind my eyes but managed to keep it together while we moved into the hall and took an elevator up to the top floor. Chase stayed at my side the entire time. I couldn't help but touch him over and over, to reassure myself that I was back with him.

"You should tell them what Laous told you," Chase urged, when we were close to the helicopter. "About his father."

Even though it disgusted me, I quickly relayed the details to the group. Daniel, again, was the one to react. "That must have been what he did with my father," he said slowly. "When he killed him, he absorbed his energy, and that allowed the network to find him worthy to be overlord."

"Did you know your uncle suffered like that?" Callie asked. "When he was a child?"

Daniel shook his head with force. "I had no idea. It would have been before I was born, and I knew my dad and Laous were never close, but I had no idea of his past."

He looked both disturbed and upset, and I wondered what was worrying him the most. Fraizer? Rao? Or the possibility that Laous had suffered worse than any of us?

Before any more could be said, we were filing into the helicopter. Tommy handed Chase a familiar red kit. I knew my guy wouldn't be able to relax until he had patched me up.

"Buckle in," Tommy said. He was manning the chopper as well. He was very useful in these situations. "They have some manpower."

Lexen, who was near the open door, leaned out and said, "I'm going to make it a little harder for them."

Dark clouds burst across the sky, drifting in from way out at sea. It took him seconds, maybe less, to fill the air around us. As Tommy lifted the chopper up, blades loud, we took off with the dark clouds around us. Bullets fired, but thankfully none of them hit their mark, except one that lodged in a side panel.

Chase wasted no time disinfecting and bandaging me up, and by the time we arrived at the safe house, I was a walking mummy. The new place was not on Lanai, but instead on the bigger island of … O'ahu, I was pretty sure. Tommy set the helicopter down on a basketball court, which was at the back of an estate of about twenty beach shacks. When we all filed out, he took off into the air again.

"He'll stash it somewhere so we can't be easily traced," Xander told us as he strode toward one of the generic white Hamptons homes. I expected him to lead us to the front door, but instead, he moved to some bushes off to the side and pried open a double door that led down into a basement.

It was dark inside. Really dark. And as the doors closed behind Daniel, who was the last through, I could barely see anything. Chase kept a steadying hand on me as we made our way down the stairs. When we reached the ground level, Daniel lit a flame in his hand and a room came into view. "Come on," Xander said, waving a hand. "This is just the decoy."

"How do you have houses like this everywhere?" Emma sounded as confused as I felt. "I mean, you four have only been on Earth for a year."

Lexen answered: "Our families have been here for years, and we have safe houses for Daelighters scattered around. This is a Royale one. They tend to dominate the island areas."

We came to what looked like a wall, until Xander pressed a button and it swung out. Stepping inside, we were suddenly in a very high-tech looking elevator. The wall shut again, and then we were moving. I'd expected it to move down, but instead it went sideways. When it finally stopped, Xander was the first out, and I followed him into what looked like a state of the art control center. *Wow*. I had not expected that.

"This is where we are going to rest tonight," Xander said, taking a seat in front of a set of twelve or more monitors. "Tomorrow, we're going to find that girl and end this all." He flicked a switch and images appeared across all of them. Many different images.

"This is how we'll keep an eye on Laous and his army," Daniel said, sitting next to Xander. "We're hooked into the most powerful government satellites. It can't track Daelighters, but it can track those armed assholes Laous has teamed up with."

Emma held up the necklace, which she had not let go of. "And this is how we'll find our last secret keeper and join the four of our energies together."

As Chase wrapped his arm around me, and I sank back into his warm embrace, I realized I was ready for this. Having the starslight stone back put us in the dominant position to end this war. Laous picked the wrong humans to go up against. The clock was counting down now, and he was about to find out his days were numbered.

HOUSE OF ROYALE

Don't miss out on the stunning conclusion to the Secret Keepers Series. House of Royale. Out the 1st September 2018.

ACKNOWLEDGMENTS

Thank you to every single person who has ever taken a chance on my books. I write for you. Always.

Thanks to Alerim for the amazing cover. You captured my vision perfectly. Thanks to Tamara, who makes graphic design look effortless, and is so talented that I have a little envy. Thanks to Lee, from Ocean's edge Editing, for always polishing my story and making it shine. Thanks to Jamie Holmes, from Holmes Edits, for proofing the story so quickly for me.

Finally, thank you to my review team for the final touches you add.

I am blessed to have so many wonderful people as part of my team!!

ABOUT THE AUTHOR

Jaymin Eve is the USA Today Bestselling author of 25+ YA and NA fantasy/romance novels. She lives in Australia with her husband, two beautiful daughters, and a couple of crazy pets. Since 2013 she has sold over a million ebooks, and has no plans to stop writing anytime in the next 30-50 years.

ALSO BY JAYMIN EVE

Secret Keepers Series

Book One: House of Darken

Book Two: House of Imperial (1st July 2018)

Book Three: House of Leights (1st August 2018)

Book Four: House of Royale (1st September 2018)

Curse of the Gods Series (Reverse Harem Fantasy)

Book One: Trickery

Book Two: Persuasion

Book Three: Seduction

Book Four: Strength (2018)

NYC Mecca Series (Complete - UF series)

Book One: Queen Heir

Book Two: Queen Alpha

Book Three: Queen Fae

Book Four: Queen Mecca

A Walker Saga (Complete - YA Fantasy)

Book One: First World

Book Two: Spurn

Book Three: Crais

Book Four: Regali

Book Five: Nephilius

Book Six: Dronish

Book Seven: Earth

Supernatural Prison Trilogy (Complete - UF series)

Book One: Dragon Marked

Book Two: Dragon Mystics

Book Three: Dragon Mated

Supernatural Prison Stories

Broken Compass

Magical Compass

Louis (2018)

Hive Trilogy (Complete UF/PNR series)

Book One: Ash

Book Two: Anarchy

Book Three: Annihilate

Sinclair Stories (Standalone Contemporary Romance)

Songbird